THE
SKY
ABOVE
US

ALSO BY NATALIE LUND

We Speak in Storms

THE
SKY ABOVE US

NATALIE LUND

PHILOMEL

PHILOMEL BOOKS

An imprint of Penguin Random House LLC, New York

First published in the United States of America by Philomel,
an imprint of Penguin Random House LLC, 2020.

Visit us online at penguinrandomhouse.com.

Library of Congress Cataloging-in-Publication Data is available.

Printed in the United States of America

ISBN 9780525518037

1 3 5 7 9 10 8 6 4 2

Edited by Liza Kaplan.
Design by Ellice M. Lee.
Text set in Stone Serif ITC TT.

FOR THE WOLVES,
WHO ALWAYS HEAR

CHAPTER ONE

JANIE

....

The day of

THE SUN BREAKS over the horizon, glistening off the Gulf. It's the only time the Gulf manages to look beautiful, to shake off her muddy cloak and stand, broad and shining. The summer party ended hours ago, but nearly twenty of us are still here, sprawled across the beach like seals. Warmed by the new sun, scratching the sand out of our scalps. In the breeze, empty beer cans skitter toward the ocean and a few more of us wake.

I woke near Cass and Izzy—though not with them. They try to pretend they like me for more than just my supply of weed, occasional free snacks at the movie theater where I work, and rides in my Honda hatchback, but we all know that's not true.

When I try to sit, the world spins and I taste stomach acid in my throat. I watch the sky instead, the sand cold and hard against my back. The tide is out, the waves a distant hiss. Beside me, Cass sits, brushes sand from her skin, and squeezes her bronze curls. She reminds me of the palms, tall and curveless but wild on top. Izzy is on her stomach with her arms stretched above her head and her legs straight out, sleeping. Awake, she's so careful to stack herself like a model—chest up, shoulders back, hands on hips, ankles crossed—that it's strange to see her free-falling, a skydiver.

The newly risen sun disappears behind a cloud and the world turns gray and lavender, transforming our beach into something from a war—the dead and injured strewn as far as the eye can see. Izzy, the corpse. Cass, the mad. Me, the paralyzed. In the shadows, the ocean returns to her muddy brown. Adventure Pier, a mile to the southwest, has been cast in black— the Ferris wheel, roller coaster, and pirate ship now silhouettes.

Somewhere above the beach, we hear the hum of a prop plane, distant at first but growing louder and louder. It's too early for the planes that tow banners across the sky, and this plane sounds like it is flying far too low. I tilt my chin up and look to the seawall behind us as the plane clears it. There are gasps. There is scrambling. Izzy shouts Cass's name. I watch the white underbelly of the plane, lift my hand as though I'll be able to skim it with my fingers. And then it is over us, over the flat expanse of beach, the scuttling crabs, the sand-bedded mussels, the skipping gulls.

I rub my eyes, forgetful of the sand, and then try to blink away the grit, the stinging.

"Israel?" Izzy says to the plane. It has a red stripe and is bigger than the planes that spray for mosquitoes, though not by much. If her twin is inside that plane, Shane and Nate must be too. They've been an inseparable trio since freshman year.

My heart hammers in my chest, up my neck, behind my eyes. Last night I watched Nate and his braced knee limp from group to group, Solo cup in hand, his hair pulled back into its bun, occasionally giving that half smile that has made me melt since seventh grade. No one at school knew we were friends— not just friends. Something more. He was the one who invited me to the party, but he barely acknowledged me, and something finally snapped. I marched up to him to ask why—right in front of everyone. He pulled me away from the fire and told me he was scared that he couldn't escape it. *Escape what?* I asked. *This double life you've built?* I told him I couldn't pretend anymore, that I was finally done.

I started drinking—something I usually avoid because of my dad—to numb my pain. And once I felt loose, I dragged my heart around after Izzy and Cass—the closest to friends I had at that party—laughing when they laughed, dancing when they danced, though my limbs were jerky, my bounce off-beat. I had to keep a smile pasted on my face because the smile was the trapdoor holding back the feral thing inside me that wanted to growl and kick sand over Nate, to bury him. He'd drifted off early, his sweatshirt cinched around his face, his arms folded in so he appeared even smaller than usual.

Now, in this dim light, all I want to see is Nate's small limping form, his bunhead, his half smile.

The plane begins to climb, slower than it should and at

an impossible incline over the waves, which run their morning laps obliviously. Around me, everyone is awake. On their elbows, their knees, their feet, looking out at the Gulf. I manage to stand despite the rocking sensation inside my stomach.

The last time Nate and I were on this same beach, we were alone, our lips swollen from kissing, the moon illuminating the neat surgery scar along his knee—my dad's work. I told him I was applying to an ivy-walled northeastern college to study literature and screenwriting, and he said, "I want to be up there," and pointed at Orion's Belt. I laughed, didn't I? Even though he had been checking out a lot after the knee surgery, his face emptying when we were in the middle of conversations.

The plane is as high as the distant roller coaster now, higher.

It stalls, hovering, and we stop breathing; even the gulls hush, a collective holding. Then there's a sound coming from my throat: a high whine turning shriek. It's echoed across the beach. We all seem to sense what comes next: the plunge. In the purple-gray light, our awe becomes ghastly. Like disgust. Cass grabs my hand and Izzy's. I imagine we must look so small to the boys in the plane—if it's really them—a chain of sand dandelions.

"Israel!" Izzy shrieks. *Nate?* my heart asks.

I wonder: Does what goes up have to come down? Can you climb higher? Can you free yourself? Can you shrink to tiny specks and disappear from our sight? Can you—would you really—leave us behind?"

CHAPTER TWO

CASS

·····················

The day of

THE PLANE HITS the waves nose-first with a sound like a transformer blowing. The water rises in a curtain and folds over it. And as fast as it appeared, the plane—as a plane—is gone. Severed wings bob where it disappeared.

Izzy runs for the water. "Israel!" she screams, clawing at the waves. She's half doggy-paddling, half climbing as though it's a hill. Again, she howls his name.

Why would her twin brother be in the plane? I last remember him sprawled next to the charred ring of the firepit near Shane. Where's Shane?

He asked how I was at the beginning of the party. I lied when I said, "Okay." He replied with the same "okay" when I returned the question. I guess that probably wasn't true either—though I believed it. He *did* look okay for the first time in a while. He'd shaved his hair back to fuzz as he always did for the summer. He shotgunned beers with Nate and Israel. He did a keg stand. He poured people drinks and threw cans into the bonfire. Generic high school happiness. It was all a step—a baby step—from calling me a bitch in a packed cafeteria.

"Shane?" I yell, scanning all of the dawn-lit faces around me. No one answers. He's at home, I tell myself. Or he snuck off with another girl and is finally moving on without me.

Everyone's heads swivel from Izzy, still screaming, to where the body of the plane disappeared amid the waves, about two football fields from where we stand. I can hear the whispers: *What makes her think he's in there? They probably went home. I saw them right here before I passed out.*

"What are you waiting for?" I yell at the swivel-heads. "Why isn't someone calling the police?"

Janie bends and starts to rake sand with her fingers. She's making a sound over and over like *guh, guh, guh.* Jesus, this girl. I toss her my phone and take off after Izzy.

I can't think about the way the plane tilted to one side, fell, and spun. Or the smack of water. Or the screams. But Izzy? I can think of Izzy.

I make it to her easily and bear-hug her to my chest. The water is still bathwater warm from yesterday's heat. She slaps at me, rakes her fingernails across my forearms. She's strong, but I am too.

"Let me fucking go," she gasps. "He's in there." She gulps in salt water and then heaves. I feel her deflate, hacking and gagging, but it only makes her angrier, like the cat I found in the alley behind our condo. I'd wrapped my arms in towels and tried to bathe him with flea shampoo. Each time I thought his small drenched body was giving up, he thrashed and clawed. Finally he got me, right across the cheek, and I let go. And, if anyone is alley-cat tough, it's Izzy.

"Izzy, stop, please. How do you know it's him?"

"I felt him."

"You felt him?"

"And I fucking heard them talking about it."

"About what?"

"Flying." The word wails out of her.

Shane. His name flares inside me like a blinding light. A migraine. I close my eyes, try to extinguish it. But I can't hold back the image of him—lanky, long-armed. I can't think of him, who I've loved since seventh grade, and restrain Izzy at the same time.

"Izzy," I say, to remind myself what I'm doing. "Izzy, you have to calm down. You don't know for sure."

When Theo Pratt stole my stuffed skunk in kindergarten, Izzy dragged him by the hair across the playground pebbles. Later I waved to her as she sat outside the principal's office, and that was it. We were best friends. Only Israel was closer to her— by default of sharing her birth. No. Israel *is*. No past tense yet.

Marcus, our best swimmer, is already out and treading water near where the body of the plane sank. His head a dot on the waves. Tien, a surfer, makes it out there next. She dives, kicking up her legs. I hold my breath, but she reappears a moment later with nothing. She kicks her legs into the air again. Returns to the surface alone. Over and over.

I keep imagining Shane's sandy hair breaching the waves. Tien would flip him onto his back, hold him under those long arms, and kick him in. As soon as she dragged him onto the sand, I'd press my mouth against his and breathe for him. Please let me do it, Shane. *Shane. Shane.*

Something sharp—an elbow?—catches me in the stomach and I double over, gasping. Izzy slip-scrambles away from me. The water is to her chin before she stops, her long black hair fanned and floating, and screams, "Israaaaaaaaael!" It's the loudest thing I've ever heard. Behind me, everyone is sound-struck. Immobile. Like we're living in a terrible dream.

Last night, before I fell asleep, I caught Shane looking at me from across the fire. The flames lit his nose, but cast his eyes in the shadow of his brow bone. His face had an expression I couldn't put my finger on. Not anger. Not hurt. Something else. Determination?

Izzy's wailing brings me back to the beach, back to the moment. I am still breathless, but I want to give her hope, want to assure her that they weren't in there, that they couldn't be that stupid. But it feels like there's an avalanche inside me, like the ground is breaking away. Shelf after shelf plummeting.

CHAPTER THREE

IZZY

....

The day of

"ISABELA, SWEETIE?"

I don't know the woman leaning over me. She has a hawk nose that is far too close to my face.

"Isabela?" she says again.

What the fuck was Israel doing? Flying? When I overheard the boys talking about it, I was sure it was bullshit, but when I woke to the plane roaring overhead, I felt my twinsense, like something was scalding me along my right side where I've always felt his pain.

I'm sitting on some sort of flat stretcher thing. Sitting is wrong, though. I'm supposed to be standing. No, swimming. I push the foil blanket off. But it's back on my shoulders again. Was it the hawk woman? Or did I just think I'd pushed it off? Where is Cass? She'll explain what's happening. She'll get me away from this hawk woman.

"Izzy, do you need anything?" It's not Cass, it's Janie, who was following us around the party all night. There's something wrong with her face, like it's a mask. Her pupils are huge, ringed in green. She's on the ground, and I'm on something higher. A medical room, with its mouth open to the beach. An ambulance?

"Israel," I say. "I need Israel." Her mouth becomes a line. "My brother," I add. Sometimes it's like she's on another planet. "Get Is-ray-el." I say it slowly, drawing out the syllables. She covers her ears. Am I shouting? Hawk woman reappears next to me.

"Your parents are almost here."

"I don't want my parents. I want Israel."

"I know," hawk woman says, in that way that adults talk to kids, like, *Yes, I know that the world isn't fair.*

"Israel is not gone." I say this to the hawk woman, to Janie, to whomever is listening. If Israel were dead, I'd feel it, like I feel his pain with my twinsense. Simple as that. There'd be something cut. Severed. You can't just lose a person you've always had and not be told by the universe.

Behind Janie, there are police and coast guard boats in the water. I can see divers falling backward off one deck. They won't find him.

"Where's Cass?"

Janie points, and Cass is in her own foil wrap, looking like someone tried to drown her. She's talking to a man—a cop?— and gesturing at the sky, drawing a rainbow from seawall to sea.

"Cass!" I shout, and wave.

She looks at me, crying, and shakes her head. Everyone is so sad. They don't know that he's still here. That it has to be some kind of sick fucking trick.

One of the divers is dragging something to the surface. There's a collective sound from the beach—a cry? It looks like Nate, maybe? A small figure with long dark hair. They haul him onto the boat. Another diver appears, hauling another limp body, skinny and tall. Shane? The police are shooing everyone back, telling parents to take us home. When did all the adults arrive? I hear sobbing, wailing. Cass has sunk onto the sand, has disappeared inside the foil wrap like it's her shell.

"They're just unconscious," I say to no one. Janie has started vomiting; Cass is a turtle; hawk woman is busy with my parents; my mom sounds shrill. She keeps grabbing fistfuls of her dyed-blond hair and pulling on it. My dad is wearing his steel-toed boots. His face is stony, but his mustache twitches every few seconds like something is dragging at his lip. Israel is going to be in deep shit.

"Don't worry," I call to everyone on the beach. "You know these boys. They're just shitting us."

People look away, but I can tell that they want to look *at* me, that they're fighting their eyeballs.

The third diver appears, hauling a body that is blocky like Israel's, like our father's. The wet hair is black and wavy. The body's clothing is drenched and only visible for a moment before it's hidden by the boat, but I see a flash of green. Israel was wearing a green shirt last night. Still, my body—the right side, where we were pressed together in the womb—is silent. Only my eyes are telling me this is Israel. And eyes can't be trusted. My twinsense is stronger. It's under the skin. It's like my body communicating with its own limbs. Israel is not— Israel cannot be—

The police boat makes a sweeping arc and starts for the pier. A few dorsal fins appear then—one, two, three—along with the smooth curves of the dolphins' spines. They're racing the boat. They cut left, then right, as though they've made a plan, practiced a dance. One leaps out of the water. It glimmers gray with a purplish sheen like a soap bubble. The smallest dives under the boat and reappears on the other side. The third drops behind to ride the wake.

I blink. And blink again.

Israel started having a dream when we were little that he'd lived before, that he'd been a father who died in a car accident. My parents thought he was nuts because, even then, Israel was usually the rational one. Yet he believed that what he'd dreamed was real, that reincarnation was possible and that he'd been someone else in a past life.

Those dolphins . . . They have to be them, right? Shane, the show-off. Nate, the small. And my Israel—steady, careful, an anchor.

You fuckers. You fooled everybody—except me.

TRANSCRIPT

....

INTERVIEW WITH ISABELA CASTILLO

Officer Reynold: I understand you're all very upset, but we have to ask Isabela some questions.

Luis Castillo: Now?

Officer Reynold: I'm afraid so. When did you last see your brother?

Isabela Castillo: At the party.

Officer Reynold: Can you be more specific?

Isabela Castillo: At the party on the beach.

Officer Reynold: Mr. Castillo—

Luis Castillo: Isabela, please. They're trying to help.

Isabela Castillo: I don't know, okay? I fell asleep, but he was around before that. *<cries>*

Luis Castillo: Shh, Bela.

Officer Reynold: Around what time did you fall asleep?

Isabela Castillo: I don't know. Two-ish maybe.

Officer Reynold: To your knowledge, had your brother and his friends been drinking?

Isabela Castillo: Probably. We all were. Sorry, papá.

Officer Reynold: Did your brother say anything that would lead you to believe he was going to take a plane?

Isabela Castillo: *<shrugs>*

Luis Castillo: Answer him, mija.

Isabela Castillo: No.

Officer Reynold: Was there anything strange about his behavior last night?

Isabela Castillo: My brother was always acting strange.

Officer Reynold: Was there something *particularly* strange about his behavior yesterday?

Isabela Castillo: I guess he was acting weird yesterday morning. Like nice to me at first and then he got mean all of a sudden.

Officer Reynold: What did he say?

Isabela Castillo: He wanted me to leave him alone.

Officer Reynold: Where did he go after you spoke?

Isabela Castillo: To his room. I could hear his voice through the wall like he was talking to someone, but I couldn't hear what he was saying.

Officer Reynold: Anything else?

Isabela Castillo: I don't know. I don't know. I don't know. Is it okay with you that I didn't know everything about my twin brother?

CHAPTER FOUR

IZZY

....

The afternoon of

OUR HOUSE HAS become a cry fest. Our family from the mainland—two tías and tíos and several primos—all take turns holding me against their chests, combing my hair with their fingers, calling me *Bela*. Their doting makes my skin crawl.

I suppose it's unfair of me because even though he's not *gone gone*, he's not here. I can't climb onto the roof and find him, a cigarette already lit. My eyes swim at that thought, but I swipe them on my sleeve before someone spots me and pulls me into another suffocating hug.

Our next-door neighbors, the Centenos, have taken over the kitchen, accepting the plates of food that our visitors drop off, arranging serving spoons, and filling the coolers. Magdalena clicks her tongue at the sight of me and hands me a pumpkin empanada from Lulu's panadería. She doesn't realize I stopped eating sweets in middle school to lose what my

15

mom calls *lonjas*—the extra flesh above the hips—but people don't bring fresh salads to a— What is this even called? A grief gathering?

Someone has removed last year's school photo of Israel from the wall and set it on our dining table. There are already flowers surrounding him, grocery store carnations and potted lilies. He, of course, is staring from the frame with dark intensity. I've always been jealous of his eyes, sure that I could make it as an actress if we'd shared that trait. Instead I have our grandfather's expressionless cow eyes. And we both inherited our mom's round, flat face and wavy hair.

I stare back at him because he should be the one being interrogated—not me, not our mom, and not our dad, who is with the police now.

What did you do?

How did you do it?

Will I ever see you again?

That last question gives me the spins like when I'm drunk and trying to fall asleep. He's my twin. I *have* to see him again.

Or—

Or—

I stagger to the bathroom, narrowly escaping a cousin who keeps saying *qué lástima* and calling it an unfortunate accident. I drop the barely nibbled empanada in the trash can, sit on the toilet seat cover, and pull out my phone. I zoom in on the map and trace the long flat side of our island—the beach where the plane went down. If I were going to disappear, I'd pick the side of the island that broke off from Texas. So many nooks and inlets, places for fish—or mammals—to hide.

Dolphins migrate, right? I remember that from science class or Animal Planet. In a few days' time, they might be swimming down the curve of Mexico before flicking up toward Cuba. And then down to Venezuela, where our parents were born. Who knows after that?

I did not mention any of this to the police, of course. I didn't need anyone saying: *Poor girl. Lost her twin and her wits.* I left out the part about what I overheard from the hallway outside my brother's bedroom, too.

I pull up Israel's social media. It has turned into a tribute page, filled with post after post about how sad everyone is. What a #tragedy. It's all garbage. I scroll past, looking for his posts before the accident. There's a video of the boys at a soccer practice, a few selfies of Israel and this sophomore he's been flirting with, a story that hasn't expired yet showing a game of flip cup Shane tagged him in during the party. I save what I can—just in case—but there's nothing about where he was headed, what he was going to do. Israel always held his cards close to his chest.

Someone knocks on the door.

"Está ocupado."

"Bela?" It's my mom. Her voice scratchy like she's recovering from a cold.

"¿Qué?"

"Are you—" She doesn't finish the question, but in the crack under the door, I can see her feet. She's just standing there. There's something about the twin dark shadows of her shoes that makes me dizzy again. The bathroom swings back and forth, swirls of floral wallpaper, mauve towels, rose-scented soaps—her feet a pendulum now.

Are you— Are you— Are you, I repeat to myself. *All right? Afraid? Sick? Still a twin? Brokenhearted? Just plain broken?*

Which words will make the bathroom stop swinging?

Are you— Are you— Are you—

I let out a sound that is part groan, part sob, and I guess it's the right answer because her feet disappear and the room stops swaying.

My phone is still in my hand, his face framed in overgrown curls, his eyes on me.

Would you leave without telling me?

I have to find those dolphins—it's my only chance at finding answers.

CHAPTER FIVE

JANIE

....

The afternoon of

NO ONE NOTICES me, sitting on the sandstone blocks at the base of the seawall, after the bodies have been pulled from the ocean, after the sand has been cleared of concerned parents and wailing teenagers. After the news helicopters have stopped hovering overhead. After the coast guard and police have begun to tackle the problem of the sunken body of the plane.

No one thinks to call my dad, because he doesn't attend PTA meetings or soccer games or tourism board elections. I lost my phone in the sand, but I doubt he's texted to see where I am anyway. He's on call this weekend, so his silence probably means there was a bone sticking out of someone's skin that required emergency surgery. On scheduled surgery days, he's usually out by two p.m., which gives him four hours of drinking in bars before he arrives home, asks me if I've done my homework, and drops onto the couch to watch TV. If I have a shift at the Adventure Pier theater, he's beer-snoring by the time I get home.

It's responsible alcoholism, he says, because he drinks beer rather than liquor, which apparently keeps his hands steady. He started drinking when Mom left. After five years, he's had to make accommodations to still get drunk, which means drinking more and eating less. I'm usually on my own to make a box of mac and cheese or eat the leftover theater popcorn that Neil, the manager, gives me in black plastic trash bags. For both Dad and me, these habits have resulted in tires settling around our midsections. It's not tough to hide, though, in worn-soft T-shirts from Goodwill. It pays to be frugal in more ways than one.

I leave the hatchback at the beach and search downtown for an ATM and Timmy, a homeless vet Izzy told me about, who loves making cash off teenagers who need alcohol. He stood on the seawall through two hurricanes, so he's not afraid of anyone's incensed parents.

I withdraw money from my dad's account—he's got plenty and I'm saving what I make for college, my dream of writing workshops in redbrick buildings and crossing a campus in the snow. I like the idea of earning my own way there.

My stomach is still queasy from last night. Cass and Izzy dried my pot supply at the party and I don't know that I can stomach food without it.

I ask Timmy to get whatever liquor is best for losing someone, and he emerges with a handle of vodka.

"If it's good enough for the Russians," he says, and I wait, thinking he'll complete the sentence, but he turns and walks away from me, stuffing the change in his pocket.

Vodka in hand, I wander to the bayou, where a few fishermen are packing up for the day. Across the brackish water, my dad's boat is docked at the marina. It was a gift for my mom that was supposed to help ease the move to the island. *You got me a boat? A boat is supposed to make up for the job and home I left?* I remember her shouting.

I sink under a palm tree, prepared to sweat it all out: the alcohol, the memory of Nate, the ache I've carried with me since I moved in next door to him that summer before seventh grade. I take a swig of vodka, but the handle is too heavy and it plows into my lip. The vodka is cheap—Timmy wanted a bigger share of the change. It tastes like nail polish remover and burns the scabbed zit on my chin.

At school, Nate was distant, as though we were acquaintances. That first day of seventh grade after I moved to the island, I thought I must have the wrong person—there was no way the neighbor kid who invited me to perch behind him on his bike was the same one who barely nodded a hello. But quickly, I learned that it was the nature of our relationship. At school, he was a star on the soccer field, surrounded by athletic boys who wore silken cloaks of assuredness, of dominance, who were uninterested in an awkward girl like me.

But, after school, behind our houses' doors, he was interested and open and kind. Every time I felt upset or hurt and wanted to say something about the two Nates, I got scared I'd lose him, the one person on the entire island who knew me before my mom left, who knew the truth and still liked me.

So we never talked about it. Until last night, when I upset the perfect balance because I had the nerve to think that an invitation to a party meant I deserved more. Why did I have to open my mouth and allow those to be my last words to him?

The sun is high now, but without my phone, I can't tell the exact time. My clothes smell like campfire and seawater and sweat. The vodka raises my temperature and I feel trapped in my own body, nauseated. Bile pools in my throat. I scramble to the water, lean over, and vomit. But there's nothing left. Just yellow, stinging acid. Small fish dart to the top and gobble it up.

I rest against the tree, allow my head to loll to the side. The day I moved into our blue bungalow perched on stilts like a squat flamingo, Nate was riding his bike in loops, pretending not to notice me while I pretended not to notice him. Maybe we would have gone on like that if I hadn't sneezed, a huge achoo right as he swung by. He almost fell off his bike.

"Who are you?" he asked, skidding to a stop. His hair was short back then but gelled into a neat ridge at the top of his head.

"Janie."

"Nate," he said. "I live there." He pointed at the canary-yellow house next door. "Want to go to the beach?"

I nodded, enthusiastic to see this beach my father had bragged about while my mom seethed with anger.

"Hop on," he said.

I stepped onto the pegs and put my hands on Nate's shoulders. I could feel the dense knots of his muscles through the fabric of his shirt. He took me on a tour, pedaling past the factory where they made saltwater taffy to supply gift shops; the Rusty Kettle Diner, where they made the best cheese grits; Lulu's, where you could get chocolate-filled churros; and the haunted McAllister mansion.

When we reached the seawall, he dropped his bike onto its handlebars and climbed up. He offered me his hand.

"You ever been to the Florida side of the Gulf?" he asked as he pulled me up.

"Once, with my mom's family," I said.

"The beach and water are prettier there, but do you know what we have that they don't?"

"What?"

"Magic." He gestured at the beach as though unveiling a great trick.

The water was a mossy emerald with swirls of brick red and smelled like all those tiny sea deaths—fish and clams and crabs. The beach was stamped with bright towels and puffy, sunburnt Texans. Was he joking?

"Do you see it?" he asked, and there was something about his voice, eager, yearning, that made me say yes.

I'm not sure how much time has passed when I wake to a man shaking my shoulder. "Hey. Hey, girl, you okay?" I open my eyes, which I have no memory of closing. My cheek is pressed against the bark of the palm. I have to squint because everything is bright, glinting and hot. My face and throat burn.

"I'm okay."

"Strange place to sleep," the man says. He's so close to my face, I can smell his breath, spearmint barely masking the scent of chewing tobacco. His eyes sweep my body, and I sit up abruptly, knocking my forehead into his. I gather the handle of vodka, dragging it like a resistant pet.

A few feet away I trip onto my knees, the handle clunking the pavement beside me. I can't make sense of any of this. The stinging. The trickle of blood. The small rock buried in my knee. This—the way things end and people leave.

My mom left that same summer we moved to the island. Back in Maryland, she'd been a nurse at a women's clinic that performed abortions as one of its many services and had to wear a bulletproof vest to and from work. Once, a protestor had thrown a chunk of concrete at her while she walked to her car with a security officer. Once, she had to change her cell phone number because a person had programmed a system to call her every ten minutes and play a recording of babies' wails. Once, someone followed her home, someone who came back and left bloody pig intestines on our doormat. That's when my dad started looking for other jobs and found one at a small-time hospital on this dinky island. He convinced her to move by saying it was for my safety.

The night before she left, my parents had been up late arguing, my mom about how she'd already had to give up medical school when I was born and now she'd given up a job and home she loved, my dad about how she didn't have her priorities straight. It was nothing new, so I slept with headphones, dozing until the heat from the summer sun forced me out of bed. I was planning to eat breakfast and ride to the ocean with Nate, but there was a letter on the kitchen counter with my name scribbled on it. I don't remember the exact words—I only read it once before running it through my dad's shredder—but I do know it said she was sorry and she loved me. She promised to call, to arrange for me to visit as soon as it was feasible. And she did call every week after that; I'd hear my father whisper-shouting at her in the bathroom. When it was my turn to talk to her, he'd emerge—his cheeks red and shiny, his eyes wet—and I'd refuse to take the phone. I was afraid to hear her voice, afraid that it would reopen the wound, that the bleeding would never stop.

Through my dad, she invited me to visit her at her new apartment back in Maryland, but I refused that, too. My dad only half-heartedly tried to convince me. I think it gave him some satisfaction that I'd cut my mother out so completely after she'd walked away.

I didn't speak to my mom for an entire year after that. It was a year of punching walls in my new school. Of glaring from lonely corners of the cafeteria. Of sleepless nights that left me delirious, unsure what was a dream and what was real. Of ignoring a counselor who advised me to hit pillows and silent scream, as though that could somehow stitch me closed.

I think that first year on the island is part of the reason I have so few friends now.

Nate was my only companion that year. Being with him felt like a vacation from the real world. After school we'd collect sea glass, eat taffy until our teeth were gummed up, poke dead man-o'-wars with sticks, and watch for dolphins. He never asked about my mother, or my outbursts at school. He pretended, simply, that we didn't attend the same school, that he never saw me in the hallways. The aching hole inside me was happy to be filled—if only a little—by this conditional friendship.

And I destroyed even that.

Somehow I make it to the hospital nearly a mile away, but my dad's Camry isn't there. Maybe his surgery is finished, and he's parked at one of the ice houses. I try Seashells first, and then Landry's. Each stop brings me a nearly empty parking lot and a *Sorry, kid*.

I sit on a curb next to Landry's dumpster, sipping from the handle. My stomach bucks and reels, but I swallow more, force it down. And when it comes up, I let it burn all the way up my nose.

The handle is light enough now that I can lift it over my head and chuck it across the parking lot. It shatters and I want it to relieve some of the pain, but it doesn't feel any better than punching pillows. All it does is earn me the attention of a security guard in a small golf cart, and I'm forced to leave, to wander our island utterly alone.

CHAPTER SIX

CASS

....

The afternoon of

I DON'T REMEMBER much about the trip home from the beach. I know my mom forced me into the shower because I wake in bed with my hair braided, my eyes burning as though I cried myself to sleep. I pull off the hair ties to loosen the pressure behind my ears. She always makes the braids too tight.

My laptop faces me from my desk. It's open, the screen dark. Before the party, I'd been making a spreadsheet, listing the application requirements for each school. They were ranked, my dream schools in green, my next preferred in yellow, and least preferred in orange. Today I'd planned to start my personal statement. I was going to write about chemistry—the field I've always wanted to study and the kind between people: me and Izzy; my mom and dad; me and Shane. How bonds form and split. I won't be writing that essay anymore.

Right now I can't imagine writing anything again.

I check my phone and have over one hundred notifications—texts, messages, posts, and tags.

```
Thinking of you, Cass. <3 <3 <3
```

```
We miss you, Shane, Nate, and Israel.
#flying @casswithsass_49 @Izyoureal_02
@dancer_in_a_box @mels_meows
```

```
How could you?
```

The last was from Shane's older sister, Meg, and I have no response. She's right, of course. How could I break his heart? How could I show up at the party last night when I knew he'd be there? How could I sleep half the day after I saw them pull him from the ocean?

A cry erupts from my mouth. I press and hold on each social media app to delete them and then chuck my phone across the room.

My bedroom door swings open and my mom is there. She wraps her hands around my head and holds me to her belly, like she wants me to go back inside.

"Oh, Cassie," my mom says. "Sweetie, I'm so sorry."

"Can I see him?" The words don't sound like they're supposed to, but she understands.

"I don't know, honey," she says, grasping me again.

"Sometimes, the family doesn't want to have an open casket. It depends on how—" She stops herself.

The memory of the plane plummeting into the ocean shudders through me. That crash of water. Izzy's scream. I sob a wobbling, anguished *"Mom."*

She rocks me and makes a shushing noise. I can tell she's crying now too, by the way her stomach heaves against my ears. My mom has so much empathy that she'll cry simply because you are crying. When I finally told her about why we broke up, she kept saying, "Poor Shane. Poor you." She's the only one who thought "Poor me," I'm sure.

I've known Shane since we were in diapers. In seventh grade, he started walking me home every day, ignoring Izzy, who'd lean out the bus windows, screeching: *How's your pet Shane? Does he realize his knuckles are dragging?* But Shane didn't ever seem to hear. He'd turn down this street and that, unconcerned about which direction we were headed. While the rest of us had our hackles up like street dogs, Shane could laugh off a teacher accusing him of cheating, his sister letting him take the fall for her weed, a goal scored on him during an important game, my protective best friend's jabs. And he could make me laugh too.

It was his idea to sneak into the beach houses they were building on the southern end of the island and play house—even if we were too old for it. Each of them could fit two or three of my mom's condos inside, and it was fun to imagine they were all mine. Shane pretended to be my chef, making dishes he'd seen on TV cooking shows: scallops with pea puree, red snapper with lemon pepper and salt, brisket with coffee BBQ sauce. Back then he had the confidence to be anything, anyone. And I broke that.

I groveled across the cafeteria. I groveled up his driveway. I sorried up and down the whole seventeen miles of our island. But I would have said sorry again. And another time after that. And again and again if that's what Shane needed to fly further, climb higher.

My fingernails are digging into my palm. I'm my fists. Balled and tight.

My phone vibrates on the carpet near my closet. Mom retrieves it and looks at the screen. "It's Izzy," she says softly.

I grab it from her and answer. "Iz?"

"Cass, meet me at the Kroger." She hangs up without another word.

"I have to go. I need to borrow the car." I'm already out of bed, scrambling to put on clothes. I pull my jeans over my pajama shorts and zip up a hoodie even though it's hot out. I want to be covered, to have bulk and substance.

"I don't think that's a good idea, Cassandra." My mom has always been wary of Izzy because of her sharp edges, but she doesn't get to see how fiercely loyal the girl is.

"She needs me." I meet her eyes when I say this, try to appeal to her endless well of empathy. "Izzy has got to be feeling ten times worse than me."

"This is not a grief competition. She feels heartbroken. You feel heartbroken. There's no need to measure your grief against hers."

She's right, of course. Measuring grief is impossible, but what you *can* measure, what I've already started to measure, is guilt. It had to be me, the reason Shane was so determined in the firelight? The reason he fell from the sky?

REMEMBERED SOULS FORUM

....

GULF COAST

ElGranZambini: In my last life, I was a blue heron. I didn't know I was a blue heron at the time, but I've looked at plenty of bird books, and I know that's what I must've been.

I remember having this feeling that I was at home in the swamp, and that this particular tree was mine.

One day I dropped from my tree to snap up water bugs when I saw the two humps of a gator's eyes breaking the surface of the swamp. It set my wings to beating, but I was too late. Those things can jump, let me tell you. The jaws closed on my leg, like when you slam the car door on your finger. That's the last thing I remember: the sharp clamp of teeth and fighting for the sky.

Anyone else remember being an animal?

LittleLambo: I think I may have been a plant or a tree. I don't remember sights or sounds like you, but I do remember warmth and vibrations

that felt like they were inside me, like I was
buzzing from the inside out. There was a ticklish
feeling too, like the kind that sends goose bumps
all up and down your body. At the end, though,
there was a sharp, screaming feeling, like being
torn in two.

AlphaHOU: I was a whale. The day I died,
I was following the coast north to the bays
where I was born. I knew I'd been on that
route before, that the path was carved in
my brain.

I couldn't keep up with the pod,
though they were mine—children and
children's children and even further down
the tree. I called out in our language, long
and mournful followed by a fast chitter.
My first daughter answered. She floated
in the distance, waiting for me. The sun
cut through the water, illuminating the
black slick of her head, the white streaks
above her eyes, the gray saddle patch we
all share.

I knew that it was my time—knew it
as well as I knew the water around me, the
path before me. I called to her again, and
while I can't put human words to what was
communicated between us, I like to think that

I told her I was going to be okay. That she
should go on without me and lead our pod, as
I probably did when my own mother finally
allowed herself to sink, to settle onto the ocean
floor, to become food for all the tiny creatures
that surrounded us.

CHAPTER SEVEN

ISRAEL

....

Thirty-one days before

ISRAEL'S ALARM BUZZED at six a.m. He rubbed his burning eyes. His dream had first woken him up an hour before, bathed in sweat and croaking, like he'd been trying to shout. It had taken a while for his heart rate to slow and the adrenaline to drain enough for him to doze off again. Just in time to wake up for his early-bird class.

Sometimes he didn't remember a single thing from the dream. He only knew he'd had it from the way he'd been dragged into the waking world gasping like a fish out of water. Sometimes he remembered all of it: the pavement, shimmering where slick. The slip of the tires. A woman, whose mouth made an O, in the oncoming car. The agonizing pain in his right leg, the nothing feeling of his left. The black smoke billowing from what used to be the hood of his car. Sirens. The shouts from outside the car. Someone calling for *jaws of life*.

The heat from flames. Frantically tugging at a seat belt that wouldn't let go. Someone saying *hold on*. Trying to hold on by thinking of his wife, Lara, and son, Peter, who was in need of medicine. And when he, Israel, finally woke up, he had the haunting feeling that the person he'd been in the dream hadn't.

His pit bull, Luna, thumped the bed with her tail. Her wet nose burrowed under the covers and found his hand. He scratched her ear and threw his legs over the side of the bed. His whole body ached like he'd been to the gym.

He had to be at school by 7:05 a.m. for early-bird AP Econ. He needed those weighted GPAs if he was going to make it to the top 10 percent of his class like his parents wanted, so he'd signed up for every AP class he could fit into his schedule. Freshman Israel had really screwed over now-junior Israel with all those Cs. Hell, two years ago, Israel hadn't even thought about college. He was just a nervous, quiet kid who'd started hanging around Shane—the sun of the school—because if you were in Shane's glow, you were seen and golden.

Back in freshman year, it was Shane who'd said so casually, *You should try out for soccer.* Israel had played in a few recreational leagues as a kid, but he'd never played traveling like Shane and Nate. Still, Israel made junior varsity, along with Shane. Nate, who had talent and a soccer player's compact yet muscular frame, made varsity. Their school was small, so JV and varsity practiced at the same time and played games back-to-back. Each evening, Israel sat across from Nate and

Shane on the team bus, talking instead of doing the next day's homework, which was why he'd had all those Cs.

Israel opened his door, bracing himself to find Izzy there, which she often was unless she'd already put herself back to bed. Sure enough, his sister was curled into a ball, her bony knees drawn to her chest. At the sound of the door, her face scrunched and one brown eye popped open to peer up at him. She uncurled, stretching out like a starfish before pushing herself into a sitting position against the doorframe. Her hair, which she usually straightened, was limp.

"You're in the way."

"Sorry, sorry," she said, yawning as though she wasn't actually sorry.

He stepped over her knees and slammed the bathroom door behind him. It irritated him that, on top of everything else, his distress and pain called her to him—even when they were both asleep. The whole twinsense thing made him feel like she was draped on him like a scarf. A wet, woolen scarf knitted by your abuela who doesn't remember you live in Texas, where you can drink the air it's so humid.

He wet a comb and tried to work it through his hair, which was the sort of texture that humidity made look both greasy and frizzy. He plucked a few hairs from between his brows and rubbed shaving cream onto his cheeks. He wasn't nearly as vain as Izzy, but he had to spend almost as much time in front of the mirror just to battle back the hair that sprang from his ears, his nostrils, and practically every part of his face.

As he was rinsing off, he caught a whiff of coffee and heard the scrape of a kitchen chair downstairs. His father would be sitting, crossing one ankle onto the opposite knee to lace up his work boots. Usually their dad was gone by sunup, and Israel only saw him in the short sliver of time between dinner and his father's early bedtime—even less now that Israel often ate dinner with his friends. Israel missed his dad, but lately every conversation with him had turned to his plan for Israel's future: he'd go to college, intern in New York, and then start a job in the financial industry. His dad imagined him in slim-cut suits and mirror-glass high-rises.

"It's a different kind of money," he always said when Israel pointed out that their family had plenty of money now. Israel understood what his father meant, that this other kind of money came with security and respect—the kind of respect a small island contractor would never earn, no matter how many houses he built for rich people. The kind of money that didn't take your body to make it.

But Israel wasn't sure what he wanted for himself.

"Buenos días," he said as he descended the stairs, Luna on his heels. No response. "Buenos días," he repeated, louder; his dad's hearing was starting to go.

"Buenos días, mijo." He smiled at Israel, a chipped-tooth grin crowned by a mustache. Israel had chased that smile as a boy, trying every antic from marching in his mother's heels to singing songs he'd heard on the playground.

Jingle bells
Batman smells
Robin laid an egg

It was hard to get noticed when your dad worked at all hours and your twin plowed through life like a hurricane.

Israel let Luna out as his dad brushed his thinning salt-and-pepper hair forward with his palm and settled a baseball cap on his head. He was aging poorly, and noticing it made Israel's chest ache as though he were short of breath. His dad's shoulders—always so square and lifted—were starting to cave inward. His skin was that of a much older man: thick and dimpled like an orange rind. There was a slight tremor to his hands as he fixed his hat. Only his thick brush of a mustache remained the same.

"Need help after practice?" Israel asked, though he knew the answer.

His dad shook his head. "My father didn't move us here so his grandson could one day work construction."

"He didn't move here so you could work construction either," Israel said.

"That's why I'm the jefe now." His dad stood and poured coffee into a thermos. He took a mug down from a cabinet and poured Israel only half a cup. "Porque todavía estás creciendo." *Because you're still growing.* It was sweet to be cared for like he was that little boy who thought smiles were the gold at the end of a rainbow.

"I don't want you to get stuck, Israel, just because business is good now. It won't always be," his dad said. "And there are bigger things to think of."

Here it was. The conversation about his future. Again.

"How are your grades? Only a couple weeks left."

"They're good. I think I'll get straight As if I nail finals."

His father beamed, and Israel couldn't help smiling back. He wanted to go to college and achieve this dream for his dad—for both of his parents. But lately, between the exhaustion from his dreams and the pressure of trying to improve his GPA, he'd been feeling as thin as tissue paper. He carefully patched and pasted together the self that he brought to school, that played soccer, that he allowed his parents to see, but one breath of wind or drop of rain, and he was sure he would tear apart.

"How about you take a Saturday off? Make mandocas like old times. You look like you could use a rest," Israel said. When they were little and it was too rainy for their dad to work, they'd wake to him mixing the dough, rolling and shaping it into individual teardrops, dropping them into hot oil, and serving them with a freshly squeezed lime drink called papelón con limón.

"Your sister doesn't eat those anymore. Tiene miedo de engordar." He patted the slight paunch of his own stomach and laughed. "Plus, I'll rest when I'm dead." It was his favorite Americanism.

"But when you're dead, you can't eat mandocas."

"There better be mandocas in heaven or I'm not going," his dad said before hugging him goodbye.

Israel sat at the counter in the empty kitchen sipping coffee and scrolling through his phone. He didn't want to wait until he was dead to rest. He'd begun to feel the paper thinness in the fall when he'd had four tests in the same week for his AP courses. He'd tried to fight off the dream by staying awake, chugging caffeinated drinks, blasting music in his headphones, and pacing his room with note cards to study. It had been hell at school. He'd snapped at everyone, he hadn't had any energy on the field, and he'd barely stayed awake through the physics exam.

Even some sleep was better than none, he'd decided. For midterms, he'd tried over-the-counter sleep aids, and they'd certainly kept him asleep, but he'd experienced his dream death on a loop. It had made him jumpy, cringing away from loud noises and afraid to drive.

If he was going to go to college in a little over a year, he had to figure out how to live with the dream or get rid of it altogether.

He couldn't ask his parents for help. When he'd told them about the dream as a kid, his dad had looked at him like he was a disappointment. It was the kind of moment that you remembered forever: his father, shaking his head, his eyes squinted and hard in the rearview mirror. No sympathy, no concern, and certainly no belief. After that, Israel had begun to curl into himself, quiet and protected like a snail. He'd vowed never to talk about it again.

So this spring, when he'd started having the dream more frequently, he began doing research, reading every book he could find about past lives—from the anthropological to the religious to new age to psychology. The most helpful had been the group he'd found online, Remembered Souls. It was filled with people who recalled past lives just like he did. He'd been lurking on the page for months, and then a few days before, he'd finally been brave enough to break his vow and write what he'd been dreaming every night.

People had responded to his post asking for details about the make and model of the car, if he remembered what state he was in or Lara's and Peter's ages. He didn't have many answers.

He took a sip of his coffee and logged on. Overnight, someone had replied with a link. Israel clicked it, aware of the heartbeat in his temple.

He inhaled sharply when he saw the headline. It was an old death announcement:

Randolph A. Ryerson, 42, of Honore, TX, died February 17, 2002. A funeral service will be held at VanDyke Funeral Home, officiated by Deacon Harvey Jenkins. Cremation will be accorded and a private inurnment held at Beachtree Cemetery. He is survived by his wife, Lara, and son, Peter.

Israel rubbed his eyes and reread it. He read it again. February 17, 2002? It was his birthday. That was impossible. Wasn't it? His pulse was racing, hammering now in his head and jaw. This was the closest to proof he'd ever found that his dream was true. He had been Randolph.

He glanced at the time. He'd be late to econ, but he couldn't stop now. He googled Randolph Ryerson, his fingers slipping and sweaty on the phone screen as he typed. There was nothing except the death announcement. He tried the website of the local newspaper in Honore, but they didn't have online archives from that time, and it was so long ago that Israel couldn't find any social media accounts. Israel kept searching and found a few documents on a family history database. A birth certificate dated 1960. A marriage certified to Lara Ripple.

Israel looked Lara up first and found a social media page that hadn't been updated in months. She had dark gray hair cropped to a puff around her face, sharp eyes, and a stony expression. She never posted about herself, only shared other people's posts—sentimental videos of soldiers surprising their children at school and dogs singing while their owners played the piano.

He searched Peter Ryerson next. The son—now a grown man—lived in the same town his father had. His social media accounts were private, but the public cover photo showed a thin blond man with pink-splotched skin, a short beard, and beady blue eyes. Israel wasn't sure what similarities he'd expected to see—something behind the eyes perhaps—but he didn't have anything in common with the man except, perhaps, a car accident that had changed both of their lives.

Israel found Lara's address on the map and stared at the white line of her street, the highway nearby, stretching all the way to their island. He slung his backpack over one shoulder.

He couldn't just ring her doorbell and say, *Hello, I'm your dead husband*, but he couldn't do nothing, either. If he was going to succeed in college and be the suited man his dad imagined instead of a paper-thin person stuck to someone else's shoe, he had to do something—and soon.

CHAPTER EIGHT

NATE

....

Thirty-one days before

ISRAEL WAS WAITING for Nate outside his precalculus class so they could walk to the cafeteria for lunch. He had a textbook pinched under his arm, his hair was untamed like he hadn't combed it, and his dark eyes had purple smudges beneath. The kid didn't sleep, Nate knew, but he looked wired—like he'd swallowed a bunch of caffeine pills.

He tried so hard at everything—at school, at soccer, at being friends with Shane and Nate. At first the constant striving had been laughable to Nate, but now it had become almost admirable. If there was a student in their school who was actually going somewhere, it was Israel. Nate sometimes wished he felt motivated to be better like his friend. The only thing he was good at was soccer and, for that, he didn't have to try or practice. He'd always been fast and the game was instinctual for him: he understood where the ball would go and how the players around him would move.

"I have something for you." Israel pulled a pamphlet out of his econ book and handed it to Nate. "I got this in the mail and thought you'd be interested."

Two soccer players fought for the ball on the front of the pamphlet, the University of Maryland's name on their jerseys. Inside, the brochure raved about the diversity, the rich student life, the ample opportunities for internships.

"Maryland?" Nate asked, raising his eyebrows at Israel. "Do they have a good team?"

"Yeah, and it's a good school, too. I heard they send scouts to that camp you're going to this summer. You might get noticed."

Between Israel and Janie, Nate had been hearing about college all year. *It's where you'll find your people*, Janie had told him wistfully. For Israel, it was sleek city streets and skyscrapers. For Nate, who didn't really *want* anything except soccer, college was only a path to playing professionally someday.

Nate and Israel passed the library, which had recently been remodeled with floor-to-ceiling glass walls, so it sat in the heart of their school like a fish bowl. Janie was in the stacks, her friend Marisol beside her, running a finger over the spines of the books. Janie's brassy hair was wound back in its usual braid. She was dressed in light-wash jeans, white tennis shoes, and an orange bowling shirt that she'd probably bought at a thrift store. Nate hated to wear clothes that someone had worn before him—part of having an older brother and years of hand-me-downs.

He looked at the pamphlet again. Maryland looked so green—not a dark tropical green like their island, but a cool green. An Atlantic green. Janie had grown up in Maryland, but she never spoke about it—probably because her mother had moved back there when she left. It would be so easy for him to stop and show her the pamphlet, to ask her if she thought he could fit into that faraway place, but there was still a wall between their two worlds.

That summer Janie moved in, Shane had been away at camp and Nate's brother, Aaron, had grown out of what Nate called their *adventures*: riding bikes to the ocean, digging in the sand for crabs, collecting sea glass, riding the free ferry, and net-fishing jellies. Nate was starting to feel left behind. Everyone else his age was strutting laps around the public pool, identifying new crushes, and eating Pixy Stix until their tongues were bright shades of blue or purple.

But Janie was different. She smelled like dusty cotton, like the T-shirts at the bottom of your drawers. Her green eyes were large and round, her chin got lost in her neck, and she was a few inches taller than him. When she stuck out her bottom lip to blow her bangs off her forehead, he had a strange desire to climb her like she was Jack's beanstalk. Best of all, she was eager to ride with him to the beach, to stand at the seawall and marvel at everything he still found beautiful.

One morning they'd woken up early and he'd biked them to the point with a half watermelon tucked under his arm. They waded ankle-deep into the tide pools and he told her all the names his father had taught him.

Banded sea star.

Sea anemone.

Red sea urchin.

Lined periwinkle.

False limpet.

Blue crab.

After, they sat on the sand, scooping watermelon out of its rind with salty hands. Nate had rolled onto his stomach so he could see the curve of her bang-covered forehead, the upward slope of her nose, the rise of her chest. He wanted nothing more than to *know* her.

"Tell me a secret," he'd said. "Something you've never told anyone."

She was quiet for a moment. "My mom doesn't like us very much," she said.

"Your mom? What do you mean?" Nate had met her mom a few times. She was a petite woman with a blond pixie cut. She was almost always sitting on their back porch with a book or a newspaper, her bare feet up against the slats of the railing. She never seemed to read—just stared at the house behind theirs. If he said hello, her eyes focused quickly on him, and she'd smile—sadly—and say hello before returning to her stare.

Janie had rolled onto her stomach too, so their noses were inches apart. He could smell her breath, sweet from the watermelon. "I hear them fighting," she'd said, looking down at her hands. Nate could see a few tears clinging to her eyelashes.

"My mom always brings up how she had to drop out of medical school when I was born. My dad kept going, and she worked at a bank for a while to pay for his school. When he was done, she did a nursing degree."

"Well, that's not your fault. She could have finished medical school if she'd wanted, right? Maybe she wanted to be a nurse."

She looked down and picked at her cuticles but didn't answer.

Two weeks before the end of the summer, her mom left. Nate didn't see Janie for days after that, and when he finally coaxed her out of her house, she stared at everyone in this outright, uncomfortable way—like they were aliens and she was trying to understand their culture—to the point that Aaron said, *Take a picture; it will last longer.* This had made her burst into tears—the gasping kind where he thought she was going to hyperventilate.

She began acting more erratically, too, like a cornered stray. His mother had asked her if she was doing okay, and she'd practically shrieked that she was fine, that everyone should stop worrying about her. Once, when she was borrowing Nate's bike, she'd start pedaling fiercely and glancing over her shoulder at him, a wide-eyed look of terror on her face as though he were chasing her. She wouldn't slow, even when he called after her. When he finally found her, she was kneeling in the sand, digging with her fingers.

He was out of breath, but he knelt next to her and started digging too. "What are we looking for?" he asked.

"I lost something," she said.

"What?"

"I don't know." She practically wailed the words. Nate stopped digging and brushed off his hands, watching her. The mad scramble of her fingers, the sand coating her knees and thighs, the way her pupils seemed loose in her face.

He hadn't intended to cleave his two worlds so cleanly that first day of seventh grade when the new school year began. He'd simply asked his mom to drive him early so that he could catch up with Shane. And when Janie had walked through the school doors a little later, her hair frizzing out of its braid, her eyes roving wildly, he'd looked away. Marcus had snickered and whispered something to Shane. Nate hadn't heard what he said, but it was enough to embarrass him. What if she told everyone that he'd spent his summer going on *adventures*, like a child? That he'd called the ocean *magic*? What if they thought he was dating her? His popularity afforded him everything—teachers favoring him more than he deserved, an easy circle of friends at lunch, coaches letting him run drills.

Now, as though she knew he was staring at her, Janie's eyes lifted from the bookshelf, looked out the window into his. And just as he had that day so long ago, Nate looked away.

CHAPTER NINE

SHANE

....

Thirty-one days before

SHANE CLIMBED THE stairs to Cass's condo and rang the doorbell. He heard her mom from the other side of the door: "Cassie! He's here."

For the better part of five years, Shane had walked Cass to school. There were a few months where he'd driven her, before he totaled the car his parents had given him for his sixteenth birthday and they'd gone back to walking.

He'd known her his whole life, but he hadn't really noticed her until that first day of school in seventh grade. She had returned from volleyball camp with lean triceps stretching from her shoulders to her elbows. She wore a band of stretchy fabric that flattened her gold-tinted curls at the top of her head and behind her ears, but allowed them to explode on the other side like licks of flame. She'd grown gloriously tall, taller even than Shane at the time. There were boobs, too, of course, and black stretchy volleyball shorts that made him want to pull her hips against his own. That year, he'd vowed that he would walk her wherever she needed to go for the rest of their lives.

"Hey," Cass said as she stepped out. He felt like an antenna tuning to her. She was even more beautiful than she'd been back in seventh grade. Her jeans were high-waisted and tight, and her floral top had tiny pearl buttons down the front that gapped and gave him peeks at the lace of her bra.

"Hi, gorgeous."

She flushed slightly, which made her cheeks glow. "Did you study for history?" she asked.

He shrugged.

"Shane."

"Whatcha going to do?"

"Yes, what are *you* going to do?"

They were having this argument more and more often now. His sister, Meg, had left for college this past fall. Cass was heading there too, to study chemistry, probably on a path paved with scholarships. And Shane? Cass thought he should go to a community college for two years before transferring to a university near wherever she ended up. The thought of two to four more years of homework and tests made him nauseated, but what else was there? The navy, like her dad? Becoming a fisherman like Nate's? Constructing houses like Israel's? Would any of that be good enough to keep Cass? It certainly wasn't good enough for his parents. His own dad was a geologist for an oil company and his mom had studied art in

New York before becoming the floral designer for all the big tourist weddings at the historic hotel downtown. They'd both come from money, and their expectations were even higher than Cass's. The real problem was Shane had no clue what he wanted to do with his life.

"Cass, my lass," he said in his Irish accent, which was informed more by Lucky Charms than any actual knowledge of Irish people.

"Yeah, you're not allowed to do that accent."

"Okay, I'll add it to the list."

"Great, put it right after 'don't keep trying to look down my shirt.'" She was smiling now.

"Oh no, I cannot, in good conscience, put that on my list."

"It's not like you haven't seen them before."

"Are you ever like, 'I've seen the ocean before; I never want to see it again'?"

She laughed, and that—more than her looks, more than her intelligence—was what he loved most. It rang through him, and he was always trying to find new ways to inspire it.

It was for that laugh that he'd first stopped at the Seabreeze Cove construction site the second week of seventh grade.

"Let's go inside," he'd said, pointing to a vacation house that was just a skeleton, perched on pilings. They'd had to wrap their arms and legs around the pilings and shinny up, like climbing a palm tree. But once they were up, they'd slipped between the studs and found a room that seemed like a promising kitchen.

"Sit. I'll make you something to eat," he'd said.

Shane had pretended to cook them dinner, and she'd waited for her plate, cross-legged on the floor. The way she'd pursed her lips to blow on an imaginary spoon before taking an imaginary bite had made him tingle from neck to knees. She'd asked Shane about his day and he about hers, and they'd invented jobs for themselves: chemist, professional basketball player, deep-sea diver, architect, international lawyer, cartoonist, psychic hotline operator.

"You want to be a phone psychic?" she'd asked.

"What else am I going to do with these?" he'd said, flexing his long skinny arms.

She'd laughed like it was a surprise—a huff of voice and breath and gravel and bells.

He wished they could go back to the days when he didn't have to be more than a phone psychic to make her laugh like that.

Izzy was waiting for them on the corner a block from school. When she saw them, she tossed her smooth dark hair over one shoulder and smiled. It was fake, like she was posing for a selfie.

"Hey, Cass," she said cheerily. Then: "Shane."

He nodded back.

Izzy was like a terrier who guarded Cass and sunk her needle teeth into him at every chance. *Peahead*, *Neanderthal arms*, *skinny bones*, *paddle ears*, and, if Cass wasn't around,

Reading Rainbow, which never made sense to him because, as far as he knew, the whole point of the old TV show was that the guy liked reading. And, while Shane wasn't illiterate, he certainly wasn't a good reader. He could look at words on a page and understand them. The problem was that once he started stringing the words together for longer and longer stretches, he lost the map and had to wander. It took tracing every single word with his finger as though he were pinning them into his brain, memorizing them really, to get through a page and have any idea what he'd read. And if he was assigned a whole book? Forget it.

In early elementary school, reading specialists had pulled him from class, tested him for dyslexia—which they'd determined he didn't have—and told him to work on reading comprehension and fluency, as though he knew what that meant and could somehow will himself to get better. He saw the looks on other kids' faces when he had to sit at the half-moon table with Mr. Bern and read a picture book while everyone else had moved on to chapter books. He'd been in conferences when Mrs. Palmer told his parents that he needed to try harder and apply himself. It made him feel like a small fist of charcoal, burning with shame.

So he'd started cheating off Nate. And once he'd started doing better on quizzes and tests, Mr. Bern and Mrs. Palmer had left him alone. His parents were so proud. Shane quickly realized that fitting in and surviving school meant collecting more willing friends like Nate, so he started paying attention to kids—popular and unpopular alike. He complimented them, gave them expensive clothes his mom had picked for him, invited them over to his pool, and bought them doughy cafeteria cookies with his over-abundance of allowance. It had worked; here he was, about to be a senior.

But Cass wouldn't understand. She'd tell him he should have advocated for himself more, talked to other teachers, asked for a different kind of help—not understanding what that would have taken from him, how small he'd be now.

Izzy and Shane had the same first period, English, so they dropped Cass off together. He kissed Cass, who was a force to kiss, like locking lips with a tropical storm: salt and rain and power. Izzy stood beside them, making a hairball sound in her throat.

"Oh, you're next," Cass said, pulling Izzy toward them so they were in a weird three-way hug.

"Ew," Izzy said.

Cass stepped into her classroom, giving them a bright smile over her shoulder.

"Shall we, m'lady?" Shane gave a mock bow and offered his arm to Izzy. She rolled her eyes.

Shane had taken Israel—a moody, thin-skinned kid—under his wing at the beginning of high school to get Izzy on his good side. Despite the fact that Israel was now a prince of the school on his way to taking over Wall Street, Izzy was still not impressed with Shane.

When they walked into first period, Shane noticed that Mrs. Gutierrez had written *Vocabulary Quiz* in green letters on the whiteboard. That meant he'd have to sit behind Kyle, whose football bulk could hide Shane from the teacher, and near Javi, a teammate who was happy to tilt his paper.

But Izzy was watching him with a smirk as he settled into the seat. "I don't know if I'd pick Javi," she said.

"What do you mean?" he asked.

"For a vocabulary quiz? He knows, like, three words. *You're-blind-ref.*" She ticked the words off on her fingers.

"I don't know what you're talking about," he said, though he knew his neck was flushing. It always betrayed him. Sometimes he wished he had long hair like Nate to hide it.

"Yeah, you do."

He shrugged. "I just need to stay on the soccer team for our last game. Not get an A."

"Suit yourself," she said, and took a seat in the back corner of the room.

As Mrs. Gutierrez distributed the quizzes, he glanced over his shoulder. Izzy wasn't looking at him, but she did seem to know he was looking at her. Her lips curled up slightly, like she was thinking about something that made her happy. And Shane wondered, uneasily, if she could be thinking about his secret that he couldn't read well. Knowing her, she'd hold on to it and lob it like a grenade into his relationship.

CHAPTER TEN

IZZY

....

The evening of

I CHOOSE THE Kroger right off the public beach as a meeting place because no townies will recognize me and coo about my loss. It's full of summer tourists: flip-flops, board shorts, and bottle-blond hair as far as the eye can see. I order an iced coffee from the Starbucks inside and chew on the straw until Cass shows. She looks terrible and fucking beautiful at the same time because she's Cass. Her hair is a half-braided nest, but she's wrapped a frayed piece of purple silk around it. She's got deep blue half-moons under her eyes and her lips are chapped, but she's in these jeans and a thin black hoodie that make her seem willowy and strong at the same time, like some video game avatar. For a while I thought Israel had a crush on her, but he's always been loyal to Shane, who plucked him from a life of unpopularity. And, despite the one slipup, Cass has always been loyal to Shane, too. What it is about that noodle-armed court jester, I will never know.

Cass wraps her arms around me and squeezes. I squeeze back.

"Why are we here, Iz?"

"Because none of them know us." I nod to the shoppers in their mesh tops and sleeveless man tanks, strolling by with carts of hard lemonade and margarita mix. I can tell she's waiting on me to elaborate, giving me time and space to answer the real why. So patient, that Cass.

"We need to go to the beach," I say. "To where it happened."

Her face hardens until she's all sharp angles. "No," she says quietly.

"Cass, I know you won't understand this, but they're not gone. Israel and Shane and Nate are still out there." I leave out the dolphins for now.

Cass cups my cheek with her palm, and it's simultaneously the kindest and most patronizing gesture she's ever made. "Izzy," she says, looking me straight in the eye. "They pulled his body out of the ocean today, hon. Your parents identified him."

I shake off her hand and gesture at the sliding glass doors. "Just trust me, okay?"

"Izzy, I can't go back there."

"Don't you want to talk to Shane one more time?"

She flinches at his name. "Of course I do."

"You want to know why they were flying that plane, don't you?"

"I do. I just don't believe that going to the beach will help

59

us figure it out," Cass says. "I don't think I'm ready to see it yet," she adds, her voice quiet—almost angry. "Have they even pulled the wreckage out?"

"Okay, you don't have to come." I know that if I start walking, she'll follow. I give her a hug, pretend to say goodbye, and march into the humidity.

I cross the parking lot toward Ocean Drive. Out of my periphery, I see Cass lingering by her mom's car, and I can see it flickering in her face. Love for me. And hurt. Because those fuckers left.

I walk to the light, cross Ocean, and head a block north to confront the memorial that has already been erected. Someone has printed their junior year photos and put them in cheap plastic frames. Israel's smoldering gaze now in black and white. There are more flowers wrapped in shiny paper. Teddy bears, crosses, saint candles, hand-drawn posters with their names. I step over the shit and climb onto the seawall. Police vehicles are still parked on the sand and a large portion of the beach and the water has been cordoned off with a network of cones and buoys. In the distance, outside the orange buoys, a coast guard boat is anchored, bobbing.

The sun sinks behind me, warm on my back. Yesterday, I sat on a blanket beside Cass and watched the sky swirl with colors as the same sun set. Not far from us, Israel was standing ankle-deep in the ocean, holding a Solo cup. Nate was beside him, and Shane was telling a story with his hands, glancing toward Cass every few seconds.

Who knew that sunset would be the last where everything was normal?

"Why were they so stupid?" It's Cass, predictably, at my elbow. Tears are welling in her eyes. She always knows what I'm thinking; she always has.

"They aren't," I say. They are assholes, but they aren't stupid.

"Izzy." Cass grabs my wrist and spins me so I'm facing her. "You know that I love you. More than anything."

I nod.

"Which is why I have to say this to you again: Israel is dead."

Cass is not an ugly-crier. She cries stoically, face immobile, tears shedding freely, silently. But poor, lovely Cass has never felt something that can't be explained rationally. She's never had to. Things just come so naturally for her.

I face the water again, looking for any boats zipping across the waves. I spot one, train my gaze on its wake, and there—one dorsal fin cutting through the wave. Another. A third.

"That's them." I point.

"What?"

"Look behind that boat. The fins."

Cass's jaw drops. She opens her mouth. Shuts it again. Opens it.

"Shhh. Just watch."

And she does, but I can almost feel her disbelief.

"Iz, I think I should take you home." She sounds worried.

"Cass." Now it is my turn to grab her by the wrist. To turn her toward me. I know her better than she knows herself. "You have to believe me. Because the alternative is—the alternative is—" I can't finish because the tears are trying to drown me: hot and gurgling in my throat. I grab my side where I last felt him, pinching the skin so hard I bite my tongue. Cass wraps an arm around my shoulders and walks me back across the street.

CHAPTER ELEVEN

JANIE

....

The evening of

IT'S DARK WHEN I get home—although I'm not sure where the day went. My dad's car is parked under our lofted house. I climb the stairs and peek through the window. He never bothers to shut the flowery curtains that look and smell like they've been there since the seventies, just as he hasn't bothered to replace them. He's snoring in our plaid recliner from Goodwill—I get my frugality from him—with his glasses perched on top of his head and his hairy belly peeking out over stretchy pants.

I open the heavy storm door and let it smack against the siding. He doesn't stir.

His red-blond beard is slightly damp around his lips like he's been drooling. Did he even notice that I was gone?

"Nate died," I say.

Snore.

A little bit louder: "Nate died." Now I'm almost shouting: "Nate died."

Dad snorts awake, snuffles, and grapples on the coffee table for his glasses. Not finding them, he squints at me and tries to swallow a yawn. "What's wrong?"

"Nate died." It's the fourth time now. What charm is naming it four times? What will be kept safe now? What is there left to keep safe?

"What?" he asks.

"Our neighbor."

"I know who he is, Janie." He's irritated. "What happened?"

"Nate, Shane, and Israel. A plane." The words come out jumbled and lumpy. "It was in the air. Ocean. Probably the impact, right? Not drowning. How have you not heard about it? You work at the hospital, for God's sake." Now I'm near tears again. "I tried to find you."

He stares at me, and I can't tell if he gets it. "Oh God. I'm so sorry, Janie-bug," he finally says, sounding shocked. "I heard there was a plane crash, but they weren't saying the names on the news. Poor Roy and Sofia. I can't even imagine."

I hiccup.

"Are you drunk?" he asks.

"You are." I say it like an insult, but he nods. If he's anything, he's an honest drunk.

"You didn't drive, did you?"

"No," I say.

"Where's your phone? Why didn't you call?"

"I lost it at the beach. Why didn't you try to find me?" I want to collapse and nestle beside him in the recliner like I would when my mom read to me as a child—*Little Women*; *Black Beauty*; *The Lion, the Witch and the Wardrobe*—but I feel my stomach surging again. The heave of nothing that still manages to hurt like hell.

"Janie?"

I jog to the bathroom, wrap my arms around the porcelain basin, and lean into the bleachy smell of toilet water. One heave. Two. Nothing comes up, but my stomach, my throat, everything is seizing.

A cold, wet towel is around my neck, and a hand is on my back drawing clumsy circles. "Oh, sweetie," my dad says softly. The towel smells pleasantly of lavender—certainly not because of my dad or me, but because our housekeeper, Lori, comes once a week to clean and do laundry.

"How did they learn to fly a plane?" Dad asks.

The question is gentle, possibly rhetorical, but I snap: "Clearly they didn't."

He pauses briefly, perhaps stung, but resumes the lazy circles on my back. I spit into the toilet.

"The better question," I say, my throat raw, "is why they were flying a plane in the first place."

CHAPTER TWELVE

NATE

·······························

Thirty-one days before

COACH MANTLE HAD put out the mesh jerseys after school, which meant they were scrimmaging. He tossed the jerseys at the varsity starters, including Nate, and waved the second string onto the field. Shane and Israel jogged onto the field together, laughing, and Nate felt a quick tug of jealousy. They'd been friends with Israel since freshman year, but Shane had been Nate's best friend since before he could remember. His mom had pictures of them at daycare together, covered in finger paint.

Nate sat on the bench, smoothing his hair back into a tight ponytail.

"Bryan and Colby, you're strikers. Nate, Javi, and Aiden, I want you at midfield," Coach called. "You have one game left, so make today count."

As a midfielder, Nate's job was to be everywhere at once,

to fill gaps in his team's defense, to punch holes in the opposing team's defense, to set up goals, and his favorite—to chase down opponents. When an opponent got a breakaway, Nate could feel the kick of energy in his calves, the horsepower in his quads. He was the fastest on their team, and probably on all the teams they played against. As long as he stayed in game shape this summer, he was certain he'd impress the scouts at camp.

Nate took position, pinning one arm across his chest to stretch his shoulder before switching sides.

Shane was pulling on his gloves. He had been the varsity second-string goalie since sophomore year, and occasionally Coach had him start for low-stakes games. He had the height and a huge wingspan, but he wasn't as aggressive or scrappy as their starter.

Israel took his spot on the midfield line. He was striker for the opposing team, which Nate thought was a poor choice. Israel liked to play offense so he could score, but he was a much better defensive player. Lately he'd been asking Nate to come practice penalty kicks with him on weekends. He'd been hungry for Nate's shooting tips, which was flattering, but also strangely competitive—as though he were chomping at Nate's heels.

When Coach blew the whistle, Travis tapped the ball to Israel, who immediately started dribbling, a selfish move this early in the game. Nate began jockeying him, forcing him toward the field boundary.

"That's my Jack!" Coach shouted. He'd nicknamed Nate after a Jack Russell because he could be obsessively persistent, dogging a forward until he stepped out of bounds or made a mistake.

Nate could tell Israel was getting anxious, that he was knocking the ball farther and farther in front of him as he moved down the sideline. Nate positioned himself to block off Israel's passing lanes, so when Israel stopped, shielding the ball with his body, and tried to pivot, Nate was already there. Israel set the ball up for a desperate pass, and Nate dove in.

He took the ball easily and was off, dribbling as fast as he could, his T-shirt flapping against his skin. In his periphery, he could see his teammates advancing with him, positioning themselves so they were ready for his pass. He could hear Israel behind him too, panting. Nate squared up with Danh, a big defender who was a little too slow for first string but could be a mountain when you needed it.

"Me, me, me," Nate's striker, Colby, said, from the top of the box. Shane had stepped out of the goal, and was hunched slightly, arms out—ready for a leap. The angle was right—Nate could pass to Colby, who'd knock it right behind Shane.

But Nate couldn't pass because he was suddenly on his side, cheek planted in the grass. There was a searing pain in his right knee, like someone had peeled his kneecap clean off. Nate tried to think, tried to remember what had happened, but there was a blinding white light behind his eyes. He was dizzy with it. He rolled onto his back and tried to clasp his knee to his stomach, but the motion made him retch. He turned his head to the side and spit stomach acid into the grass.

There were figures standing above him. Shane. Israel. Some of the others.

"What are you doing down there, little doggy?" Shane asked. He was trying to make Nate laugh, but his expression changed when he saw Nate's face. Israel stood beside Shane, a shorter, stockier shadow. His heavy brows were drawn together, like he was trying to puzzle something out. Nate felt dread pooling at the base of his throat. The pain was bad. Too bad.

"Talk to me, Nate." This from Coach. "Do you need to go to the trainer?"

Nate found his voice, forced it out through his teeth. "I just need a minute."

"Get him inside, boys," Coach said.

Nate pushed himself up on his elbows and looked down at his leg. His knee looked fine, didn't it? Israel and Shane crouched, each sliding an arm under his and pulling him up onto his good foot. Nate tentatively put weight on his injured leg, but it immediately buckled, pain sawing through him. He groaned at the shock of it, bit his lip to feel pain somewhere else in his body—to misdirect his mind.

Shane and Israel helped Nate hop across the student parking lot and into the school. "I'm so sorry, man," Israel said.

Nate grunted. He remembered feeling a cleat against his right ankle. Israel's cleat. The slide tackle had driven his ankle in one direction, while momentum forced his weight—and his knee—in another.

Janie was sitting on the bench outside the front office with a stopwatch as they approached. She appeared to be practicing something—probably the speech for Mrs. Gutierrez's English class, which they had during different periods.

The trainer's office door was closed.

"Fuck, he's not here," Shane said.

Nate was starting to feel a little dizzy. He pointed at the bench where Janie sat and the guys shuffled him over there.

"We'll go find him," Israel said, and started toward the gym. Shane took another hallway toward the track.

"What happened?" Janie asked as soon as the guys were out of sight.

"My knee," he said, and then gritted his teeth again.

"Should we go see my dad?" she asked. "I can drive you." Her braid was crooked, and she was wearing a gray PE uniform T-shirt like she'd forgotten to change after the class or had lost her real shirt in the locker room, which wouldn't have surprised Nate.

"Where's your shirt?" Nate asked.

Janie looked confused.

"Your shirt," he said again, insistent. "You were wearing that orange bowling one earlier."

Janie paused a moment. "You noticed what I wore to school today?"

Nate felt the contents of his stomach rock back and forth. He imagined a wave pool. Up one side. Down the other. He must have moaned because Janie stood.

"We'll call him from the car. Come on." She slid under Nate's arm and lifted him to his feet. She was strong.

Israel rounded the corner, shaking his head. "I couldn't find him. Shane's still looking?"

Nate felt Janie freeze beneath his arm. They'd never been caught together before. His stomach rocked again, but this time it wasn't from the knee. What was he supposed to say?

But Janie spoke first, directly to Israel. "Can you help me get him to my car? My dad's a doctor."

Israel took his spot beneath Nate's arm again, without seeming surprised at Janie's involvement. Nate felt a flash of relief, which was quickly erased by the pain in his knee.

They hobbled back out of the school and into the parking lot where Janie's hatchback was parked. Nate's knee was pulsing now, the pain blinking on and off and becoming brighter each time. Now he felt cold, too. The vomit surged up his esophagus.

He wiped his mouth and realized that Janie's shirt was splattered yellow. "That's why you changed it," he said, his throat burning from the bile. "Because you knew I'd throw up on you."

Janie laughed and pulled her gym shirt off—right there in front of Israel. She was wearing a blue stretched-out sports bra, and her belly was the softest, palest thing Nate had ever seen.

She blotted his mouth with the clean inside of the shirt and tossed it in her trunk.

Israel reclined the passenger seat all the way back. "Keep your right leg as straight as you can," he told Nate. "Pretend you're doing a one-legged squat on your left and lower yourself down. Sit sideways and we can lift your legs in." Nate tried to keep all the instructions in his head at once, but they slipped out. He practically dove headfirst into the seat, and pain shot all the way up his body. It made him squeeze his eyes shut and utter an *Uhhhhh* sound.

When Nate opened his eyes again, Janie's dad was leaning into the car and rubbing his beard. They were in the roundabout in front of the hospital where people dropped off patients.

"Your mom is almost here," he told Nate.

Nate's brain seemed to only be able to think in colors— red every time his knee pulsed and the cool leafy green of that Maryland soccer field—when he thought about what he might lose.

"Will I play soccer again?" Nate asked.

His tongue felt like rubber, but Janie's dad smiled sadly at him as though he understood. "Let's figure out what's going on with your knee first." Nate let his head roll back onto the head-rest. Dread the color of ice was expanding inside him, pushing outward on his windpipe. Choking him.

REMEMBERED SOULS FORUM

....

GULF COAST

BTS4U: Hi! New here. Jumping on this thread to introduce myself. I'll follow suit and share my death.

I think I was a teenage boy—17 or 18. I made it on time for the 3:07 from Jasper. I jumped the fence and stuck to the tree line along the tracks. I assume I needed to stay hidden so they didn't get me on trespass. The 3:07 was going to be my chance to get away from my bastard of an older brother, Charlie. I don't remember what he did to me—just that I hated his guts.

I heard the 3:07 sounding its horn as it crossed through town. Once it cleared town, it sped up, so I had to be ready to catch it before it got going too fast. It chattered and roared up to where I crouched. The conductor was oblivious to me, so I took off running. A livestock car flew by first. It smelled of pig and wet hay. It was followed by a few closed cars—probably coal. The first empty one I saw, I flung my bag and ran hard like back when

I raced in school. But the fall leaves were slick from rain, and they churned under me like I was a cartoon character on a banana peel. I slipped and that was it. I must have gotten caught under the wheels.

Here's my question for the group: Why do I remember? Why do *we* remember?

CHAPTER THIRTEEN

ISRAEL

....

Thirty-one days before

ISRAEL COULDN'T SHAKE the sinking feeling in his stomach as he unlaced his cleats and slid them off. It was a perfectly legal slide tackle—he'd gone for the ball, not Nate. But now Nate could barely walk. He'd thrown up. It was serious. And accident or not—Israel was to blame.

He opened a group message with Nate and Shane.

`Hey, Nate. You okay?` he typed. `I'm so sorry.`

Shane was talking with some teammates a few feet away. His blond hair was wet with sweat, and he was stretching one of his quads, pulling his foot behind him and balancing with a hand on Javi's shoulder. He made it look so easy—to gather people around him, to let himself be admired.

He must have heard the text message notification because he dropped his foot and pulled his phone out of his soccer bag.

The doctors say anything yet? he texted to the thread, and then looked up and met Israel's eyes.

"You wanna come over?" he called out. "Cass is bringing a pizza."

Before Shane and Nate, Israel hadn't had many friends. Just a few bookish kids who were in Mr. Swanson's board game club. One day in eighth grade, he'd been walking home alone—Izzy was in detention—wearing new headphones and Js his dad had bought him. Something hard had struck him at the base of his skull. He'd tripped forward onto his stomach, scraping his chin on the gravel. When he'd tried, dizzily, to push himself onto his knees, someone had kicked him in the side. He'd curled into a knot, but the pendejos had ripped his headphones from his head and pried off his shoes.

Someone had shouted and he'd heard the scuff of gravel as his attackers ran away. It was Shane who'd yelled, who'd helped him to his feet and loaned him his bike so that he could ride home shoeless.

"Do you mind not telling anyone about this?" Israel had asked, embarrassed, when he returned Shane's bike the next day. Izzy had known, of course, because she'd felt his pain in her side and sprinted home from detention, earning herself an in-school suspension.

"No problem, man," Shane had said, shrugging like it wasn't a big deal.

"Is there anything I can do to thank you?" Israel asked.

"Hmmm. Not really. Just buy me one of those doughy cookies at lunch."

So Israel had, expecting that that would be it, but when he'd delivered the cookie to Shane's table, Shane had scooted closer to Nate and offered Israel a seat. Shane had never stopped giving, and Israel did what he could to give back: answers to test questions, rides, and plenty of distance from Cass—who he'd had a crush on since Izzy adopted her as her best friend back in kindergarten.

Israel stuffed his cleats into his bag and shook his head at Shane. He couldn't eat pizza with Cass and Shane and pretend everything was fine. "I'll give you guys some space," he said.

Shane frowned slightly. "Are you sure?"

"Yeah. I'll text you later."

Shane nodded. "See ya."

Israel slung his bag over his shoulder. Truthfully, he wanted to go home and lie down, but his exhausted body would probably fall asleep immediately, cueing the dream. And, undoubtedly, Izzy would be home and want to know what was wrong.

Her twinsense had started to bother him in elementary school. Their teachers had kept them in separate classes—it was supposed to inspire them to be independent—but it hadn't stopped Izzy from showing up to save him. Like the time Carmen Mendoza had teased him for a dried mustard stain on his shirt during the class party for her birthday. Israel's old house didn't have a washer and dryer, so he and Izzy had to re-wear their uniforms in between weekly trips to the washeteria.

Not a minute after Israel had teared up at the insult, Izzy had barged into the room.

"What's wrong?" she'd asked.

He'd dropped his eyes, blushing, but she'd pried the story out of someone else in the class and then popped every single one of Carmen's birthday balloons with the tip of her pencil. As she was being ushered out by Mrs. Anderson, Israel had tried to shrink into his desk and disappear.

After years of being told that her twinsense was an invasion of his privacy, she'd mostly stopped coming to his rescue—except in her sleep. She still knew when he was upset, though, and always asked about it, so if Israel needed space, it was just easier for him to stay away.

He pulled up Lara's address on his phone again. Even looking at it on a map made his heart flutter with nerves. It was on the mainland, only an hour away. There'd be no harm if he just went to look.

Unlike the lofted homes of their island, Lara's house was low and flat. It sat in a subdivision of new ranch-style homes, which seemed to come in just four models, each a different shade of tan. Some had kidney-shaped pools and others had pergolas that seemed useless for blocking the sun. Lara's house had neither, but it did have a two-car garage and two large aloe plants standing like sentries on each side of the path leading to her front door.

Israel parked down the block and sank in his seat. This seemed like the kind of neighborhood where someone might notice him and call the police. He pretended to be busy on his phone, keeping one eye on the house. There weren't any texts from Nate yet; he would have written by now if everything was okay. Or would he only write if it wasn't? Israel tried not to think about it.

Though Shane was the one who'd ushered Israel into popularity, Nate and Israel had more in common with each other. Nate was clever; he could deliver a joke so straight-faced, you weren't entirely sure if it was a joke. Once you got it, though, he'd give a lopsided smile—like he was half sad it had taken you so long. Israel was convinced that, if Nate applied himself even a little at school, he'd probably be near the top of their class. The thing about Nate was that he didn't seem to care much about school. He wasn't pretending not to care like so many other people in their grade—he simply didn't. Soccer was it for him. Israel had given him the University of Maryland pamphlet trying to be a good friend. He had thought that if soccer got Nate into college, he might start to care about doing something else. Israel may as well have ripped the pamphlet back out of his hand.

Israel glanced at Lara's house. Still no movement, so he opened Remembered Souls and scrolled to see if there were any new posts.

There was a user he'd been following since he'd joined a few months back. Unlike most, OtherPlanes remembered more than one of his past lives. In one, he'd lived as a wolf on the Great Plains, before the white settlers. He said the memories were less clear than when he'd had a human consciousness, but that he remembered a lightning storm and the stink of his pack's fear. He remembered his pack cornering an injured buffalo, and the sound of its bellow. And he remembered howling, a cry that sprang automatically from his throat when he heard other howls. *There's something magical about being part of a collective*, OtherPlanes had written. Israel had never forgotten that line. He felt the same way about Shane and Nate. As a little kid, he'd been bullied for being poor, for being chubby and hairy, for being too serious and meek. He'd never imagined that someday he'd have friends like Shane and Nate.

Israel appreciated that OtherPlanes didn't just write about his past lives or deaths, like the other users; he shared his theories, too.

Earlier that day someone had responded to a thread asking why people in the group remembered their past lives. OtherPlanes had been quick to offer an explanation.

> **OtherPlanes:** My theory is we have restless, hungry souls. While everyone else waits their turns for a blank slate body, we badger our way in and try again.
>
> **BumblerX9:** But why are we restless?
>
> **OtherPlanes:** I think we can't seem to get

it right. That's why we remember: so we can
try again.

What if Israel could figure out what his soul hadn't
gotten right in the last life? Could he fix it? Would that
finally stop this awful recurring dream?

Motion caught Israel's eye ahead. A silver pickup was
backing out of Lara's garage. He ducked lower in his seat. The
driver—a light-haired wiry man with a barely there beard—
never glanced his way. But Israel could see that the man was
cringing at the road in front of him like it was too bright out.

Peter.

Israel put his car in drive and followed, hanging back a
few hundred feet. Peter turned out of the neighborhood and
drove to a grocery store near the highway. After he parked,
Israel chose a spot on the other side of the lot. In the rearview
mirror, he watched the man climb out and gather reusable grocery bags. He glanced once toward Israel's car, and Israel froze,
heart thudding, but Peter continued to the entrance without
another look.

Following this man wasn't going to help him fix whatever
his soul had gotten wrong. He had to talk to Peter and Lara and
gain their trust. Israel pulled up their photos again. Lara, with
her solemn face, almost dared him to fool her. There was something gentler about Peter's expression: not so much gullible as
hopeful.

It wasn't hard to find the man's email address with a quick

search, or to come up with a white lie about why Israel was emailing. It was much harder to press send, to take the shot in the dark.

Dear Mr. Ryerson,

I'm a student at the University of Houston working on a thesis on trauma and grief. I'm especially interested in studying people who have lost loved ones to a traumatic incident. I saw your father's accident referenced in newspaper archives. Would you mind answering a few questions?

Israel J. Castillo

CHAPTER FOURTEEN

SHANE

....

Thirty-one days before

SHANE STRETCHED OUT on his back, hanging his head over the edge of his bed so it was beside Cass's. She was sitting on the floor, leaning against the bed with his chemistry book in her lap. He kissed her cheek, a purposefully slobbery one, and she wrinkled her nose and shoved him away.

"What are covalent bonds?" she asked, sounding bored. She was in AP Chemistry, so this was just basics to her.

Shane searched his memory. *Covalent bonds. Covalent bonds.* Something about electrons? "What do you want to do for the long weekend?" he asked her instead of answering.

"I have a volleyball tournament in Austin, remember?"

"Oh. Yeah." He felt a throb of disappointment. Weekends were starting to feel like a precious resource that was evaporating. How many more easy days would he get to spend hosting Cass, Nate, Israel, and the rotating cast of peripheral friends at his house? His parents turned a blind eye while they sprawled on towels by the pool, blared music from his dad's sound system, drank everything in the house, and snuck quickies in the humid garage, legs tangled in swimsuit bottoms, heads buzzing from the smell of motor oil. He loved being the center of it all, filling Solo cups with rum and pineapple juice, grilling hot dogs, orchestrating water volleyball and flip cup, keeping smiles on everyone's faces. Especially Cass's, which, after hours outside, shone like she was a sun lion.

"So, covalent bonds?" Cass prompted.

He rolled onto his stomach to see down her shirt. Her breasts bloomed over her bra cups.

"Why don't you come up here?" he asked, letting his voice drop drowsily. It was the wrong move.

She twisted around, practically knocking skulls with him. "Shane, Jesus."

"What?"

"First of all, your mom is downstairs. Second of all, I'm trying to help you study for this test. Please don't waste my time. You know I can't afford college without scholarships."

"I didn't know I was such a waste."

She rolled her eyes. "I didn't mean it like that. It's just that we weren't all born rich."

He shrugged. What really seemed like a waste was all this time he had to spend worrying about staying eligible for the soccer team and going to college and planning out his entire future. Was he the only one who felt his youth beating impatiently inside him? The only one who could taste it, buttery on his tongue? "I wish this were easier," he said.

Her eyes fell. "I know," she said softly. She didn't, though. No one thought Cass was anything less than perfect. Cass, the kind. Cass, the generous. Cass, the intelligent.

"Don't you want to get better at it? On your own?" she asked.

That "on your own" bit made him wary. Had Izzy told her about him cheating to keep his grades up? "Sometimes I just wish we could go back to seventh grade. Don't you?" he said. "We didn't have a care in the world when we played in those houses." He reached for her arm and traced the vein from her wrist up her forearm to make her smile.

That's what he'd done the first time they kissed, inside one of the under-construction houses. She'd shivered under his finger and he'd pulled her toward him. He hadn't been prepared for her gale-force kiss in return, the way she'd slipped her tongue into his mouth and raked her teeth against his lip. He'd grown hard instantly.

Heart stopped.

No air.

Died in love.

Unfortunately, he'd had to pee. The annoying pressure in his bladder brought him back and, frankly, saved him from shuddering against her and coming in his jeans right there. That probably would have altered history.

But this time, she pulled her arm away and scooped him

out of the memory. "No," she said. "I like where I'm at now. I feel more comfortable with myself." She closed the book, shifted onto her knees, and pecked him on the lips. "I'm going home."

"Please stay. Are you mad at me?" A little whine crept into his voice. He couldn't help it. Lately he'd felt the gravity weakening between them. She could easily spin off into her own galaxy, leaving him with all her insignificant moons. It made him want to hold on to her that much tighter.

She shook her head. "I have to study for calculus. I need to focus."

When he heard her say goodbye to his mom downstairs, he rolled back over and closed his eyes. She deserved everything she dreamed of. He just wished he deserved it too—or even knew what he wanted.

His phone buzzed. It was Israel, checking on Nate again. Shane pulled up Nate's social media, which was usually flooded with hilarious videos and memes he shared from other accounts. There were no new posts. Shane messaged Aaron, who was a freshman at the same university Meg attended.

```
Hey, dude. Just wondering if your bro is
okay.
```

```
Mom said he has a torn ACL. Has to have surgery
```
once school is over, Aaron wrote.

`Fuck`, Shane texted back. What else was there to say? They'd been playing together on traveling teams since fourth grade. Nate was a wonder to watch—the way he drove his body down the field, precise as a blade.

`Think he's home yet?` Shane asked.

`Yeah, he is.`

Shane jogged down the stairs. His dad was offshore, but his mom was at their dining table, which had become a craft station littered with rolls of floral tape, pins, and green foam. The blooms for tomorrow's event were in the kitchen sink. Their house always smelled like greenery. "Gotta go to Nate's," he told her.

"What about chemistry? Cass said you have a test." She was carefully trimming the thorns off a yellow rose and didn't look up.

"Not as important." And it wasn't. Shane's friends helped him survive school, and he owed them all that he could give in return.

She pressed her lips like she was blotting lipstick. It was something his sister always did too, especially on the volleyball court when her team was losing. "What's your plan, Shane?" she asked. "Cass told me she's applying to my alma mater."

Columbia? Cass hadn't told him that. It was far, but what did he expect? That she'd stay close enough to see him on the weekends? Maybe. A little.

"Mom, Nate's knee is broken. I don't have time to talk about college plans."

"Soon, then. We'll do a few visits once you're out of school."

He couldn't imagine a worse prospect than trailing behind his mom on college tours, her posing questions about dining plans and course requirements and him wondering if he could do it—make new friends all over again and cheat his way through more school. What he said was, "Yeah, maybe."

When Nate's dad swung the door open, Shane was struck by the stench of fish and sweat, his scent during the long tourist season. He wore his usual uniform for fishing tours and charters: a T-shirt that advertised an island surf shop, and holey jeans.

"Hey, buddy. Good to see you." He gave Shane a quick squeeze on the shoulder.

"How's he doing?"

"Not great, unfortunately." He waved Shane inside. "Warning: he's on some painkillers."

Nate was sprawled on the couch, his leg propped up on throw pillows, his body relaxed like he was asleep. A pair of crutches leaned against the arm of the couch.

"Hey, man," he said sleepily.

"Hey."

"My leg's fucked." He laughed, a loud cackle Shane had never heard before. Usually, his friend bottled up his laughs, kept them contained behind a tight-lipped smile so they wheezed inside him and shook his shoulders. This laugh was loud and almost villainous.

"How are you feeling?" Shane asked cautiously.

"Like a million bucks."

At least there was still that sarcasm Shane knew. "I'm sorry this happened."

"Me too." Nate closed his eyes. "I don't know what I'll do after senior year now."

"You've got a long time to figure that out."

"Nah. I don't," Nate said. "You don't either."

"God, did my mom call you?" Shane asked with a laugh. "Or Cass?"

"Yeah, they've got me saved as a favorite. Always texting me like, 'Hey, you up?'"

Shane laughed. "I think we're both fucked."

"At least your knee works."

"Yep, me and my golden knee are going to rule this crumb of an island."

"King of the crumb," Nate said, lifting his hand as though he were going to cheers Shane with a drink.

"*Kings* of the crumb," Shane said back, knocking his imaginary cup into Nate's. Shane held his grin—for Nate—but he was starting to feel like everything was teetering. If the world tipped an inch more, he was going to lose his grip.

CHAPTER FIFTEEN

NATE

....

Thirty days before

JANIE CAME OVER after school wearing battered Birkenstocks, a tie-dyed T-shirt that said Camp Karankawa, and a gray skirt that fell to the tops of her ankles. She had a canvas tote bag hanging over her shoulder, a yoga mat across her back, and a paper plate wrapped in plastic in her hands. He opened the door and tried to smile like this was any other day.

"Brought your books," she said, lifting her shoulder with the canvas tote bag. "You know, so you can study for finals."

"Study? That sounds awful. I'm supposed to be convalescing," Nate said, trying to keep his tone light.

She laughed and pushed the plate into his hands. It felt unusually heavy. "Mmm. Hockey pucks. My favorite."

"Oatmeal raisin, you ass."

"Gee, thanks," he said. "I'll call up Nana and tell her you made her some cookies."

She put her hands on her hips in mock anger. "Nana Herschel wishes she could eat my cookies."

"Well, she certainly needs the fiber."

Rolling her eyes, Janie pushed aside the coffee table and then unrolled the yoga mat for him. Dr. Dennis had scheduled Nate's surgery to repair his ACL for summer break and sent Nate home with crutches and some prehab exercises to strengthen his muscles. Yes, he might play soccer again, Janie's dad had said, but it could be a year or two. And even then, his knee may never be like it once was.

Janie read from the packet of exercises her dad had printed: "Okay, for the first one, you have to lie on your back and slide your heel toward you and then away."

He set down the cookies, hopped to the mat, and lowered himself. It smelled like a hot day at the beach, like brine and dried seaweed.

"Count," she said, and he did, exhaling each number with a grimace. His knee ached, and the dread was still there, tight against his throat. A pinprick and it would all leak out.

What was he supposed to do without soccer?

He tried to push away the question. To forget about the scouts at camp this summer. The cool green grass of Maryland. The dream of standing on the field, hand on his heart as they played the national anthem before his first professional start. But there was nothing else to think about. Not with his knee throbbing so much it felt like there was a bright light behind his eyes.

"Tell me about Maryland," he said.

She flinched at the name like he'd thrown it at her. He braced himself for her to snap, but she didn't. "Maryland," she repeated softly.

"What was it like?"

She was quiet a moment, and Nate wondered if she was thinking of her mother. "It could be hot and humid in the summer like here, but it never lasted as long," she said finally. "And, in the winter, it would snow. Sometimes a lot."

He smiled at this, imagining snowflakes falling from the ceiling, kissing his skin—light and cold. It never snowed on their island.

"Next one," she said. "Bridges."

He dug his heels into the mat and lifted his pelvis. "Did you live near the ocean?" he asked through gritted teeth.

"Not that close. We'd go to Ocean City sometimes, though. They have these french fries on the boardwalk that they serve in paper cones with malt vinegar."

Nate could taste the sourness and salt on the back of his tongue. He dropped his hips with a gasp. "Let's watch TV," he said.

"You've still got to do the glute ones," she said.

"Yeah, yeah, you want me to get a good ass."

She blushed, but still managed to throw it back. "Everyone wishes you had a better ass, Nate. It's flatter than our island." She grew serious again. "Don't you think you should follow my dad's instructions so you won't regret it after the surgery?"

He shrugged. "It doesn't matter what happens after."

Janie could miss social cues sometimes, but she didn't now. She helped him to the couch, then dragged the coffee table back over and positioned a pillow on top so he could prop up his knee. Once seated, she kicked her feet up next to his and wiggled her toes unselfconsciously. They both sank down, their heads pushed back into the cushions, which had long ago become dented with their bodies. While he waited for the apps on the TV to load, he stared out the window, which faced the front porch, the street a story below, and the beach—if you managed to see beyond blocks of interceding houses.

"You wanna drive to the beach? Just sit on a blanket or something, for old times' sake?" Janie asked.

When he was younger, the beach had pulled at him the way the moon pulled at the ocean. Maybe he'd grown out of it later than everyone else, but he *had* eventually grown out of going on adventures there. Now he only went to the beach for the occasional party.

"Nah. It feels like a hot, damp washcloth out there," he said. The joy of going to the beach was something he'd lost without even noticing. Was that all life was? A string of losses— both unnoticed and deeply felt—that you dragged behind yourself like a broken tail?

The dread crept from his throat and settled cold and heavy on his chest. Thinking about it was only making it heavier, compressing each breath into a quick gasp. He felt like he wasn't getting enough air.

"Are you okay?" Janie asked.

Nate nodded and tried to inhale slowly and deeply like the instructors in the yoga videos his mom did each night. He just needed to empty his brain and lose himself in a TV show he'd seen a million times before. He scrolled through the episodes of an old show about a group of disgruntled employees in an office. The show always made Janie cackle—an eruption of sound that shook the couch.

He pressed play and pasted a smile on his face, pretending like nothing at all had changed. When, in fact, everything had.

EMAIL THREAD

From: IsraelJCastillo@youremail.com
To: PRyerson984@LyteCorp.com
Subject: Research Question

Dear Mr. Ryerson,

    I'm a student at the University of Houston working on a thesis on trauma and grief. I'm especially interested in studying people who have lost loved ones to a traumatic incident. I saw your father's accident referenced in newspaper archives. Would you mind answering a few questions?

                    Israel J. Castillo

From: PRyerson984@LyteCorp.com
To: IsraelJCastillo@youremail.com
Subject: RE: Research Question

    Ok. What do you want to know?

                    —Peter

From: IsraelJCastillo@youremail.com
To: PRyerson984@LyteCorp.com
Subject: RE: RE: Research Question

Peter,

Thank you so much for your willingness to participate. Can you tell me what you remember about the accident?

Israel J. Castillo

From: PRyerson984@LyteCorp.com
To: IsraelJCastillo@youremail.com
Subject: RE: RE: RE: Research Question

I was 12 so I don't know much about the accident. It happened on a curve a few miles from our house. My mom said it was rainy and he was going too fast. His car slipped into the lane of an oncoming car. There was a vehicle fire and the rain wasn't heavy enough to extinguish it.

From: IsraelJCastillo@youremail.com
To: PRyerson984@LyteCorp.com
Subject: RE: RE: RE: RE: Research Question

Peter,

Thank you. Can you provide a little more context about your father? What did he do? Do you have a photo of him I might include in my paper?

Israel J. Castillo

From: PRyerson984@LyteCorp.com
To: IsraelJCastillo@youremail.com
Subject: RE: RE: RE: RE: RE: Research Question

He was a country veterinarian who specialized in farm animals. We lived on a ranch outside Honore, so we always had a ton of goats, pigs, chickens, dogs, and barn cats.

<Attached photo shows a small boy in the lap of a tall man with a pencil-thin mustache. The boy is holding a chick in his cupped hands and the man is leaning over his shoulder, angling his face toward the boy, so you can't see much of his expression.>

—Peter

From: IsraelJCastillo@youremail.com
To: PRyerson984@LyteCorp.com

Subject: RE: RE: RE: RE: RE: RE: Research Question

Peter,

Would you be willing to meet in person so I can ask more questions? I need to know more about your relationship to analyze your response to the trauma.

Israel J. Castillo

From: PRyerson984@LyteCorp.com
To: IsraelJCastillo@youremail.com
Subject: RE: RE: RE: RE: RE: RE: RE: Research Question

Who is this really? Why are you so interested in my father?

CHAPTER SIXTEEN

IZZY

....

Two days after

LUNA PACES OUTSIDE my room. She's looking for Israel.
I get it; I am too. But it makes me feel like there's a centipede
under my skin because every time her nails click by on the
tile, I'm reminded that he's gone.

I fling open the door. "He's—not—here!" I yell—even
though she can't hear what I'm saying and wouldn't understand me if she could. She wags at me, lifting her head so that
I'll scratch under her chin.

"I'm not Israel." I nudge her away with my knee and
knock on my parents' door. My mom hasn't left her room in
twenty-four hours.

"Hey, mami, are you . . ." But I can't finish the question.
"Can I come in?" I say instead.

"Sí," she finally says, her voice hollow. I push open the

door and Luna springs in, probably excited to have a new room to search.

"La perra hiede," my mom says—though the room smells far worse than Luna, like sweat and sleep breath. She's curled under the blankets, her spine to me, her hair a stiff nest.

I swing open the French doors that lead to their balcony. It's hotter outside, but the air is fresh at least and you can hear the ocean several blocks away. I step out and Luna follows, sniffing the ground as though she's on his trail. It feels like we're on top of the world in this house. It's two stories stacked on a garage that our old house could have fit inside.

I inhale and try to imagine that Israel, wherever he is, is hearing the same crash of waves, smelling the same mix of dead fish and salt and seaweed. Like we're characters from our favorite childhood movie—*Fievel Goes West*. When Fievel and Tanya are separated, they sing "Somewhere Out There," and it comforts both of them to know that they are wishing on the same bright star. I think of Israel and me, wishing on the same ocean right now. The thought settles the centipedes under my skin a little.

"It's too bright," my mom calls from inside. "Shut it."

I shoo Luna back inside and climb into bed to spoon my mom, but she's radiating so much heat I scoot back to the edge of the mattress. Who knew grief could feel like fire?

"Mami, do you believe that our souls can live inside other things, like animals?" I drag my fingers through her streaked-honey hair, working out the small knots at the ends.

She rolls onto her back so she can see my face, and I realize she hasn't looked at me since Israel disappeared. For our entire lives, our parents invested their hopes and dreams in Israel. He was the hard worker, the quiet, responsible one. I have always been the loud troublemaker. I shouldn't be surprised they're disappointed that I'm the one who's left.

"Catholics don't believe in reincarnation," she says.

"Well, we're barely Catholic," I say. "I'd call us Catholic-lite." What I don't say: Israel was definitely an atheist.

"Dile a tu abuelo." *Tell that to your grandfather.* Her father is one of our few relatives who still lives in Venezuela. He comes to stay with us for a month every few years, and, when he does, it's Mass at the Cathedral Basilica twice a week.

There are creases beneath my mother's eyes that I've never seen before. They make her skin look brittle, like it might snap to pieces if she smiled. Not that she would.

"Why do you ask?"

"I was thinking about how Israel would have that dream," I say.

She covers her face with her arm.

"¿Recuerdas?" I prod.

"I remember," she answers, her voice muffled.

Israel and I couldn't have been more than four or five, belted in the back seat of my dad's pickup truck. He was tracing the path of a rain droplet down the car window. I'm not sure why I remember that detail.

"It was raining like this when I crashed," he said casually—almost dreamily.

"You crashed, Israel?" our mom responded from the front seat. She was applying makeup using the mirror on the back of the sun visor while we drove to some event. A birthday party? A baptism?

"A long time ago," he said. "I was getting medicine for my son, Peter."

My parents glanced at each other, and our mom turned around in her seat to face us; one eyelid was plain and the other had been shaded in blue. "What an imagination you have," she said. My dad's eyes kept flicking to the rearview mirror so he could see us. He has dark, expressive eyes like Israel's, but in those short flashes, I couldn't tell what he was thinking.

"We'll be careful driving," our mom said.

"That's what I told Lara," Israel said. "My wife."

I don't remember if the conversation continued, but I do remember his nightmares did. Back then we shared a walk-in closet my father had converted into a bedroom. In his dreams, Israel rolled back and forth like he was on fire, and mumbled nonsensically. Was it this Lara person he was talking to? Or his son, Peter?

I'm guessing we didn't have money or insurance for a shrink at the time, so my parents took him to see a friend who was a doctor on the mainland. They moved him onto the pull-out couch in the living room so he wouldn't wake me anymore.

But I could still feel his terror—sharp along my right side—as we were getting ready to go to bed. After the move, I'd wake spooning him on the couch with no memory of having gone to comfort him. Once we had our own rooms, he'd lock the door to keep me out, and I started waking up right outside—sleepwalking to be near him.

It's why Janie's script got my attention last fall in film class. I'd picked her for our group because she'd told the class she wanted to be a screenwriter, and I thought she'd do most of the heavy lifting, leaving Cass and me to act. She surprised me by turning in a script about an old man who takes his granddaughter to the aquarium after his wife dies. The man sees an orca and believes the whale has been inhabited by his wife's soul. He thinks he can tell her everything he always meant to say. In the final scene, the viewing room is black, the man a silhouette against the glass, the water on the other side a deep blue. The man splays his fingers against the glass. At first the orca is a distant dark shape in the tank, and then it swims toward the man, looming large, until the whale's shadow swallows that of the man. And *Fin*.

"How on earth are we supposed to film that?" Cass said, probably pissed because her grade was on the line. "Do you have a trained orca we can borrow?"

Janie looked stunned, like the thought hadn't even occurred to her.

We ended up doing a basic drunk-driver-on-prom-night story, but Janie had hooked me. The script was far weirder and more interesting than anything else in the class—the kind of movie I loved. Plus it made me wonder if Janie knew something about whether this thing Israel experienced in his dreams was real. It was enough to motivate me to hang out with her here and there.

"It gave me the chills," my mom says, interrupting my thoughts. "How sure he was."

"But you didn't believe him?"

"The doctor said it was nightmares."

I'm not surprised my parents believed that their treasured son was simply afflicted by bad dreams. They also don't believe in my twinsense, even though it's gotten me into trouble for years.

"Is your dad home?" she asks.

I shrug.

He made all the funeral arrangements and spent last night loudly directing the kitchen renovation of a beach house on the north side from the hallway outside our bedrooms. He's one of the few contractors who anticipated the upswing in tourism, the shifting of our island from seventeen miles of cheap hotels to a rich Texan playground with shiny condos and beach mansions.

"Why don't you just stop?" my mom had called from the bedroom.

"Mis clientes no viven aquí, Victoria," he'd said. "They don't know what happened."

"I envy them," she'd said.

And I do too. Since I was young, I tried to channel the way the tourists barreled into a place as though they owned it, and gave so little of themselves in return. Israel complained about the tourists like everyone else on our island. Of course, he seemed perfectly happy to live in our new house, drive around in his car, and play soccer—all paid for with money our father earned from tourists.

Mom's phone buzzes on the nightstand and she reaches over me to grab it. I can tell by the way she pinches the bridge of her nose with her thumb and forefinger that it's the police.

"I see," she says. "Have you learned anything from the instructor . . . ? Wait. What?"

What do they want? I mouth.

She shakes her head, but her jaw drops open and her eyes fill with tears.

"I understand. . . . Okay. . . . I'll be there in an hour."

She hangs up and clutches the phone to her chest, letting out a sound that is as much a birdcall as it is a sob.

"What happened? What did they say?"

"They—want—to—interview—me—again," she says, each word punctuated by a wet heave.

"That's probably normal, right?" Honestly, I don't know what's normal but it's not this. She answers with another shrieking sound. I feel like I should duck in case the room fills with feathers and beaks and wings.

"Tell me what's wrong, mami."

"They said—they are still trying to determine if it was an accident or—"

Or if they were trying to become animals? I don't say that aloud.

"Suicidio." She whispers the word.

The crawling sensation intensifies, like my skin is shivering from the inside out. I bolt out of bed, wanting nothing more than to pull the blankets off her, to pry the pictures from the wall and shatter them on the floor, to roar like a lion over her bird noises. I don't know if I'm mad at the police for suggesting it or at my mother for falling apart over it or at myself for not considering the possibility or at Israel for putting us all through this.

Luna leans against my thigh. The weight—her solid bulk—helps. "It wasn't," I say. "It couldn't be." If he was dead, for real, I'd know. And if it wasn't a death, then it wasn't a suicide. Simple.

"Do you know that?" my mom wails. "Because I don't."

"I know him." It's a lie, but I stalk out, Luna eager at my side, and slam the door on my mom's hothouse of grief. In the hallway, I can't stop it: the crawling in my throat, under my eyelids, down my forearms. I scratch furiously at my skin, leaving pink tracks from my nails.

Luna heads for the stairs, back to her hunt. She's right not to stop.

I won't either.

I pull my phone out of my pocket and text Janie. She has

given me plenty of car rides since the project, so maybe she won't think it's too weird if I ask her to take me out in her dad's boat.

I will find the dolphins again, up close. I will confirm that Israel is out there. That there's some logical explanation for all of this. There has to be.

CHAPTER SEVENTEEN

CASS

....

Two days after

EACH TIME I start to fall asleep, I feel his arms around me, and it's so familiar—the tightness, the pressure, the way he folds me into him—that I sit up, certain he's in the room. Then I have to confront the truth—again and again—that he isn't. That my brain is missing someone into existence.

I pick up my phone to distract myself but immediately remember why I deleted all those apps. I turned off the notifications for my text threads, too, but I still check for messages from Izzy. We haven't talked since we stood together on the seawall and sobbed.

You awake? I text.

She doesn't answer, though I doubt she's asleep. Her energy can be manic—especially when she's upset. I'd be surprised if she wasn't stalking up and down the island, power walking like the middle-aged women at dawn.

When gray light eventually peeks through my curtains, I climb out of bed to start some coffee. I turn on the kitchen TV and keep the volume low. The local news is about to start. There's a teaser about the crash with video of the plane being drawn out of the water. Then a clip of a man in a cheap suit at a podium responding to reporter questions.

"At this stage we cannot determine if they died by suicide," the man says.

My heart thuds in my ears, and I realize I'm holding the screen, gripping the hard plastic edges and tilting it toward me, like you'd hold someone's face. It's a commercial now. A chipper voice lists all the cars in stock while a red-and-white banner screaming SALE flashes across the screen. It's replaced by an insurance commercial with a calm, fatherly man telling you to protect your loved ones. When the news returns, the anchors smile warmly, but their smiles drop almost immediately. The plane is up first.

The screen goes black.

"You should stay away from the news right now, love." My mom puts down the remote. "You have to protect your heart above all else." It's something she says often: how the heart is a precious resource to be guarded.

She's wrapped in her robe, and she pulls me into a fuzzy hug. I'm much taller than her now, and there's something about the height difference that makes me feel like I should be more mature than I am, that I should need her less. My chin is on top of her head like I'm the one comforting her.

"Do you think they—" I can't get the words *died by suicide* out, but she hugs me tighter, like she understands.

"I don't know," she says softly. She pushes me away from her so she can look up at my face. "I know it's hard, Cassie, but you should go express your condolences to his parents in person. I can go with you if you want."

Tammy and Travis opened their home to me on countless occasions. I spent summers swimming in their pool, dinners at their table, and movie nights on their couch. I have no idea what Shane or his sister, Meg, told them about our breakup, but Mom is right. At the very least, I owe them a visit.

Mom pulls a box of brownie mix from the cabinet. It was Shane's favorite and the only kind we keep around—dark chocolate with chocolate chips.

"It might help," she says, but it doesn't. The smell of chocolate feels like his arms around me all over again.

As the brownies cool, I hear the familiar ring of Skype on my laptop down the hall. It can only be my dad, who is stationed in Hawaii now. He was raised in Louisiana and enlisted in the navy right out of high school. When my parents met, my dad was at a base in Texas and my mom was living nearby with her parents. He got deployed abroad not long after I was born. Since then, he's been stationed several other places—Florida, Bahrain, California, Virginia, El Salvador—and we've never followed him. My mom said she kept us on the island because she'd grown up a navy brat herself and knew how moving every few years could feel for a kid.

Izzy, though, thinks there's another reason. *Who doesn't put family first? People who aren't a family anymore, that's who.* It's brutal, but that's Izzy, and I'm not saying she's wrong. When my dad visits us or we visit him, my parents are affectionate and lovey for the first few days. By the end they're squabbling like roommates. Mom seems relieved when the visit ends. If I ask her about it, she swears up and down that they're fine, that the fighting is part of getting used to each other again. She is honest with me to a fault, but I'm not convinced she's very honest with herself.

"Mom!" I yell. "Did you tell him to call?" She's always trying to force us to talk more. She feels guilty he's not in my life enough—not that he couldn't make more of an effort too.

"Of course!" she calls back.

I groan but jog to my room to answer the laptop. "Hi, Papa." He is hunched over his own computer, too tall and broad for the frame. The walls behind him are blank, sterile like a hospital's.

"Hi, Cassie, cher." Even after years away, his New Orleans accent is thick. "Your mama told me what happened."

"Yeah." I stare at myself in the tiny corner video. I look washed-out, like crying has drained me of blood and sleeplessness has bruised me.

The image of him turns pixelated and his voice stutters.

"Shane was a goo-goo-good boy," he says. "Real good." My dad always emphasized how boyish Shane was. On the phone call after our breakup, he said I'd be able to find a real man when I was ready to find a real man. My mom and I left out the part about me cheating on Shane. He would think it wasn't behavior befitting *nice girls*. *And you're a nice girl, ain'tcha, Cassie?*

"Yeah, he was good," I say, trying not to burst into tears at the past tense: *was*. I'm not sure why I feel the need to be stoic for my dad. Because we don't show strangers our grief?

"Pass along my condolences to his folks, won'tcha?"

"I will."

My mom steps into the frame behind me. "Bernard, maybe it's time for a trip home." I have a feeling they've talked about this recently—argued, probably—and my mom thinks he won't be able to say no if I'm on camera looking like I've been drained of all life.

"Kitty—"

"Your daughter needs you."

It's like I'm not there, seated right between her and the screen. "Mom, I'm fine."

"You're not fine, Cass," she says, her hand on my back.

"Don't speak for me," I say sharply, though of course she's right. I'm not fine. I don't think *fine* will be a word I use to describe myself ever again.

I slip out of the chair. "I'm gonna go see his parents now."

"I'll come with," my mom says.

"No, I need to do this alone. You two finish"—I wave at the computer—"whatever this is."

It's the first time I've been to Shane's house in weeks, and it feels as automatic as ever, as though I'll climb the stairs to their wraparound deck, open the always unlocked front door, shout a hello to his parents, and then head up to his bedroom and find him on the bed, listening to music.

But there are cars I don't recognize in the driveway—one that has dash lights and looks like an unmarked police vehicle. The house blinds are down. The door, I'm sure, is locked.

When I muster enough bravery to ring the doorbell, I hear voices and the soft tread of bare feet. There's a pause; someone has seen me and is deciding whether or not to open the door.

It's Meg who finally swings it open. We were on the volleyball team together before she graduated. She's athletic and tall like Shane—only an inch shorter than me—with Shane's same thin, straight hair. Without makeup and with her hair back, her face looks like his too: a high, flat forehead and broad cheekbones. His ears protruded like he was a character in a child's drawings, but hers are as delicate as seashells.

Behind her, there's a voice I don't recognize and can't make out. Her dad's voice booms back.

"It has to at least be negligence," he's saying. "Teenagers shouldn't be able to just take a plane."

Meg glances back before stepping onto the deck and allowing the screen door to shut behind her.

"What do you want?"

"Oh, I, um, I just wanted to offer my condolences to your parents." I hold out the brownies.

"They're busy, and I doubt they want to see you."

It feels like a playground pinch—something small enough to swat away but big enough to bruise. "Can you just please tell them I'm here?"

"No, I know what they'll say, and I'd prefer to protect them from any further pain."

This feels like a blow to my temple, but I get it. "Okay. Listen, Meg, I'm so, so sorry for your loss. Shane was—"

"I don't need you to tell me anything about Shane. I've known him his whole life."

"Okay." I push the brownies toward her hands. For a moment I think that she won't take them, that I'll either have to return home with the brownies or allow the plate to shatter on the deck. Who, I wonder, would pick up the shards?

But she reaches for them. Mom says people can feel intent, that sometimes you need to exude all the positive energy you can and will it into the space around you. In the few seconds both of our hands are on the plate, I hope Meg feels how much I love him, how we are united by the fact that we'll both remember him for as long as we can.

She steps back into the house, allowing the screen to slam between us, but she pauses before shutting the front door. "If you loved him so much, why did you cheat on him?" she asks, as though she's heard my thoughts.

"I don't know. I shouldn't have."

Instead of the fury I'm expecting, she looks weary—a weariness I've seen on the faces of old commercial fisherman who've long ago accepted the dwindling populations of their fish, the dwindling value of their work on this island. Without another word, she closes the door. The lock clicks.

I can't blame drugs or alcohol or coercion. Even if I hadn't fully admitted it to myself, I was starting to realize that Shane wouldn't be going to college near me, if at all, and that that distance might be too difficult. But he and I didn't have a fight. We didn't fall out of love. I stayed at UT for an off-season volleyball tournament. I met Kendall, an athlete on one of the Austin boys' teams. He was tall and Nigerian, and when he smiled, it felt like the world cracked open and sunlight poured through to the mantle. We flirted in the hotel hallways, lingering as long as our chaperones allowed. And on the last night, long after the coaches had finished room checks, I lay in bed burning with—desire? Curiosity? Self-destructiveness? It was easy enough to sneak out of my room and down the hall to his. His roommate pushed his headphones into his ears. Kendall lifted the covers on his bed for me, as though he were a gentleman opening a door, and smiled the whole time.

I didn't love Shane any less afterward. I didn't want him any less. And strangely, I didn't feel much guilt. I had simply made a small tick on the ruler of my life. As in, *there*, that tiny line is Kendall, who taught me about light and impulses.

I may not have even told Shane if it weren't for Karen, my

tournament roommate, who is terrible with secrets and wasn't going to keep quiet about my disappearance. He'd have found out eventually. And so, as soon as I got home, I told him. Maybe it was naive, but I thought it would be okay—that he wouldn't think I didn't love him anymore, and we could go on to have a senior year filled with trips, prom, graduation parties.

Obviously, I was wrong.

My phone buzzes as I walk back to my car. Izzy, finally, responding:

> `We gotta get a boat. Meet me at the movie`
> `theater. Janie's working.`

Oh God. Is this about the dolphins again?

It's Janie's Whack-A-Mole script that got Izzy into this, convinced that her brother—that all of them—are still alive in the bodies of fucking dolphins.

When Janie first moved to the island years ago, it was like she'd been raised by alligators and had never been in public before. In high school she traded the growling and snapping for awkwardness. She swings between confidence and self-consciousness with an energy that makes me jumpy. In class you're never sure if she's going to argue with the teacher or sit silently with her eyes on the ceiling.

`I don't know if that's a good idea,` I type back—a response that's as much about the implausibility of dolphins as it is about keeping Janie at arm's length.

I want you there just in case. Please. I
need you.

Just in case what? I wonder. But I don't ask. I get into the car
and head for the movie theater.

CHAPTER EIGHTEEN

JANIE

....

Two days after

I GO INTO work today, even though I still feel hungover—not as much from Sunday's alcohol binge as from the long crying jags, the kind that make you feel scraped out inside. It was Dad's idea that I go to work. He stayed home yesterday with me, but he had a surgery today, and he said I'd be less alone—read: less of a danger to myself—at work.

So here I am, sticky-handed from the soda syrup, filling popcorn bags and trying not to listen to the voices of people in line.

It was that Foster boy flying it, you know Tammy Foster's kid?

She won't be so full of herself now.

How'd they get the plane?

Stole it from some flight instructor on the mainland.

So irresponsible of those parents, if you ask me. I heard they didn't even know the boys were taking lessons.

That poor twin sister. I can't even imagine.

Nate Herschel. Wasn't he that kid in the paper all the time for soccer?

At his name, my mind flutters, mothlike and hovering, over memories of him. The tight knots of his shoulders under my fingers as he pedaled me to the ocean the first day we met. His shirt damp with sweat and clinging to his skin. That gleam of fondness? Appreciation? Inspiration? As we looked at the ocean. His smile—as impish and quick as his jokes. His long hair curtaining my face, brushing against my ears and neck, the night we finally kissed.

He was proud that he'd grown his hair to his shoulders—not that he ever wore it down. He seemed to be cultivating an image with the bun and the light dusting of stubble, with the slim jeans and graphic-print button-downs. Something more Euro than Gulf Coast, and it suited him—especially when his dream was the British Premier League and backup was the MLS. Before the knee injury, that is. After, he'd simply pointed at the stars.

I look up from sliding Junior Mints across the counter and see Cass and Izzy outside the theater. I can tell they're having an intense conversation by the way Cass is gesturing, waving to the ocean and then pressing her hand to her chest. Izzy, who you'd expect to be the emotive one, seems calm, like she's waiting it out rather than listening. Cass crosses her arms, and her shoulders bob up and down. Crying for sure. Izzy pulls her into a hug.

I have to turn around to pump butter into popcorn and when I turn back, Cass and Izzy are inside. Standing in my line like when they want me to sneak them a free treat before a show. Cass isn't crying anymore, but she hasn't bothered to wipe the tear streaks off her cheeks, either. Her hair is tied back tight, drawing her eyebrows high and emphasizing the puffs under her eyes.

Izzy, on the other hand, appears surprisingly well-rested—bright-eyed and almost perky. She's scanning the theater with interest, clearly unbothered by their fight.

"You never answered my texts," Izzy says as soon as the person in front of her steps out of line.

"I lost my phone when it—when the plane—"

Cass flinches, so I don't finish the sentence.

"You have a boat, right?" Izzy asks. Cass gives a slight disapproving shake of her head, but I can't tell if it's a signal to me or if she's just irritated at Izzy.

I say nothing.

"Come on—you don't know if you have a boat or not?" Izzy asks.

I look at Cass again, but she sighs and avoids my eyes, staring at the candy case instead. A few preteens have lined up behind them. One whines, "Hurry up," and Izzy shoots them a look.

"My dad has a boat," I finally say.

"Can we borrow it?"

"Um, I don't know if he'll let you."

"Not me, us," she says, nodding toward me. "You'll be there too." Izzy's attention always makes me feel like I'm about to become prey or a predator myself. It's unsettling.

"What do you want a boat for?" I ask.

Cass bites her lip like she's stopping herself from saying something.

"I need to see where it went down," Izzy says. "The plane. To say goodbye."

It wouldn't take a genius to detect from Izzy's urgency and Cass's annoyance that there's something else going on here. What is she hoping to find? Does she know something about the crash? About why it happened?

If there's anything I've learned from spending time with Cass and Izzy over the past several months, it's that I need to make myself valuable to them if I want something in return. In this case: answers about why Nate was in that plane.

"Okay. I'll try," I say, though there's no way my dad is going to let us borrow his boat.

Izzy narrows her eyes at me. Trying isn't enough for her.

"I'll get it. I promise," I say with fake confidence.

"When?"

"I'm not sure yet. I'll let you know."

"How? You don't have a phone."

"Jesus, Izzy," Cass murmurs. "She probably has a laptop or something."

I nod, grateful to briefly have Cass on my side.

"Okay," Izzy says firmly, like we've just shaken on a

deal, though I'm not sure I completely understand what I'm agreeing to.

I wait with Mickey for a movie to finish so we can sweep up the scattered kernels and M&M's before the next showing. He's a rising junior and football-player huge, but he prefers the company of the old bridge ladies on the island.

"Have you seen this?" he asks, leaning close to show me something on his phone.

I haven't gone on social media since the crash. Unlike most people at school, I only have one account—something I opened because Izzy once asked me in film class, *Don't you want to be normal?* with her lip drawn in a sneer. I do, but I rarely post because I don't like the idea of people looking at me any more than they already do.

Mickey plays a video message from one of his senior friends, a girl named Layla who hangs out with Cass and Izzy sometimes. He has it muted, so I can't hear what she's saying to the camera, but it's clear she posted it from the party. The video filter gives her a pair of round purple sunglasses. Behind her is the beach volleyball court and Shane handing out hot dogs. Nate would have been nearby—maybe at the keg or seated on the coolers. I almost slap the phone out of Mickey's hand before the camera pans to him, but I catch myself.

"I don't want to see," I manage.

"Wait, were you there?" he asks.

I nod.

"You were?" His eyes widen. "Damn. All right, party girl. Tell me everything."

"Everything?"

"Yeah, like from the beach. Everyone is saying it was some prank that went wrong. So were they showing off? Or was it"—his voice drops—"a suicide pact?"

Suicide? The word stalks through me—huge and stark. It's the first I've allowed myself to think the word. I shake my head so hard I see stars. I've heard about plenty of their pranks from Nate—like the time he and Shane turned the soccer team's backpacks inside out, replaced their contents, and zipped them back up from the inside using a bent paper clip. Or the time Shane took over the AV system before a school assembly and played goat scream videos. A prank—a stupid fucking prank—seems far more likely.

But.

In the weeks since the soccer accident, Nate had been different. He lost his sport, the thing that made him strong and popular and fast, the thing he'd tied his future to. There were days I'd find him collapsed into the couch, greasy-haired and watching the weather through half-lidded eyes. He seemed far, far away.

Mickey is staring at me, and I realize I'm hugging the broom to my chest and crying.

"God, I'm so sorry," he says. "I didn't know you were close with any of them."

"Nate was my best friend." I've never said it aloud before, but the words spring out easily.

Mickey, though, looks doubtful—like I invented the friendship. To him, of course, I have. "You should go home," he says softly, resting his large hand on my shoulder. His kindness only makes me cry harder. I have to find out what happened.

I tell Neil that I'm sick and ask to call my dad with the theater's phone. I punch in the extension for one of my dad's nurses. "Candy, it's Janie," I say.

"Oh, hon, how are you doing? I heard your neighbor friend was one of the boys. I can't even imagine what you're going through. I'm so sorry."

My dad told her?

"Yeah," I say, aware that I've paused too long, and it isn't quite the right response. *Is* there a right response?

"How can I help you, doll?"

"Can you tell me when he's in surgeries this week?"

"Let's see. He has something on the schedule tomorrow, Thursday, and Friday." Friday is perfect; it will give me a few days to figure out how to get the boat from the marina without him knowing.

"Okay. Great. Thanks."

I hang up, realizing too late that I probably should have waited for her to say *you're welcome* and said goodbye. Fortunately, I have enough sense to know it would be even more awkward to call back and say it now.

• • •

In the late-afternoon heat, the marina is a ghost town. No deep-sea fishing tours or boat renters clogging the docks. The waves throw quick glints of sun, and everything else is hazy, the heat and pollution hanging low and yellow. Seeing the tree where I passed out on Sunday—was it only two days ago?—makes me feel queasy all over again.

Dad and I take the boat out once a month, usually when he sees the marina's invoice and remembers it exists. He's talked about selling it, but I think he's fond of it. It probably reminds him of the family we were supposed to be.

I get seasick, so I have to take an anti-nausea pill before we go out, which makes me drowsy. I spend the hours on the boat half dozing, rocked out of consciousness by the waves, the coconut scent of my sunscreen, the soft *scree* sound as my dad casts. Despite a few lessons with Nate's dad, he's a terrible fisherman and rarely catches anything. I think he does it so that his hands don't feel so empty.

Generally, he calls ahead and they get the boat ready, but you have to pass through the marina's bait and tackle shop to access the dock. They're bound to notice three high school girls marching through to take a boat.

The bell clatters as I walk into the shop. "Can I help you, miss?" It's an older man I've seen before—short and lemon-shaped. I take a deep breath, channeling Izzy's confidence.

"I'm looking for someone from school. I think he works here."

"Theo?" the man asks.

"Theo," I repeat, relieved he supplied a name. There's only one Theo in school, a rising senior like me. We were lab partners in geology class together last year. We aren't friends, but he was nice enough to me. Was he at the party? I picture the beach, the fire, trying to scan the faces in my memory. But I can only see Nate—his cheeks chapped from the wind and bonfire, his eyes locked on something in the distance as Shane told a story with wild gestures. It was after our argument, and I was downing a terrible cocktail I'd mixed without really knowing what I was doing.

The man looks at his watch. "He should be in soon. He took off the morning because—well, I'm sure you know."

I nod, but my face must be doing something on its own again, communicating my pain without my knowledge.

"You knew those kids too?" he says. "The ones who stole the plane?"

I nod again, and his face pinches. "You can't just fly." He's indignant, like I'm trying to sprout wings right before his eyes. I nod again.

The man's face softens. "I'm real sorry," he says. "Sometimes there aren't any answers."

That's what my dad said when my mom left.

"You're wrong," I snap, and the man's eyes widen in surprise. "There are answers."

My mom left because she wanted a different life. She didn't want the boat or the island or my dad or me.

There's a reason Nate barely acknowledged me at school.

A reason he was in that plane. There's a reason it fell from the sky, too. And I need to know the real reasons—no matter how much they hurt.

I wait on the bench outside the marina until a black SUV parks at the back of the lot. Theo climbs out, his forehead shiny with sweat and a flare of eczema across his cheeks. He *was* at the party. I remember him now, slinging his arm around Cass's shoulders and running a hand through his prematurely thinning hair while she was tapping the keg. She had shrugged him off.

"Theo! Hey!" I call, practically jogging to meet him.

"Janie?" He's puzzled, I can tell. I'm eager to ask about the boat, but there are formalities now. Grief calls for it.

"How are you?" I ask a little impatiently.

He squints at the bay. "I'm okay, I guess. How are you?"

I ignore the question. I'm sure my red eyes and tearstained face tell enough of the story. "Listen, I have a favor to ask. I need to get my dad's boat out in a few days. It's a surprise, so I can't tell him about it."

"You're surprising him with his own boat?"

He's right. It doesn't make any sense. I've heard he doesn't like Izzy because of something that happened in kindergarten, so I go for a half-truth instead. "It's actually for Cass," I say. "She's clearly having a hard time. She needs to go to where it happened, you know?"

He nods as though he understands, and I feel a wash of relief and shame.

"How about Friday?" I ask.

"Nate's funeral is that day."

His funeral? I hadn't heard anything about it, and the thought makes me feel as though I'm collapsing inward, folding into myself, until I am a dot of concentrated, inky sadness. I'm making a sound, I realize, mewing like a kitten.

"Okay," Theo says. "Okay. It's fine. Friday, after the funeral. I'll make sure the boat is ready."

I turn to leave without saying thank you or goodbye, but I have no idea where to go.

VIDEO

....

SHANE FOSTER TRIBUTE PAGE

<MEG SITS IN her childhood room, facing the camera. Behind her, there's a white dresser topped with volleyball trophies. One of the drawers is open, and you can see clothing spilling over the top. On the wall, there's a plaque carved with MVP *and her name.>*

Meg: My brother—you know him as Shane, but I called him Sandy—he wasn't like other people. If you're on this page, you know this already. He loved you. He loved everyone. I'm not even kidding. When we were little and my mom tried to run errands with us, he'd smile and talk to everyone. The mailperson. The woman checking us out at the grocery store. Any salesperson. Once my mom thought she'd lost him in this clothing store, so we did one of those announcement things. Turns out, he'd found his way into the dressing room and was, like, giving advice to this old woman on her outfit choices. He was probably flattering her shamelessly. It got to be so my mom would hire a babysitter just so she could get shit done faster without him.

<Meg laughs and tears up.>

I've never been as nice as him. No one can be. It's a high bar. But I know that I could still be nicer.

<Meg grabs a Kleenex from somewhere off frame and blots her nose.>

Today was a hard day. But Sandy wouldn't have used that as an excuse and so I won't either.

If there's anyone on here who needs to hear it: I'm sorry.

And for everyone else: be like Sandy.

CHAPTER NINETEEN

NATE

....

Twenty-nine days before

AFTER DINNER, NATE'S dad helped set his bedroom up for the night with his tablet, a stack of pillows to prop up his knee, and the textbooks Janie had brought over—not that he planned to study. There was no point if he wasn't trying to get a soccer scholarship.

"Got everything?" his dad asked. He smelled strongly of his favorite green bar soap, which you could find in hair-speckled slivers throughout their house. He said it was the only one that took away the stench of fish.

"Yeah," Nate replied, eager for his dad to leave him alone.

But his dad seemed to have other plans. "Listen." He cleared his throat and sat in Nate's desk chair. "You know how I played baseball in college?"

Nate nodded.

"Well, I had this buddy who hurt his knee. Just like you.

He couldn't play, but he did equipment management and stat keeping for the team for a couple seasons. And you know what he does now?"

It was rhetorical, Nate knew. He kept quiet.

"He's head of baseball operations for the Mets."

"Is that supposed to inspire me?"

"It's supposed to remind you that there's so much more after this. You don't know where your path will lead."

His dad seemed to want him to be over the injury already, to make plans for a new, soccerless future, but he didn't have the first clue where to start. And what's more, he didn't *want* to imagine a life without soccer.

The doorbell rang—saving him from further lectures—and he heard the murmur of his mother's voice and two sets of footsteps down the hall: Shane and Israel.

"Hi, Mr. Herschel," Shane said, practically bursting into the room. "We wanted to surprise Nate. We promise not to stay super long."

Nate's dad squeezed Shane's shoulder. "All right. I'll leave you guys to it."

Shane grabbed Nate's desk chair and pulled it next to the bed. Israel stepped into the room, but still hovered near the door. His hair—somehow always perpetually overgrown—curled over the tips of his ears. He kept his eyes down, but he shot looks at Nate.

"Dude, it's Saturday night, and you're in bed," Shane said.

"It's Saturday night and you're here," Nate responded. "Why aren't you with Cass?"

"She's at a volleyball tournament in Austin for the long weekend." Shane glanced around the room. "I'll get another chair. Is, take this one." He bounded out of the room with as much energy as he'd entered it.

Israel sat in the chair. He held himself so stiff and upright, Nate thought it was a miracle he wasn't the one to break a knee.

"I'm sorry," he said.

He'd always been jealous, though. Nate remembered how Israel would sit across the bus aisle from him and Shane after games freshman year, listening hungrily to their conversations as though there'd be a test on how much he'd learned. The next day he'd show up to practice with a favorite snack or song on his phone that Shane had mentioned in passing.

"Nate? I said I'm sorry."

The thing about painkillers was that they only worked for short intervals, which Nate was beginning to think of as sweet valleys between massive hills of pain. He was nearing the top of his pain hill, and he had to wait to take the next dose so that he could sleep through the night. It was his last dose too. Dr. Dennis wanted him on over-the-counter meds as soon as possible.

Nate pushed his fists into the bed and tried to shift so his knee would hurt a little less. "I heard you before," he said with a grimace.

Israel's shoulders dropped—a jerky motion, like even

relaxation was robotic. "For what it's worth, it *was* an accident," he said.

With the pain returning, Nate felt like a ball of raw nerves. "Was it?" he asked.

Israel's eyes widened at the question. "Of course," he said. "Why would I want to hurt you?"

"To be a starter maybe?"

"Nate, I like soccer, but I only play to hang out with you guys and have another activity on my college apps. I don't need to be a starter."

"Right, you don't *need* it because you are the model student with good grades and community service and teachers who worship you," Nate said.

"That's not what I'm saying."

"That's exactly what you're saying," Nate said. "And, well, I *do* need it."

Shane returned, dragging a chair from Aaron's room. "Hey," he said. "How's it going in here?"

Israel stood. "I should go," he said. "Can you walk home, Shane?"

"Yeah, but—" Shane looked at Nate and raised his eyebrows. *Ask him to stay,* his face seemed to be saying. Nate started browsing for a web series on his tablet. "Do you want me to go too?" Shane asked.

"Up to you," Nate said. Israel was standing in the hallway, hovering outside the room.

"It seems like you might be tired," Shane said.

Nate shrugged, aware he was testing Shane. If Shane was really his friend, he'd stay.

"Okay," Shane said. "See you at school?"

Nate didn't answer. Shane paused in the doorway for a moment, as if waiting for more, then closed the door behind him and left with Israel.

Nate tapped the last pill into his hand and chucked the empty bottle at the door. He didn't need his friends.

He didn't need anything now.

CHAPTER TWENTY

ISRAEL

....

Twenty-nine days before

ISRAEL DROVE SHANE home, pretending it didn't matter one way or another if Nate forgave him. But it mattered. As soon as Shane had climbed from the car, the streetlights transformed into blurry blobs. He tried to take deep breaths and stitch himself back together, but there were too many holes to repair at once: his GPA, Randolph's death, Peter catching him lying in the emails, Nate's knee.

Luna didn't greet Israel when he came in, which meant she was probably following someone else around the house, hoping to get fed instead of watching out the window for his return.

"Hello?" Israel called. "Mami?"

"She's out with Magdalena. Dad's working," his sister called from upstairs. "Are you okay?"

Israel didn't answer her, but he trudged up the stairs. Luna was sprawled on the floor outside Izzy's room. She sprang up and wagged when she saw him.

Izzy swung open her door. She was wearing sweatpants, folded over at the waist, and a soccer tournament T-shirt that she'd sliced at the neck so it fell off one shoulder. All of it had been his from freshman year, but she'd made it retro cool.

"What's wrong?" she asked, touching her side.

He wasn't sure what face he made at her, but she dropped her hand.

"I thought you were hanging out with Nate and Shane tonight," she said.

"Nate was too tired."

Her laptop was open on her bed, something paused on the screen. As popular as she was, she spent a lot of time alone watching movies.

Mostly, though, he was jealous she got to have her own hobbies. Their parents wanted Israel to succeed so badly that anytime he deviated from their plan for him—like the time he'd enrolled in the dance PE elective instead of a computer programming class—they'd freaked out. Izzy wasn't under the same kind of pressure; they'd already realized she wasn't going to follow anyone's path but her own.

"You going to tell me what's hurting you or are you just going to stand there staring?" she asked.

She wasn't going to leave him alone unless he offered her something. "Fine," he said. "Let's get the shoebox."

"That bad, huh?"

Without answering, he retrieved his stash of cigarettes that he kept hidden in a shoebox and they climbed onto the roof together. He tapped a cigarette out of the pack and lit it, handing it to her after he took the first drag.

"I'm the one who injured Nate," he said after a long exhale. It was part of the truth.

"That's no secret," she said. "Cass already told me."

"It wasn't on purpose."

"Okay," she said. She handed the cigarette back and inspected her split ends. She was always complaining about how straightening her hair damaged it, but she couldn't stop. *People expect me to have straight hair,* she'd say as though it were unquestionably true.

"It wasn't," he said again.

"I said okay. Why are you so defensive?"

Because he was used to people not taking his words at face value. His parents and their doctor didn't believe him about the dreams. But he had to remember that Izzy did, probably because she experienced something inexplicable too: her twin-sense. "Nate doesn't believe me," he said.

"Do *you* believe you?"

"What do you mean?"

"Is there part of you that wonders if maybe you did it on purpose?"

"Why would I do it on purpose?"

"All of us—even you—have been that kid on the beach poking the bird with the broken wing."

He blinked at her. "You're shit at metaphors," he said.

"I'm just saying it's human to want to watch something bleed."

"I'll admit to wanting to beat him at soccer sometimes. Wanting to win," he said cautiously. "But that's competitiveness—not cruelty. It's not like I've wished harm on the guy."

"Okay," she said again.

He shoved her with his elbow.

"What?"

"You have the most judgmental *okay*s of anyone I know."

"Fine. Fine. You work this out on your own. I've got my stories to watch," she said, and stood, brushing the dirt of the roof off her butt.

"What is it this time? Murdered orcas? Tortured artists? Child brides?" She'd been on a documentary kick lately.

"Close. Child soldiers."

"Bye, Iz," he said.

"Bye, Is," she said back.

He finished the cigarette and took out another. Was she right? Was there a tiny part of him that had wanted to hurt Nate? He closed his eyes, picturing it. He'd gotten a breakaway and had momentarily been flooded with adrenaline—enough to spur his tired body down the field—his ears ringing with his teammates' cheers. But Nate was faster and had recovered the ball from Israel easily. Israel's teammates had fallen silent, and Israel had felt the weight of their disappointment. It was only a scrimmage, but he was already carrying the weight of his parents' expectations too. He'd gone after the ball at Nate's feet with all that added weight. It was enough to bowl anyone over.

This was all his fault.

If he didn't stop the dreams, they'd continue to hurt him and the people around him. Not just Nate, but Izzy, who was already becoming more and more of a stranger. His parents, who he was bound to fail.

If he had any shot at stopping the broken record of Randolph's death from consuming him, he couldn't shy away from figuring it all out just because Peter had caught him in a lie.

He opened his email and began to type.

Peter,

The truth is that I think I'm him—your father. Since I was little I've remembered a car accident and a fire that I couldn't escape. I also remembered worrying about my son, Peter, and my wife, Lara. That's how I found you. I know this sounds like bullshit, and I'm sorry if my lies caused any pain.

Could we please meet in person so I can explain better?

Israel J. Castillo

CHAPTER TWENTY-ONE

SHANE

....

Twenty-seven days before

HEY, WE SHOULD be arriving in 20. Can you pick me up? Cass texted.

It was a relief to hear from her. She knew Shane hated texting, but she'd been especially quiet all weekend. She hadn't even posted anything on social media from the tournament, but he'd seen her in a few of her teammates' photos and videos. In one photo, a long table was crowded with empty glasses and plates, and she was grinning, cheeks flushed, an arm draped around Karen's neck.

He wanted to tell her how Nate and Israel were taking a break from each other, how Meg had come home for the long weekend to move some of her stuff back and was hogging the washer and dryer. How his mom had insisted they eat every meal together and had put him on cleanup duty, which meant he'd been dealing with smeared egg yolks on the counters, onion skins stuck to tiles, and trash that smelled of chicken carcass.

Picking up Cass would be a break from it all.

The charter bus was parked in front of the school, a pile of duffel bags beside it. Cass waited away from the other girls with a pillow under one arm and her bag over the other. It was hot, but she was in oversized sweats. Her hair was pulled back into a tight ponytail, and a stretchy green headband kept it flat to her skull. She looked vastly different than she had in the team dinner photo, her face drawn and gray. Was she sick?

"Hey," he said as she climbed into his mom's car. He leaned over to kiss her. She accepted the kiss but didn't return it. He caught some of the other girls staring at them as he put the car in drive. He was used to stares. People wanted to be him and Cass. But today Cass's teammates seemed something other than jealous.

"How was the tournament?" he asked.

"It was okay," she said. She was quiet. Quieter than usual.

"Want to come over for dinner?" he asked. "Meg's home, so my mom has been acting like it's Christmas."

"No, my mom is expecting me, but I needed to talk to you first."

This made his stomach sink. He pulled out of the parking lot and turned toward her house.

"Actually, can we go to the beach instead?" she asked.

"Yeah, okay," he said. He looked over at her, but she was staring straight ahead. He wished he could tell what she was thinking.

"So, how'd you do this weekend?" He tried to make his tone breezy.

"We won the first game but lost the second. So we just got to hang out for the rest of it."

"It looked like you were having fun."

Cass's face froze.

"I saw a photo from some dinner online," he prompted.

"Oh. It was kinda fun," she said cautiously.

"Everything okay?" he asked.

"I'm just tired."

He tried to meet her eyes, but she turned her head toward the passenger-side window.

He parked along the seawall and was about to climb out to put a dollar in the meter when she grabbed his arm. She still didn't look at him, though; her eyes were on the beach. A few surfers were sitting on their boards. A man and a boy were flying a kite.

"I just want to talk," she said. "We can stay in the car."

Now his stomach was churning. She was about to break up with him, wasn't she? Sure, they weren't on the same path any-more, but he'd thought they were going to try to make a go of it with long-distance in college. It had been her idea, which he'd thought was a little strange considering she often talked about how poorly long-distance went for her parents. But he was willing to do it because he loved her. Didn't she know that?

But maybe it wasn't about college at all. Maybe Izzy told her that he'd been cheating at school, and she'd decided she couldn't be with someone dishonest like him.

"In Austin I—" Her voice cracked. "I slept with someone."

She said the words in a rush, and Shane felt like they were being force-fed to him. They grated their way down his esophagus and plummeted into his stomach. He tried to throw them back up.

"What?" was all he could manage to say.

"It wasn't a thing," she said.

"What does that even mean?" The world was tilting again, and he was scrabbling for purchase. There was nothing to catch him.

"It means—I didn't—there weren't feelings or anything," she said. Tears fell down her cheeks, which only made him angry. Why was *she* the one crying? "It was just sex."

He blinked at her. What was he supposed to do with that information? Forgive her? "So you want me to be like, 'No biggie; it was just sex'?"

"No, I—" She finally met his eyes, but didn't say any more.

"So you threw this away—us away—for sex. Is that what you're saying?"

"I—I'm so sorry."

"*Sorry* doesn't fix it." He thought of how angry Nate still was even after Israel had apologized. He got it now.

"No, it doesn't. But I'm hoping you can forgive me someday."

"Get out."

"Shane, please talk to me."

Suddenly it all seemed funny. Here he'd been, afraid that she was going to break up with him because she found out he'd been cheating at school. And she was the one who'd cheated on him.

"Why are you laughing?" she asked, and he realized that he must be laughing out loud. He doubled over so that his head rested against the steering wheel, and clutched his stomach, where her admission had settled.

"I can't talk to you if you're like this," she said, which only made him laugh harder. *She* couldn't talk to *him*? And what even was there to say now?

The car door slammed, and she was gone.

He looked up—still laughing or possibly sobbing now— and saw her waiting at the stoplight to cross Ocean. She had her pillow clutched to her chest and was resting her chin on it like the much younger girl he'd first fallen in love with. The memory punched him. He had to get away before he said something to punch back.

Back at home, he sat in the driveway for a while, trying to compose himself so he could face his parents and sister. But each time he thought he'd stopped crying, he started again. He texted Israel and Nate.

Cass cheated on me.

What? Israel texted back. With who?

Shane hadn't thought to ask that question, but now it was all that mattered to him. Who would she have thrown five years away for?

So sorry, man, Nate texted. You okay?

There was a knock on the window. Meg stood with her hands on her hips. She was in jeans and a T-shirt with her college's name in gothic print. There was something more adult about her than there had been months before when she first left for school. Her cheeks were plumper and her skin brighter and clearer. Would he ever look that fresh-faced and collegiate? No, but Cass would. He could imagine it now—her own filling out, hips rounding instead of poking out like shelves, Greek letters stretching across her chest.

Shane wiped his face and unlocked the doors.

"Why are you moping in the car?" Meg asked, opening the door and bending to see him.

"Cass."

"What about her?"

His gut instinct was not to tell the truth, not to poison Meg against her. But why would he bother to protect her now? "She cheated on me," he said. "At the volleyball tournament."

"Seriously?"

He nodded.

146

"Wow. I never would have expected that. She seemed so high and mighty all the time. Queen Cass, you know?"

He didn't respond.

"How'd you find out?"

"She told me."

Meg rolled her eyes. "Of course she did, and I bet she expected you to forgive her because she was doing the right thing." She sighed. "Come here, Sandy." She grabbed him under the arms and dragged him into a half-seated hug. Her chin dug into the top of his skull. It was the sort of violent hug she'd given him when they were kids and their mom demanded they hug to make up after a fight. "I'm going to be real with you. You guys weren't going to make it through college. So now you get to have a free senior year. Playing the field. Banging all the ladies. Whatever it is you gross dudes say."

He laughed, and she squeezed him tighter.

"I know it sucks, but you're going to be okay." She released him from the vise-grip hug. "Now come inside so we can eat."

"Okay."

She straightened up. "What do *you* want?"

He realized she was speaking to someone else. Shane glanced in the rearview mirror, and there was Cass again, still clutching her pillow and duffel bag. She'd taken off her sweatshirt and tied it around her waist, and the gray of her T-shirt was darkened under her armpits and around her neck. She'd actually walked from the beach where he left her—not that it was a great distance.

"Leave him alone," Meg said. Even at his age, it still felt good to have his older sister's protection.

"I'm sorry," Cass said from the bottom of his driveway. Meg took his arm, and he let her pull him toward the stairs up to their front door. "Shane, I'm so sorry." Her voice wavered at this, and he was glad for it. At least she'd lost something too.

CHAPTER TWENTY-TWO

SHANE

....

Twenty-six days before

SHANE FELT LIKE glass. Like he might shatter. He hadn't gone to school in years without stopping by Cass's condo first. Today, simply walking past the turn to her complex made him tear up. He wasn't sure how he was going to make it through this last week of school filled with reminders of her—let alone the actual presence of her—without breaking.

Israel was in his early-bird class; Nate was staying home another day because of his knee or because he was avoiding Israel. Shane was being forced to try something new, step out of his routine. He headed for the cafeteria, which smelled of doughnuts and cereal milk. He sat next to Marcus and a few guys from the swim team, trying to act normal, but he couldn't remember what that looked like. Was he laughing at the right time? Could they tell something had happened?

Marcus swiveled toward Shane. People used to confuse the

two of them because they were both tall and skinny, but lately Marcus had been bulking up to get on a college team, and his shoulders were massive compared to Shane's. It wouldn't surprise him if Cass had chosen a boy who looked more like Marcus.

"Tien told me what happened. I'm sorry, man," Marcus said.

Shane managed a nod in response, but it felt like another chip in his glass. "How does Tien know?" he asked weakly.

"I think the volleyball girls told everyone."

Was that why Cass had told him? Because she knew she'd get caught? Another crack. He wasn't sure how much longer he could keep himself from breaking.

"Dude," Marcus said, jerking his head over his shoulder toward the cafeteria entrance. Cass was there, her hair pulled back into a tight bun, dark circles stamped under her eyes. Momentarily, Shane's heart ached toward her.

He turned his back, but the swim team was silent around him. She had to be walking this way. He braced himself for her hand, long-fingered and light on his shoulder. Would he be able to resist taking it?

But it was her voice that touched him first, thick with tears. "Can we talk?"

He didn't turn around.

"Shane?" Her voice rose in pitch. "Please, I'm so sorry."

One thing about broken glass was that it could cut. "Get away from me, you bitch." He said it loudly. Too loudly. The whole cafeteria froze; Marcus's spoon stopped an inch from his mouth.

"Whoa," one of the guys whispered under his breath.

Immediately Shane regretted it. He was a person who liked other people, who wanted them happy and laughing. This wasn't him.

He turned around slowly, and Cass lifted her chin defiantly at him. Shane felt his love—that injured, fragile thing—wobble to its feet. She was so proud and strong.

"You can't talk to me that way. I know I did something terrible, but it doesn't excuse—" She swallowed hard.

He almost apologized. He almost took her by the elbow and led her from the cafeteria so they could talk, but Israel was there instead. Before Shane could do or say anything else, Israel was the one guiding Cass out of the cafeteria, murmuring softly to her as they walked.

Shane stood. He wasn't sure what else to do; everyone was still watching—like they'd watched him get pulled from the elementary classroom by the literacy specialists or sit reading picture books with the teacher. He grabbed his backpack and left through the other exit. As soon as he crossed the threshold, the cafeteria exploded with sound. Laughter and gasps and whispers and their names over and over.

Cass cheated on Shane.

Cass and Shane broke up.

Did Shane just call Cass a bitch?

Shane found his way to his first-period classroom—he wasn't sure where else to go—and sat there, leaning against Mrs. Gutierrez's door. He tilted his head, hoping gravity would force the tears to run back into his head. He only had a few minutes until the bell rang and the empty hallway flooded with students, their voices pinging against him like hail.

When he opened his eyes, Izzy stood above him, her jaw working angrily back and forth. "How could you do that?"

"Where's Cass?"

"Not your business anymore."

"I know." Shane rubbed his forehead, which was pounding now. "I shouldn't have said that to her."

"Damn right. Cass deserves way better."

"Don't I deserve better too?" He knew his voice was a whine. "I mean, she cheated on me."

"I don't feel sorry for you," she said, and there was a hint of a smile beneath her glare.

"You didn't tell her, did you? About the vocabulary test?"

"I didn't have to tell her," she said, emphasizing each word like a snap.

Did that mean Cass already knew he'd cheated on tests? That he couldn't read? Before he could ask more, the bell rang and Izzy turned the doorknob, unconcerned that he was leaning against the door. He sat up and she stepped over him without another glance.

Shane pushed himself to his feet. He couldn't fall to pieces here, right in the middle of the hallway.

Outside, under a blanket of heavy clouds, Shane walked south. The island was only seventeen miles long, and their school was plopped right in the middle of it. He could walk the whole thing and be back before the final bell. He could apologize, and if Cass forgave him, they could get back together.

Shane tried to imagine their senior year. She'd probably overcompensate with sweetness, and he'd have to try to bury any distrust or resentment as he hosted pool parties filled with people who used to be his friends and were now just hoping to see a train wreck.

Then what? She'd still leave for an excellent college and be surrounded by overachieving, motivated college boys with big shoulders. It would happen all over again.

As though in response, thunder rumbled off the coast. He walked toward it, until he reached the beach houses in Seabreeze Cove. They were five years old now—as old as his relationship with Cass.

A crack of lightning lit them in icy gray. The clouds broke, and the rain fell in sheets. The wind drove it into him sideways, stinging his skin. He wrapped his arms around his forehead to shield his eyes and ran for one of the houses.

He leaned against a piling under the blue one, teeth chattering. It felt like such an insult that here he was, shattering from the inside out, battered by wind and rain, while these houses stood unaffected, uncaring. Ready to age on past him.

And Cass was nowhere in sight.

TRANSCRIPT

....

INTERVIEW WITH VICTORIA CASTILLO

Officer Reynold: Thank you for coming in today.

Victoria Castillo: You're investigating whether they died by suicide or accident?

Officer Reynold: We're investigating all options at this point.

Victoria Castillo: You said you didn't find a note when you searched his room. If it was a suicide, wouldn't you have found a note?

Officer Reynold: That's not always the case.

Victoria Castillo: Did you try their phones? They spent more time on those than talking to us.

Officer Reynold: The phones were destroyed in the water, and it will take a little while for the records to come in. Ms. Castillo, did Israel have a history of depression or mental illness?

Victoria Castillo: No. I mean—well—no.

Officer Reynold: You seem uncertain about that.

Victoria Castillo: [Pause] We took him to the doctor once because he was having strange dreams. But the doctor said that was normal.

Officer Reynold: What about lately? Did you notice

anything different about your son's behavior in the past few days or weeks? Any big fights?

Victoria Castillo: Maybe he was a little moody. A little stressed about school. He got a lower grade than usual in economics. He wants <*muffled*>. I'm sorry. He wanted to go to a good college. . . . I know you think it's our fault. That's what you're saying, isn't it? That we missed something about him—something that could have prevented this.

Officer Reynold: We're just trying to get the full picture at this point, ma'am.

Victoria Castillo: And what if there isn't one? Or what if there is, but he took it with him?

CHAPTER TWENTY-THREE

IZZY

....

Three days after

OUR HOUSE IS silent: my dad is gone, Luna—finally—is settled on the couch watching for Israel out the window, and my mom is back in her room, the word *suicide* planted in her brain.

I feel like I want to shiver out of my skin.

My dad has been returning home well after midnight. He makes himself an arepa with fried cheese—I can smell the toasty corn flour from my room—and falls asleep to the sound of infomercials. I'm not sure if he and my mom are even talking. I've heard that couples sometimes fall apart after losing a child. Israel probably knew that, too, but either he thought our parents would be different or he didn't care.

After college my dad was working in the oil industry. He got laid off in a recession and started working construction to keep us afloat, which is how he ended up a contractor. He says it was all for us, but anyone who believes that is kidding themselves. It was for Israel, so he could go to New York to make bigger, more secure money. Even now our dad is still only working for Israel—to escape his loss.

I miss Israel's music, Nate's and Shane's voices as they grab snacks from our kitchen, my mom talking on the phone to her sister back home.

"Mami, are you going to Shane's funeral with me? It's in two hours," I call through her door.

She says something, but it's too soft for me to hear.

"¿Qué?"

This time I can hear her, the words anguished but loud: "No puedo."

"Fine," I say back loudly. It's not like I want to go either. I'll go for Cass because she would—she will—do the same for me.

She's pissed at me, though, because I keep trying to tell her about the dolphins. Cass would never call it that; she'd say *irritated*. I am the irritant, that tiny piece of sand under her fingernail or the popcorn kernel in her teeth. People think I'm oblivious to their little signals—the sighs, the arm crosses, the strained voices, and the locking of jaws. I'm not an idiot. I just don't believe that I need to be a receptor for every feeling other people broadcast. I make enough of my own noise.

But Cass has loved me at my cruelest, at my neediest, at my weakest. She loves me when I don't love myself. For today, I can shut up about dolphins and boats.

• • •

The church is already packed, the whole island here whether they knew Shane or not. Meg has pulled a chair up to the head of the coffin, and she's petting Shane's hair. His cheek. His hand. The thought of touching the body that is supposed to be Israel makes me feel like vomiting.

Cass is hovering beside her mother, along the outer aisle of the church and as close to the coffin as she can be without being near Shane's family. She's wearing a black dress and has a yellow purse across her chest—something that seems so out of place on her and in this room. Her eyes are glassy and she's paler—as though she's a print of herself. She thinks she's the reason he's gone, I can tell.

"You okay?" I ask. Her mom takes a few steps away from us; considerate, but I know she's still listening.

"I'm sorry about Shane," I say. Really, I *am* sorry about what she *believes* happened to him. But I'm not sure she knows everything there is to know. A month ago I thought about telling her how I'd seen him cheating on quizzes—testing if it broke them—but she did that all on her own.

I hug her, and she drapes herself on me. The weight of her grief surprises me.

Cass won't go up to the casket now with Meg there. She keeps clutching her stomach, and I imagine that's where it hurts, where the need is clawing away at her.

I sit with Cass and her mom in an off-to-the-side pew. Tears stream down Cass's face, but she remains silent and immobile. I'm not sure where she learned to cry with such stillness.

The funeral progresses in much the same way as other funerals I've been to. There are memories and prayers shared. There are flowers and somber musical interludes. There are audible sniffles and gasps, which make me tear up too. Because my mom isn't here. Because my brother caused this pain. Because he isn't home right now, studying and being an over-achiever. Because there might be a whole ocean between us.

After the funeral, people file out of the church to attend the luncheon in the attached building. There will probably be a small window before they load Shane into the hearse for the family-only burial later this afternoon.

Cass's mom is talking to another parent, so I grab Cass's hand and pull her toward the front of the church.

"I'll run interference with Meg," I say.

"I shouldn't go up there." Cass tries to loosen her hand from my grip.

"You do what you need to do." I say it more forcefully than I intend, but she nods. Sometimes Cass needs someone else to be the decider.

At the front of the church, she cries again. This time, I can feel her stillness, the way it seems to roll over her. The only movement is her nostrils fluttering with her breath and those tears, fast and free-falling.

The Shane-in-the-box is puffy—except for his arms, which even under a suit, look bony. The makeup is caked so that you cannot see his pores, lines, or scars. A sort of ironic return to babyhood. There's something strange clumping his eyelashes, and I want to lean closer, but a sharp "hey" reminds me of my job.

"Megan," I say, spinning away from Shane.

"Isabela," she says, wary.

"You're my sister now. That's how it works, right? You lost a brother. I lost a brother. Simple transitive property."

I expect Meg to say something snotty, to get back to her task of clearing Cass away, but the next thing I know, she's hugging me, and it feels like the sisterhood I've invented is real. We get each other. If someone had done to Israel what Cass did to Shane, I would have fought the person back from the funeral too.

Over her shoulder, I see Cass in Shane's father's arms. He's patting her back and murmuring something into her hair. It must be kind, whatever he says, because she rests her cheek on his chest. He has comforted so many teenagers today that his white shirt is smudged and streaked with makeup. That strange canvas of grief guts me, and I realize I'm bawling into Meg's neck.

No saint did this.

I was in the water shouting his name. *Israel. Israel. Israel.* Not only with my voice, but with my entire body.

And he didn't answer.

He still hasn't answered.

All I know is that he's not gone.

CHAPTER TWENTY-FOUR

IZZY

....

Four days after

I WAKE WITH the sun creeping through the cracks in my blinds. It's still strange to wake under my blankets in bed instead of sprawled on a rug. Or tripped on by my brother. This has to be how everyone else feels, how Israel and I should have been feeling all along.

Of course I never thought I'd be waking up to go to my brother's funeral. If I ever let myself think about our eventual deaths at all—and that's a big *if*—I imagined we'd blink out of existence at the same time: twin lights.

But here we are. No, here *I* am.

I guess I should put on a dress and do my hair and prepare to perform sisterly grief like Meg. That is the proper, endorsed behavior.

I let out Luna and wander back upstairs, stopping outside Israel's door. I've woken up pressed against it so many times, the wood warmed by my body. I put my hand on where I imagine its heart would be, if it had a heart, but, unsurprisingly, the door is cold.

It's the first time I've been inside his room since before he disappeared. The police searched it after the crash, but clearly they missed something. Something that would explain what I heard that night Shane and Nate were over.

I'd just brushed my teeth when I walked by Israel's room. The door was open—mom's rules—but Nate, Shane, and Israel were inside talking quietly, which was what caught my attention in the first place. They were never quiet.

"—said we need more hours before a solo flight," Shane said.

"He just wants more money," Nate said.

"It's also illegal," Shane said.

"When has that stopped us before?" Israel asked. He spotted me, meeting my eyes with an expression I couldn't read. I gave him the privacy he was always begging me for and didn't think anything about the incident until I woke to the plane engine and put two and two together.

Israel is impeccably neat. There aren't piles of clothing on his desk chair or bed like in my room, or shoes littering the carpet. But the investigators left everything askew: all the drawers slightly ajar, undershirts, charger cords, and papers poking from them. I pull the closet door open and am hit by the smell of him—freshly mown grass and citrus. Tears spring to my eyes.

"Fuck you," I say to the hanging clothes. "Fuck you," to the shoes lined neatly on the shelves.

His backpack is hanging on a hook near the closet mirror. I fish inside, but it has been emptied, either by the police or by Israel himself. Not that he carried much except a few notebooks and his iPad.

I spin around. He was always on the iPad, and I don't remember seeing the police with it.

Our mom is a bit of a snoop, so if it wasn't with him, he usually kept it hidden.

I know where. I kneel on the floor beside his closet and twist the screws off the vent. They turn without a screwdriver because he opens and closes it constantly. An attentive investigator would have probably noticed the lack of dust, but our island police aren't exactly sharp. They mostly respond to noise complaints and drunk drivers.

Bingo. His iPad, in its blue cover, is on top of the shoebox where he keeps binoculars, a tin for butts, a lighter, and a few packs of cigarettes. He'd bring the shoebox onto the roof to smoke alone if he'd had a bad day.

I'd call today a bad fucking day.

I grab the box and the tablet, wrench open his window, and climb onto the roof.

It's early but the gray shingles are already hot. I sit anyway, feeling the burn on the backs of my thighs. From the roof, you can see past the vacation homes to the slate strip of sand. The water almost looks blue from this distance instead of a motley brownish green.

Sometimes, if Israel was in one of his better moods, we

would sit out here together—me always on the left, so my right side was against him. It's how we came into existence, how we were supposed to be. We had the binoculars so we could see the beach, but really, we spied on neighbors and made up stories about their lives. As far as we were concerned, Magdalena Centeno had a secret lover who was ten years younger; her grown daughter, Dolores, was selling dulces to support her magician hobby; and Magdalena's husband, Arturo, was obsessed with Japanese game shows.

These moments were rare because Israel had a way of protecting himself that reminded me of an armadillo rolling into a ball. The more you poked, the more tightly armored he'd become. What was he protecting anyway?

"Bela?" I hear my dad calling from the hallway. He's only home because today is the day.

I wake up the iPad, but it's locked. I try our birthday forward and backward. The street address of this house. Of our last house. His last few soccer jersey numbers. Nope. Nope. Nope. Nope.

"Bela, ya nos vamos." *We're leaving.*

Israel always loved using the numbers on a telephone to spell out codes for me to crack. Other twins had secret languages; we had number codes. Well, *he* did. It was a fairly one-sided game.

4-3-8 2-6-6-5-4-3 was *get cookie.*

3-6-6-8 8-3-5-5 6-6-6 was *don't tell Mom.*

I try 5-8-6-2. *Luna.*

The iPad lock screen shifts to the home screen with his apps.

I tap open his social media apps, ignoring the notifications because I know I'll just find sob stories by people who've hardly ever spoken to him—and go to the direct messages. There are a few between him and the sophomore he liked—flirtatious winky faces and sexy selfies. If this had been a week ago, I probably would have spent all my time reading these messages and teasing him mercilessly. Today I open his texts with Nate and Shane instead.

A text from Shane a day before the crash: We on?

On, my brother responded.

On, Nate said.

I wonder if any of them had any doubts when they typed those two letters, if they understood—truly—what they were about to do. If not, what did they think was going to happen?

Before those messages, there's a lot of back-and-forth about times, rides, the keg for the party. My heart thumps when I spot a YouTube video Shane sent with a plane as its thumbnail, but it's just a how-to video about attaching a tow bar—whatever that is.

"Obviously, you figured out how to steal a plane. But why?" I mutter out loud.

"¿Isabela, dónde estás?" My dad is knocking on my door now, wondering where I am. If he opens it, he won't think to look on the roof. He'll have to go into Israel's room to see the open window, and who knows when he'll get up the courage to venture in.

I keep scrolling, scanning as quickly as I can. I stop when I get to messages from the end of the school year, my brother apologizing to Nate. There's nothing about dolphins or my brother's dream. Nothing that answers my why.

I open his email. Mostly, it's ads for a shoe store and a music platform. But there's a thread that he flagged with the subject line *Research Question*. The final email, sent a month before the crash, is to someone named Peter Ryerson.

Peter, The truth is that I think I'm him—your father

"What are you doing?" My dad leans out Israel's window. "It's dangerous. Te vas a caer." *You're going to fall.* My heart is hammering, but my feet are steady. I snap the cover closed and slide the iPad under the box, trying to be casual so he won't think anything of it. He's wearing a suit I've never seen before and his mustache is neatly trimmed and combed. "We have to go, Isabela. Ni siquiera te has vestido." *You're not even dressed.*

I look toward the ocean again before climbing back through the window. Israel reached out to the boy from his dreams a month before he plunged into the water and reemerged gray and glistening? It has to be connected, and I will figure out how.

CHAPTER TWENTY-FIVE

CASS

....

Four days after

I WAKE UP early the morning of Israel's funeral and walk south to the subdivision of beach houses Shane and I broke into when they were being built. Their colors—peach, sea foam, periwinkle, and yellow—say *fun is had here.* I try to map them on my memory. The peach, I think, is the one Shane peed in when it was simply a frame. Now there's cheap furniture decorated with pineapples on the porch.

I climb the stairs and press my face to the windows. It looks empty. I'm not sure what I expect to see—a younger Shane, I suppose, with blond hair buzzed to duck fuzz, Gumby limbs.

The door is locked, but a careless renter left a window open, and, with one push, the screen pops out. In my mind, time rewinds as soon as I step inside—I remember the angry pimples that marched across my forehead and the pulsing warmth of horniness in my groin. But I am still my older self, and the house is warm and stuffy. There are remnants of people: a pair of sunglasses in a basket on the coffee table, a bottle of sunscreen on a shelf by the door, the lingering smell of cleaning products from a recent housekeeper visit.

I stop in the kitchen, looking for Shane, as though he'll be there pretending to cook and making shushing sounds with his lips that were intended to be the sizzle of a pan.

I slide open the door to the back balcony. You can see the ocean from here, a wall of gray green beneath a cloudy sky. I lean against the railing. Izzy believes their souls are still out there, that the bodies dragged from the ocean were empty shells. I've never believed we're anything but fragile clumps of matter. My father is the soul-believing one in our household, and we only go to church if he's home, part of my mother's quest to pretend we're a happy family.

I try the master bedroom next, but it, too, is empty. We dry humped here—before we understood what, really, our bodies were telling us to do. It was movement that felt good, pressure from his knee, hips, the center seam of my jeans.

I circle the room, trailing my fingers, as though I can feel the studs. Here must be where he peed. Where his DNA still lingers. Two sharp kicks and I'm through the drywall. I peel it back until I can see the blond wood beneath. It looks the same. Unaged. Like nothing has happened. Like I haven't grown taller. Haven't fallen in love. Haven't lost my virginity. Haven't become captain of the volleyball team. Haven't taken the SATs. Haven't broken Shane's heart. Haven't attended his funeral.

I feel like I can't breathe, but I hear myself sucking in air—large yawning sounds. I sink down, forehead pressed against the torn wall. I could break it all away, return the house to its bones, but time will not unroll. Shane will not come back to life. I will not become the girl I was.

Back at home, I stand in front of my mirror half in my dress, my shoulders and chest still bare. Mom bought me one black dress for all three funerals. It's elegant and silky with geometric seaming at the waist, but pulling it on after yesterday makes me ill. It smells like foundation and potpourri and sweat. Like the second worst day of my life.

Mom comes in to zip me up.

"I don't want to wear it," I tell her.

"I don't know that you have anything else appropriate, Cassie."

"I don't care."

"Okay, it doesn't matter what you wear." She wipes a smudge—drywall dust—off my cheek and rests her head on my shoulder, wrapping her arms around my waist. We both look at ourselves in the mirror. Except for our noses, which are wide at the bridge and round at the tip, we don't look related. She is big-hipped, blond, and freckled. I have the height, angular face, and green-and-yellow-flecked eyes of my father.

"I wish he could be here with you right now," she says, and for a moment I think she means Shane, but she's talking about my dad. She thinks it's her fault he isn't. This—I realize—is how we're alike. We can't forgive ourselves; we don't think we deserve it.

I wiggle out of her embrace and open my closet. I have two other dresses: one white with swirls of orange flowers and the other leopard print. I pick the leopard print.

My mom retrieves a black cardigan from her closet, but when I pull it on, my eyes burn with tears. I feel so stupid crying about what I'm wearing when Shane is gone. When I'm about to go to my second-ever funeral.

"We don't have to go, Cassie," she says.

"I do for Izzy. You know that."

"It's okay to give yourself space," she says. "You can't be everything for everyone."

She's right about that. I can't be anything for anyone, let alone for myself.

The church smells like stale incense and onionskin pages. On the walls, they've mounted several stained glass windows rescued from the old cathedral that flooded in a hurricane. Each panel depicts the stations of the cross and crucifixion, in all its gory glory. Somber, loud organ music makes everything hum.

I think everyone is going to stare at my leopard print, but then I spot Izzy, seated in the first pew, legs crossed, bouncing her foot. She's dressed in leggings, a crop shirt I've seen her wear to the beach, and leather strappy sandals. Her hair is uncharacteristically greasy and swept into a loose bun on top of her head.

Her mom kneels beside the casket, head bowed, shoulders rising and lowering in quick shudders like she's crying. Her hair is just as greasy as Izzy's, but she's actually in a dress. Her dad, dressed in a black suit, greets visitors at the door. I've never seen him dressed up before, and he appears uncomfortable, tugging at his sleeves over and over like they're too short.

Mom nudges me toward him.

"Mr. Castillo," I say. "I'm so sorry."

He looks as though he can't remember who I am, even though I've been to their house a million times. Without a word, he shakes my hand and my mother's before moving to the next person.

I round the pew and sit next to Izzy; my mom slides into a row several back from ours.

"Hey."

"Oh hey," Izzy says cheerily, like it's a normal day. "Can you believe this?" She gestures at the filling pews and the altar where her brother's profile is visible above the lip of the casket.

"I can't," I say. "Your dad seems like he's taking it hard."

"I'm surprised he's not working," she says. "Have you gone yet?" She nods toward Israel. A few visitors stand beside her mother, clasping their hands and bowing their heads.

I shake my head.

"Don't bother. It doesn't even look like him."

I allow myself a quick glance, which was longer than I could look at Shane. Israel's skin is waxy, and his face is bloated. She's right. It doesn't look like him.

"I refuse to play funeral when he's still out there," she says.

So she isn't any closer to believing he's dead—even faced with a body that medical professionals and her family have identified as her brother. It pisses me off again. If she doesn't believe he's dead, she certainly doesn't believe Shane is dead, which is why she can't see how much pain she caused me when she dragged me to the ocean to look at dolphins and to see Janie about getting her dad's boat.

When the funeral begins, my mother beckons me to join her. The service is in English and Spanish, so it takes double the time. At some point during the long service, the priest invites Israel's dad to the lectern. He tells a story of Israel sticking up for Shane during a soccer game when he got carded. *Israel was honorable*, he says. *Israel was kind and loyal.* His face remains immobile, but his voice cracks at his son's name. If my heart weren't already broken, this would do it.

When he returns to his seat, Izzy stands, and I can hear a collective intake of breath as people realize she's not wearing funeral clothes.

"Bela, Bela," her mom calls softly, but Izzy marches to the lectern.

"Israel isn't honorable, kind, or loyal," she says into the mic. "He's an asshole."

Her mother makes a sound like a surprised bird.

"But that"—Izzy points at the coffin—"is not him."

With that, her father mounts the steps to the lectern and grabs her by the elbow. She allows herself to be guided down the steps and the aisle. She winks at me as she passes.

The priest resumes the service like this happens all the time, but people are whispering: *What did she just say? Poor girl. She shouldn't have come. She needs to talk to someone.*

They're more right than they know.

"I should follow her," I whisper to my mom.

She squeezes my hand.

I find Izzy in the back seat of their car, her head down like she's praying. I knock on the window, and she waves me inside. The air-conditioning is on full blast, but her forehead is shiny with sweat.

"You okay?" I ask.

She nods and points to an iPad in her lap. "It's Israel's."

She has the tablet's browser history open, and I lean over her shoulder to read. His last search was the time for sunrise on the Sunday they died. Before that, a website for *Bradley Simpson, Flight Instructor.*

"Let me show you something." She opens the email app and hands the tablet to me.

I read the thread quickly. For some reason Israel is lying about being a researcher to a guy named Peter. At the end he claims to be the guy's father.

"See," she says, stabbing the email with her finger. "They did it."

"What is this? I don't get it."

"Since he was little, Israel said he remembered a past life. He died getting medicine for his son. Israel found him—the real, live son."

I know I'm staring at her, my mouth open. Maybe I should tell my mom what's going on with her—see if we can get her some help. I swallow and try to respond calmly. "Let's pretend for half a second that's true; I still don't see what it has to do with them magically turning into dolphins."

"He lived a life before as someone else. He's living a life after now, too."

She must read disbelief on my face. "You never trust me, Cass," she says.

"I trust you. But I'm so, so sad, and pretending they are swimming around out there only makes it worse. Izzy, it's just not scientifically possible."

"Of course. Of course. There's the Cass path, and every other path is wrong."

"That's not what I—"

A gentle rap on the window interrupts us. My mom is outside. There are others outside too, milling around the parking lot in dark clothes, blotting their sweaty foreheads with hand-kerchiefs. The funeral is over.

I take a deep breath, trying to collect myself. "I should go. I just wanted to make sure you were okay."

"I'm okay," she says. Her attention has already returned to the iPad, to whatever she hopes to find.

As I walk to our car with Mom, I think of that name I spotted on Israel's iPad: *Bradley Simpson*. Maybe they told him something. Maybe he knows whether this was an accident or something they chose.

Maybe I have to seek some answers on my own.

CHAPTER TWENTY-SIX

JANIE

....

Four days after

DAD AND I arrive toward the end of Nate's wake. A group of chairs have been moved into a circle near the back of the room, far from the coffin. I can see Nate's profile, but I don't allow myself more than a glance. There's a portrait of him—a soccer photo from last year—next to the coffin, and I look at that instead. His mouth is a line and he glares at the camera with what I'm assuming is supposed to be an intimidating expression, but he looks small in his oversized uniform jersey.

"Gavin, Janie, have a seat," Nate's dad says when he sees us, gesturing at the circle of chairs. I've never seen him in anything but the stained jeans and ratty T-shirts advertising local restaurants that he wears on fishing tours. Today he is in a slim and expensive-looking navy suit. He is clean-shaven and looks like he could be heading out to the orchestra or opera. I wonder if this is what Nate would have dressed like had he gotten the chance to become a grown man. The thought makes my heart ache.

Nate's mother has removed her shoes, and she has blue nail polish, chipped, on her toes. Aaron, Nate's older brother, is holding her hand. He used to look boyish, with freckles and dark wavy hair, but college seems to have given him a more rugged appearance, with a fuller face and facial hair. He's taller than Nate was, though still shorter than most men. The cuter brother, according to many girls in our school.

My dad tugs at his beard, which means he's uncomfortable, but slides into a folding chair. There's another neighbor, Mrs. Kearn, in the circle, and a few people I recognize as belonging to the short, dark-haired Herschel extended family.

"I'm so sorry," I say, because what else is there?

Here, among his family, I'm openly known as his friend. Tomorrow, at the funeral, there will be a million people from school. People who've rarely, if ever, seen us speak to each other. The two worlds—the two Janies—will collide.

Nate's mom notices me for the first time, and she opens her mouth as though she's about to say something but then closes it.

"Thanks for being here," Aaron says. It sounds so idiotic coming from him—this boy who was always part of the Nate and Aaron wars—but here he is being the responsible one, the family greeter.

I sit for a few minutes next to my father, who is tugging his beard so hard I'm afraid he'll start pulling it out, before I excuse myself to go to the bathroom. I don't really need to go; I'm just afraid I'll blurt out something awkward if I stay.

Aaron excuses himself too. Before I get to the bathroom, he hisses, "Hey, Janie. Come outside?"

I follow him to a small garden of concrete pavers and succulents near the back entrance to the funeral home. Aaron is the one I have to thank for introducing me to weed. He was in ninth grade the year after my mom left, and he offered it to me casually once when I was over at their house. It relaxed my brain enough that I fell asleep, right there on the couch while Aaron and Nate played a video game. After that I started asking him for it so that I could sleep at home. Eventually he introduced me to the island's one dealer, a gentle hippie named Horace, who lives in a camper trailer and manages the campground on the south end of the island.

Even though Aaron was in high school with us for just two years, he's also the only one who knows that Nate avoided me there. We've never talked about it, but I've caught him looking at me pityingly.

"How are you doing?" he asks.

Terrible. I've lost my best friend, who didn't think I was good enough for him to begin with. "It comes and goes," I say instead.

He nods at this. "Yesterday I was barely functional and today I'm keeping them functional." He gestures at the funeral home. He rocks onto his toes and back. "It's good to see you, by the way."

It's my turn to nod.

"Listen, Janie, I have a favor to ask."

"Okay."

"I'm supposed to speak tomorrow, but I have no clue what to say. The only funerals I've ever been to are Shane's and Israel's. You're a good writer. Could you maybe help me write something?" He hands me his phone, where he's written one line on a note.

Nate was an incredible brother and friend.

"I have to lie, don't I?" he says with a chuckle.

"Yeah," I say. "It's all lies." He understands as well as I do that there were two worlds. But which Janie is the real one? Which Nate? "Sure, no problem. I can come over after this ends."

Aaron thanks me and returns to the parlor, but I'm not ready to go back in yet, so I stop at the drinking fountain outside the bathroom. I hear the soft smack of bare feet on tile. Nate's mom is behind me, twisting her wedding band. She's freckled like Aaron, petite and dark-haired like her husband and sons. Her hair is streaked with gray in a way that seems too purposeful to be natural. She isn't wearing makeup—she never does because she's always out on boats for her research—and her face is lined in that wholesome, friendly way you see depicted in TV ads for arthritis medicines. I've never seen her so beautiful or sad.

"Janie, you were his best friend," she says with a hint of an

Alabama accent. I want to laugh and cry at the same time. Did he tell her that?

She looks down at her ring and twists it again. "Do you know why? Why would he do this?" She's whispering now, talking more to herself than to me, and her voice cracks on the *why*. I want to tell her I knew something was wrong with him and didn't tell anyone. I want to tell her I ended our friendship during the party. But I can't hold the tears back. They slip down my cheeks, catching on my chin before they drop to my neck, my collarbone. I swipe at them but it's no use.

"Shhh. Shhh," she says softly, cupping my cheek with her hand. "That makes two of us."

But I don't know what she means. Two of us crying this way? Two of us who don't know why? Or two of us who might?

The memories cascade, one after the other:

Nate, sunk into himself, staring blankly at the television.

Nate, pointing to the stars.

Nate, at the party with that strange look on his face when I said I couldn't pretend anymore.

"I don't know why this happened," I say. "But I'm going to find out. I promise." And I will. Tomorrow I'll get that boat for Cass and Izzy and ask them what they know.

Nate's mom gives me a sad smile and a quick squeeze of my hand, then turns to go back inside and leaves me standing there alone.

CHAPTER TWENTY-SEVEN

CASS

....

Five days after

I WANT TO skip Nate's funeral. I'm at the point where grief has settled into exhaustion, where I want nothing but to sleep until everything is muted and gauzy. Izzy texts me, insisting I go because Shane would want it.

I don't answer right away. Let her think I'm still mad. Plus I'm not sure she's right. Shane hated anything slow and morose and probably would have hated his own funeral. But funerals are for those who've been left behind: Shane's was for his mom, surrounded by floral arrangements she didn't make; for his sister, holding his hand one more time; for his dad, comforting sobbing teenager after sobbing teenager and allowing it to fuel his rage. He whispered to me, *It's okay, sweetie. I will not rest until I find out who is to blame*, which only made me cry harder.

I wear the leopard print and black cardigan again and ask my mom just to drop me off. I'm tired of the hand pats, the back rubs, the hovering to make sure I'm okay. I'm not, and no amount of hugging will change that.

Izzy meets me at the church, wearing slightly dressier clothes than for her brother's funeral—jeans and a black blouse. "Hi," she says, like nothing happened yesterday.

"Hey," I say back stiffly.

It doesn't even register. Not that I expect an apology.

She picks a pew in the middle of the church, and I slide in beside her. Janie is sitting right next to Nate's mom. Her hair is in a crooked French braid, and she's wearing an oversized skirt suit in a sober plum color. It looks like something made for a much older woman. She keeps glancing behind her, her eyes roving like she's trying to find someone but can't focus. Mrs. Herschel bends Janie's head toward her own and pets the girl's hair like she's family. It makes me unsettled, this intimacy. Janie is their next-door neighbor, but I've never even seen Nate talk to her.

Izzy is watching them too with a thoughtful expression, and just like that day in film class when Janie turned in that mess of a script, Izzy seems to see something that I do not.

"That's weird," I whisper, hoping it will prompt her to share whatever she sees.

"It's interesting," she says without elaborating.

Other people from our school have noticed too. Tien, sitting across the aisle from us, is doing the most obvious cup of her hand around her mouth as she talks to Shelly. Marcus is flat-out staring.

The pastor invites Aaron up to deliver a eulogy. He clears his throat, unfolds a paper, and smooths it out on the lectern.

"Nate was an incredible brother, son, and friend. He was the kind of soccer player who made it look easy, which you all know. But I want to tell you something about Nate that you probably didn't: he loved the ocean. When he was younger, he'd ignore how hot it was and ride his bike to the seawall. He'd climb out on the rocks on the south side and watch the waves for hours. Not even our mosquitoes could keep him away. Once, I asked him why he spent so long looking at the ocean, and he said, 'Because it's magic.'

"I think he believed in the ocean's ability to wash us clean and give us a fresh beginning. Nate was always willing to begin again. When I was on the soccer team with him a few years ago and we were facing that losing streak, he'd start every practice and game like we were going to win the championship. After his knee injury, he went to every PT appointment. His physical therapist said he was a warrior; he was right. I probably know that better than anyone. We fought all the time as kids. Nate was a stubborn son of a— Sorry, Mom."

The audience chuckles, and Aaron looks for someone in the crowd. Janie? "One time we had a terrible fight about who could have shotgun. It ended with us rolling in the grass outside and our dad dragging us apart by the collars. But, once we were in the car—with me in the front seat, of course—he cracked some wry joke that made us all laugh. Because with Nate, you could always start over again too. He gave us all that.

"I hope each of us can keep our memories of him as that sarcastic, half-smiling, hilarious soccer demon that he was, but also remember that he was a person who saw magic in everyday things."

Aaron bows his head. The crowd joins him in a moment of silence, punctuated by sniffles. When he returns to his seat, a hymn begins.

"He didn't write that," Izzy whispers to me.

"How do you know?"

Izzy is watching Janie with a slight smile on her lips. "I can just tell."

After the funeral, Janie frees herself from Mrs. Herschel and looks like she's trying to escape the church. Izzy has a shark-like ability to navigate through crowds—precise, fast, and cunning—and we intercept Janie.

"Is the boat ready?" she asks without a hello.

"Theo should have it ready by the time we get there," Janie says, tugging on her braid nervously.

After our visit to the theater, they made a plan without me, I realize. Izzy rarely surprises me. Her feelings are so big that even the secrets she thinks she has are as visible as her eyeliner. But her interest in using Janie when there's a whole town of boat owners around us is baffling to me.

It's not that Janie isn't nice enough. Or smart. Or generous with the weed that she gets from God knows where. It's the way she seems tethered to a different world, unsure of the rules of this one—how to be near people without hovering, how to moderate her tone with teachers, how to think and talk at the same time, how not to punch cafeteria walls.

"Can you drive?" Izzy asks Janie with what sounds like sympathy. Janie nods back.

They start toward the parking lot, and I hang back—not sure if I'm still expected to join this pointless expedition. Mom has warned me that I need to defend my boundaries, decide for myself if something will help or hurt me. Izzy's dolphin bullshit hurts because it feels like a lie, like something you make up so little children can stomach grief: *We took Fluffy to a nice farm.*

Janie glances over her shoulder and notices that I'm not in step with them. "Cass isn't coming," she says, but characteristic of her awkwardness, she's looking at me, talking *to* me.

Izzy turns, and I expect her to insist or cajole, but her face is impassive. Patient, even. The decision, for what seems like the first time, is mine.

And I choose my friend.

Theo begins untying the boat while we climb in. It dips with my weight, and I sit immediately, right where I stepped in. Janie is already at the helm and Izzy sits on the bench across from me. She moves her legs, presumably so that I can sit beside her, but I stay planted on my side of the boat. I know it will be too loud to talk anyway, and I want to be alone in the whirring, splashing pocket of sound.

Janie points at the bench where three life jackets are stored, and we all pull them on over our funeral clothes. The vest is damp, and I can feel it soaking my mom's cardigan.

Janie is a nervous driver, and that's no different with a boat. She taps her thumbs on the wheel, bites her lip, and glances back at Theo, who is standing on the dock with his hand bridged over his eyes. The boat glides at a snail's pace out of the marina, so there's no threat that we'll hit something. When we clear the bay and Janie hits the throttle, we're still moving slowly. This is a tourist's boat. A toddling-around-the-bay boat.

We pick up speed as we approach the southern end of the island and loop around, heading north toward the beaches, toward the party beach. My hair is whipping, curling around my neck, tickling my cheeks, dashing across my forehead. There is no order out here, no calmness.

Izzy looks right at me and says something. I cannot hear her, and I try to read her lips as she repeats it. I decide that she's apologizing.

It's okay, I mouth because my voice will get lost.

She grins, and I feel lighter. I think I can face this moment, looking into the water where we lost the boys—even if she brings up the dolphins—because our friendship is solid. Because I can be Cass and she can be Izzy, and there are years and years of us to stand on.

Janie cuts the motor to a purr, and then off. We float. And

drift. I'm struck by the vacuum of sound. My ears almost throb with it. There's only the water lapping against the side of the boat. There's only us, waiting for Izzy to say or do whatever we have come here for.

It's hard to get my bearings from this view of the beaches. Between Adventure Pier and the northern tip, it is one flat stretch. The businesses and hotels across Ocean from the seawall provide the best guidance. There's also a statue of an angel mounted on the seawall, across from the Kroger. The angel was built in 1910 to commemorate the victims of a particularly devastating hurricane. We call her Gully because of the number of seagulls that have shit on her head and dress.

The night of the party, several people stopped at the Kroger for mixers and snacks. They carried the bags across to Gully, climbed down the steps, and walked north, closer to Gilligan's, a place famous for fried oysters the size of a child's fist.

I imagine dropping a night sky over this stretch of beach. Imagine a ring of rocks with a fire inside. A keg in the shadows of the seawall. Blankets and beach towels. Teenagers in cutoff shorts, bikini tops. So much skin, dusted in sand. So much life ahead of us still.

"There. That's where we were," I say, pointing.

Janie moves to the anchor, which she heaves over the side, rocking us. She looks like she's trying to swallow something back, but then leans over and vomits into the water.

"Just seasick," she says as though we asked. She waves her hands at us, like we should continue what we're doing.

Izzy has already returned her attention to the beach.

The plane was flying so low as it roared over the seawall. Were they trying to scare us? Were they out of control? Or were they saying goodbye?

My mom has been trying to keep me away from the news, but I found an article online that showed the guys in their junior-year photos. Shane was in a black button-down; I think it was the only shirt he owned that wasn't a T-shirt, so he hated to wear it. He wasn't smiling in the photo either. It didn't capture the real Shane. But nothing about this situation feels real. The article said the plane went into a stall because they'd tried to climb at too sharp of an incline from the beach. The plane was still too low and they were too inexperienced to recover.

They were inexperienced, but they had *some* experience— lessons from this Bradley Simpson guy. I could ask him if they knew climbing that steeply would cause a stall and did it anyway.

With the motor off and the anchor down, it's ungodly hot. My hair is dampening along my neck and frizzing. Izzy's is too, but for once she doesn't seem to care. She pulls a pair of binoculars out of her purse and stands, rocking us again. Janie makes a retching sound, but pinches her lips tight.

"What is she looking for?" she asks a moment later as though Izzy isn't right here.

"For our boys," Izzy answers.

"I didn't think you knew," Janie said.

"Knew what?" I ask.

"That Nate and I—you know."

I shake my head. I *didn't* know. Is she saying she and Nate were together?

Izzy, characteristically, ignores everything that isn't relevant to her objective. "They're not gone, Janie," she says. "They've transmigrated."

"Transmigrated?" Janie echoes. That's a new word for me, too. Izzy must have been doing research.

"She thinks they're dolphins," I tell Janie.

Izzy shoots me a look. "I *believe* their souls have transferred to dolphins, yes. I *know* that Israel is still alive. It's a twinsense thing."

"But why would they want to be dolphins?" I ask, fanning myself with my hand. I can't help the irritation creeping back into my voice. "What the fuck would be the point?"

"What the fuck would be the point of a joyride?" Izzy shoots back.

"There isn't. That's why people think—" I don't let myself finish. There's no use getting worked up again or trying to rationalize with her. "We should try somewhere else. They're clearly not here."

"How about near the ferry? I always see dolphins on that side," Janie says.

She lifts the anchor and we loop back around the point of the island, passing the marina again. There's a lot of boat traffic on this side, and Janie slows down to a snail's pace.

The ferry is docked and people in orange vests direct the

waiting cars. A cruise liner is waiting too, seagulls whirling above it as though they know how much food it holds. Farther out, there's a wide, flat boat stacked with shipping containers being guided in by a tugboat.

In the wake of a small yacht, I see a fin and the quick rainbow of a dolphin's spine. "There!" I point.

Izzy whips out the binoculars. "There's only one," she says.

But Janie spots more near the ferry dock. Again, the binoculars are lifted. There are five or six of them this time.

"It's not them," Izzy says.

"How do you know? Are there any identifying features other than that there's three of them together?" I ask.

"I'll feel it," Izzy says.

For several minutes we drive, all of us looking out across the water. Nothing but waves.

Then, a splash. I glance behind the boat. There's a dorsal fin trailing us and one—no, *two more*—to the left.

"Stop!" I shout.

Janie cuts the engine, and Izzy stands. She doesn't need binoculars for how close they are now, sleek gray and shining. But as quickly as they appeared, they're gone, and the three of us swivel, trying to find them again.

"There," Janie says, and we whip around to the right side of the boat in time to see the flip of their tails before they're back underwater.

We drift, letting other boats' wakes lift and settle us. A seagull lands near Izzy, and takes off with an indignant shriek when she flaps her hand at it. Janie's plum skirt is soaked through, there's something dried in her hair that I'm choosing to believe isn't vomit, and her face is green, but she's bright-eyed and alert.

A fisherman is heading back to shore on a larger boat nearby, and I spot a dolphin in front of his bow. It keeps sinking beneath the surface and reappearing several yards ahead. There are two more, racing along the side.

"Go," I say. "Fast."

Janie looks confused. "Where?"

"Out to sea!"

Izzy grins at me and I smile back. "Go, go, go!" she shouts.

They're with us in minutes, weaving in front of our boat, breaking the surface with their dorsal fins and the smooth curves of their backs. The longest one barrel-rolls. The second skips—quick dips in and out of the water. The third is the fastest, driving straight and true. They let us catch up to them, before pumping hard with their tails, propelling themselves downward and ahead. I can almost reach out to touch them.

"It's them!" Izzy shouts over the roar of the motor. "They want us to follow!"

And I can't help it; my heart is thudding.

REMEMBERED SOULS FORUM

....

GULF COAST

49er: Does anyone else remember more than just one past life? How come @OtherPlanes remembers so many and I can only remember one?

OtherPlanes: I think it's because I've been restless a long, long time. That's why I'm trying to live this life quiet and right. Just teaching people what I know so they can do better too.

Morris9786: Your last life was bad?

OtherPlanes: God yes. I was a power-hungry politician. Shot right in front of my 13-year-old son.

49er: What? You were shot?

OtherPlanes: Yeah. The funny story is how I got to be her.

Morris9786: What do you mean? It wasn't just random?

OtherPlanes: Oh no. There's a doorway.

49er: Doorway?

OtherPlanes: Think of it like a shortcut to another life. You see, before I was the politician, Millicent, I was a pilot. Flight 4945. Look it up.

Morris9786: Whoa. 75 people on board when it crashed?

OtherPlanes: That's right. Both engines failed and then I saw the strangest thing: this black lemon-shaped tear in the sky. We fell right into it.

I have no memory of being inside that tear. My theory is that I was simply a soul at that point, without a body and its memory-making mechanisms. But I'm pretty sure that I must have chosen to be Millicent, because I'd seen her before on one of my flights. She was maybe four or five then, holding her father's hand and wearing this lavender coat and a tiny pearl necklace. I remember thinking—as this former navy pilot—that it must be so nice to be a little girl like that with nothing but opportunity ahead.

And so, one minute, I was plummeting toward the doorway, my mind flashing to Millicent, and the next I became her.

Morris9786: You serious?

OtherPlanes: Dead.

49er: So, what, you just took over her body? You can kick another soul out?

OtherPlanes: I wouldn't advise it unless absolutely necessary. It wasn't easy to jump into a fully formed body. Not like being born into one. Even at that age, Millicent's mind was already set on the track that eventually killed her. She wouldn't accept the existence of a new soul—let alone be persuaded by one to do better.

CHAPTER TWENTY-EIGHT

SHANE

·····························

Twenty-four days before

SHANE PARKED HIS mom's SUV in the guest parking lot of the university Meg and Aaron attended. Nate was in back, sitting sideways so he could extend his knee across the bench. They'd joked about Shane being a chauffeur.

"Close the window, Nigel, won't you?" Nate had said, and Shane had balled up a receipt from the center console and chucked it at him.

It wasn't hard to convince Nate to come with him on this last-minute trip to visit their siblings before the semester was over. *I have to see what college life is like*, Shane had told Nate. He wanted to see what he'd be missing. *And I think you need to see too. Now that—*

He hadn't needed to finish the sentence.

Convincing his mom had been even easier. She was downright eager that Shane was showing an interest in college—not that he could get into Meg and Aaron's. He was pretty sure his mom knew he'd skipped school that week, but they weren't doing anything in class except studying for finals he'd cheat on anyway. Unlike most of his friends' parents, Shane's gave him a lot of latitude: drinking was fine as long as no one drove, sex was fine if condoms were used, mediocre grades were fine as long as college was still on the table, and skipping was fine, apparently, if hearts were broken; his parents were almost as crushed as he was that Cass was out of his life.

Aaron greeted them in the dorm lobby to swipe them in. "Hey, dummies," he said like they were kids again. "How's the knee?" He gestured at Nate's crutches.

"Hurts," Nate said. "How are finals?"

"Hurts," Aaron responded. "I've got one left tomorrow."

He took them to his room on the fourth floor. There were two boxes beside the bed, each packed with loose clutter—a desk lamp, plates, a bleach-stained towel. Otherwise, there was no evidence that Aaron was moving out that weekend. The open closet was overflowing with clothes and there were five posters hanging—a line of models in bathing suits, all with their lips parted. Aaron's roommate's side was tidier, nearly empty except for a few textbooks piled on his desk.

"Nice decor," Shane said, gesturing at the posters.

"You like? It's my gallery."

"Of wanks?" Nate asked.

Aaron rolled his eyes.

Each side of the room had a slim mattress that could slide

into a sideboard and double as a couch. Aaron's was a tangled mess of sheets. Shane sat down gingerly on top, trying not to wonder when Nate's brother had last washed them.

Nate frowned at the other side of the room. "There's got to be, like, only three feet between you and your roommate when you sleep."

Aaron nodded. "Yeah, freshmen get the shaft here, but at least it's not a room with six of us. Some of the dorms feel like you're in barracks."

"What's the school part of college like?" Shane asked.

"This year I was just doing all the general curriculum stuff, so the classes were boring and easy. The tests were kinda hard, though." The response didn't inspire confidence in Shane.

"How about the parties?" he asked.

"Every day is a party," Aaron said. "Taco Tuesday, Wine Wednesday, Thirsty Thursday."

"Oh, perfect," Shane said. "I'm thirsty."

"I thought you were here for a school-sanctioned college visit," Aaron said with a wink. "That's what Mom said."

"Yeah, but it's not like our parents have to know."

"We want the real college experience," Nate said, though it sounded to Shane like he was forcing enthusiasm for his sake.

Meg poked her head through the doorway then. "Anybody home?"

"Hey, Moo," Shane said. Meg was with a tiny mouse of a girl in a short black dress and high heels that caused her to wobble as she walked in. Compared to her friend, Meg was casual in jeans, a gray T-shirt, and red flats. It was something Cass would have worn in her effortless way, but Shane knew his sister's "casual" was much more calculated—that everything was chosen to appear as though she hadn't thought about it at all.

"How are you doing, Sandy?" she said. She pushed her bottom lip out in a sympathetic pout.

"I'm okay," he said.

"This is Monica. Monica, this is Nate and my brother, Shane. He just broke up with his girlfriend."

Monica's makeup was a shade too light, which made it seem like her head belonged to a different body. Her hair was curled into identical tubes that hung down her back. She collapsed onto Aaron's roommate's bed and emitted a sound that was half whimper, half relief, before crossing her legs and looking, very deliberately, at Shane. "Hi," she said.

Surprised, Shane glanced at Meg, who smirked back. Was he being set up?

The thought made him reevaluate the girl. He could forget she wasn't Cass if he dragged his fingers through the curls of her hair to loosen them. If he undid the buckles on her shoes. If he lifted her so she wasn't so much shorter than him. If he drank enough alcohol.

Meg passed a flask around the room, and Shane recognized the sweet burnt-caramel flavor of cheap whiskey. Monica took out a flask of her own and passed it too—a rose-gold one with the initials *MM* set in rhinestones. It contained a cherry vodka that smelled strangely medicinal. When Shane put the flask to his lips, he made eye contact with her, hoping he was sending her the same signal she'd sent him. The vodka dribbled out of the corner of his mouth and onto the collar of his shirt.

"Did your drinker break?" Nate asked with mock sincerity.

"Very funny," he said, but Monica did seem to think it was funny, and let out a squawk. It was a good-natured, silly laugh, but it wasn't the kind of laugh that you chased feverishly. The kind that you broke into houses and cooked imaginary dinners for.

From the curb, Shane could feel the party's bass in his teeth. They were outside a stucco townhouse, three stories tall and narrowly pressed between two identical houses. Crossing the threshold was like walking into a wall made of hot, sour air. In the center of a dark living room, a crowd was shout-singing the chorus to a song Shane didn't recognize. The furniture had been dragged to the periphery of the room, and every surface was covered with Solo cups. Monica grabbed Meg's hand and danced her away. Aaron waved Shane and Nate toward the brightly lit kitchen. The room was cooler, though similarly packed with people leaning against the counters. A guy in a polo stood at the stove, frying hash browns in way too much oil. The counter next to the sink was lined with liquor and soda bottles. A cooler for ice and a keg blocked the fridge. Aaron threw cash into an empty pickle jar and took a Solo cup. Shane and Nate followed suit.

Cheers erupted from the yard behind the house.

"What's going on down there?" Shane asked.

"Cockfighting," Aaron said.

"He's joking," Nate said.

Aaron grinned. "It's either beer pong or flip cup." He tipped a handle of Jack Daniel's over his Solo cup and added a splash of Coke. He waved to someone and disappeared across the room, leaving Shane and Nate in front of the booze.

Nate poured a beer from the keg and promptly dipped his shirtsleeve in it. He'd borrowed one of Aaron's button-downs, but he had to keep shoving the too-long sleeves up past his elbows. If they were around their own friends, Shane would put down his cup and roll Nate's sleeves up like he was his dad, cuffing them so they'd stay. Maybe he would straighten his collar, too. Nate would think it was funny.

Shane poured himself a shot of tequila and downed it, sucking his teeth as it burned his throat. He then mixed ginger ale with whiskey—one of his sister's favorite drinks—and waved Nate toward the living room. Monica was in the center with a few other girls in heels, most of whom were holding a drink to the ceiling as though they were offering it to some god. They were dancing—or really, they were rocking their hips back and forth without moving their feet—probably too afraid they'd fall.

Shane sidled up behind Monica, lightly touched her waist

with one hand, and raised his cup in the air with the other. Her head swiveled quickly, but she smiled when she recognized him. She backed up so she was pressed against his groin. His body didn't respond like it normally would have; it was probably waiting for Cass to walk through the door.

Nate had hobbled after Shane to the group of dancing girls, but he bobbed at the edge of the circle. He'd always been shy around girls and had only ever kissed two—both at Shane's suggestion.

Monica turned to face Shane and tilted her head back. Her eyes were closed and her lips were parted like the women in the posters. She wanted him to kiss her, he realized.

Do it, he told himself. *You have to see.* He bent his neck and stooped to meet her face. She came alive then, her tongue hooking into his mouth, her pelvis grinding against his leg. He had to remind himself to move his own lips and tongue, to behave like a person who knew how to kiss, but inside, he felt like he was barely strapped onto a roller coaster and plummeting downhill. Every decision lately had been made without him.

At some point in the night, Nate disappeared. Shane was too drunk to care. Monica pulled him by the hand upstairs and into a bedroom. The room was spinning, but he managed to count four twin beds and four desks in the room.

"Is this your room?" he asked, his voice coming out louder than he'd expected after shouting over the music in the living room. He'd learned a little bit about her that way: she liked pineapple pizza; she was majoring in communications; she'd grown up in El Paso.

"Of course it's not my room," she said before dragging him down onto a bed and kissing him. His teeth clacked against hers. Her body felt small under him, hard and tightly wound where Cass's had been languid and easy. He broke the kiss and leaned over the side of this stranger's bed, thinking he was going to throw up. Perhaps he had? Monica's lip was curled in disgust when he turned back to her, and when he went in for another kiss, she offered him her neck instead. He kissed it obligingly, tasting something chemical. Her perfume?

She unzipped his pants and grabbed him. With Cass, he'd have been hard, but his dick sort of flopped into Monica's hand.

"What's wrong?" she asked.

"Let's just talk," he mumbled, barely able to keep his eyes open.

Someone shoved him awake, a red-faced guy with a septum ring. "Get off my bed."

"Monica?" Shane croaked.

"Do I look like a Monica?"

Shane stumbled out of the room, down the stairs, and outside. He pulled a map up on his phone to find Aaron's dorm, but the lines on the map undulated and blurred. He tried to use a bush to steady himself but fell into it instead, scratching his arms up to his elbows.

A group of college girls walked by, tightening into a knot when he staggered toward them.

"I'm lost," he said, but they changed direction all at once like a school of fish.

How could he do college if he couldn't even handle a party or kiss a cute girl or find his way back to a dorm? Let alone the reading and papers and tests. He saw himself through a college student's eyes—the tall, gangly kid floundering at the front of the classroom with a picture book when everyone else was studying differential equations or consumer price indexes or whatever.

Izzy was right; Cass deserved better.

He *was* a loser.

CHAPTER TWENTY-NINE

NATE

....

Twenty-four days before

THE PULSING MUSIC and press of people's body heat exacerbated the nausea Nate was feeling because of his knee. As soon as Shane started to kiss Monica, Nate fled the house on his crutches. Outside, it was in the eighties but it felt so cool in comparison to the party that his skin prickled with goose bumps.

He hopped down the block toward the football stadium, which hulked like an oversized dinner bowl at the edge of campus. There were plenty of people out this late, crossing the campus in small groups or walking hurriedly alone, as though trying to escape someone who was tailing them. Their voices occasionally rang out, echoing against the stone and brick buildings in a way that made it seem like they were right next to him. Unseen toads called back with their gravelly trills.

Nate heard a whistle as he neared the stadium, and his

heart leapt at the familiar signal to drive his foot into the ball or to sprint toward the opponent. Right across from the stadium parking lots was a soccer field, bathed in white from overhead lights.

There were several men playing shirts versus skins. From the looks of it, they were locals borrowing the field for a late-night game. Those without shirts glistened with sweat. They were short a few players, but they still moved easily down the field, calling out in Spanish and elegantly weaving as they passed to one another.

He would never play like he once had. The ball would never be a natural extension of his feet again. His muscles wouldn't surge with electricity as he chased an opponent. He wouldn't feel the thrill of a goal scored. Of being hugged and smacked and encircled by cheering teammates.

If he went to college, he would spend every day reminded of what he lost. Not that colleges would be jumping to accept him. What did he have to offer them without soccer? He was worthless.

As though in agreement, Nate's knee buckled beneath him and his armpit slammed into the crutch. He yelped.

I deserve the pain, Nate thought. After all, he'd been cocky about soccer—pretending that his talent was all genetic, that the sport was something that belonged to him, that he didn't need anything else. Was this injury some cosmic punishment?

I deserve the pain, he thought again.

Nate's surgery was scheduled eleven days from now, and

he knew he'd feel far worse after. For now, though, he shifted his weight onto his injured knee, until the pain sparked hot behind his eyes. The sharpness took his breath away, but filled him too, like a satisfying meal. This was how he paid the debt.

"Nate?" It was Aaron. Nate turned to see his brother lit yellow by a streetlight. "You okay?" Aaron asked.

"Yeah, I just wanted some air," Nate said.

Aaron raised an eyebrow but didn't press. "I gotta get some sleep," he said. "Last final tomorrow and all."

Nate nodded. "I'll head back with you."

"Where's Shane?"

"Hell if I know. Probably still with that Monica girl."

Aaron walked slowly so Nate didn't have to struggle to keep up. An awkward silence hung between them. For so long, they'd been at each other's throats about everything and, after sixth grade, they'd barely been acquaintances. Honestly, Nate couldn't say a single thing he knew about this newly square-jawed, adult Aaron. What was he majoring in? Was he dating anyone? What did he want to do with his life? It was embarrassing how little he knew about his own brother.

"It's kind of nice you came," Aaron said.

"It was Shane's idea."

"Oh."

What a shitty thing to say. He was a terrible brother. "Thanks for putting us up," he said. "I'll have to come back for a football game or something. Maybe in the fall when my knee is better."

"Yeah. That'd be good." Aaron tapped Nate's crutch. "This is a real shit-stick. I'm sorry it happened to you."

"Thanks."

Aaron grasped the back of Nate's neck and squeezed. It was probably the first time they'd touched voluntarily in years, and Nate's eyes welled with tears. He swiped them away before his brother could see.

At two a.m., Shane woke Nate, staggering into the dorm lounge where they were staying. He bumped into a side table, knocking the lamp onto the carpet. Nate followed Shane into the bathroom, told him to splash water on his face, and pushed him into a stall, where he immediately retched.

"How you feeling, man?" Nate asked when Shane's heaves gave way to spitting.

Shane moaned in response and leaned against the side wall of the stall, his head dropping to his own shoulder like he was a rag doll. He seemed to be asleep for a moment but he jerked awake and struggled to shove a hand in his pocket for his phone. He squinted at the screen, like he couldn't quite see it, before stabbing it with his finger. Nate snatched it from him. Cass's name was on the screen.

Nate immediately ended the call. "You can't wake her up, man," he said. "Not like this."

"Please. I need to talk to her."

"Why don't you say what you want to say to me?" Nate

suggested. "And, if you still want to in the morning, you can call her then."

Shane's pupils were swimming like he couldn't find a place for them to land. "I'm sorry too," he said. "That's what I want to say."

"For sleeping with that Monica girl?"

"No, I couldn't." He gestured at his crotch. "Too drunk."

"That's probably for the best."

"I need to tell Cass I'm sorry for not being enough." He shrugged like he'd given up. "She'll be in a place like this and I won't be."

"She'll be in a dorm bathroom trying to throw up?" Nate knew what he meant, but making a joke about it seemed better than lying to his friend, trying to assure him that he'd end up wherever Cass would go.

Shane smiled sadly at Nate's joke. "This isn't for me," he said.

"I don't know if it's for me, either," Nate said, remembering the soccer field lit up like some sort of heavenly gift he couldn't have.

Shane's chin bobbed a yes before rolling onto his chest. His breathing slowed.

Nate grabbed a pillow and blanket from the lounge and tucked it around his friend. He returned to the couch where he'd been sleeping and sprawled on his back. He was wide-awake now. He took out his own phone and scrolled through his old texts. Janie's thread was near the top.

Earlier he'd texted her that Shane was kidnapping him for a trip to visit their siblings so that she wouldn't stop by after school. Need me to call the authorities? she'd joked. He hadn't texted anything back. And now that he knew this place wasn't for him, what else was there to say? Their futures would be so different. What if she didn't want to see him when she visited from college? He didn't know if he could handle that on top of everything else.

He navigated to her social media. Her profile photo was a cartoon version of her. She only ever posted reviews of movies she'd seen at work. The tone in her posts was playful and witty, like she was someone who'd never been crushed by her mom or peers at school. He had a feeling the person posting was the Janie she wanted to be when she left their island for college. He thought she could do it—become that person—although he'd be sad to see the Janie she was now go away. No, sad to see her leave him behind.

Was there a word for missing someone before they were gone? He closed his eyes and pictured her on the day he'd been slide-tackled, pulling her shirt off. He hadn't been able to focus at the time because of the pain, but now, in his imagination, he could admire the tender, never-sun-kissed skin of the tops of her breasts, the outline of her nipples under the fabric of the sports bra. He wanted to roll it up and off her, to gather her large breasts in his palms, to push them into his mouth.

But he didn't deserve to touch her. He'd been selfish for so many years, building a wall between his two worlds so that no one knew about their friendship when, really, what was the worst that could happen? Someone would laugh at him?

Nate shifted onto his side, bending his knee accidentally. Pain sliced through him and tears sprang to his eyes. It hurt like his skin was ripping, like he was about to burst through himself—blood and bone and muscle and ligament. All torn. How he wanted that bright explosion. He deserved it.

He straightened his knee, took a breath, and then bent it again.

Again.

Again.

CHAPTER THIRTY

ISRAEL

....

Twenty-four days before

ISRAEL KEPT READING and rereading a question on his econ final about supply and demand and then staring at its accompanying graph without being able to connect the two. His mind felt like a long tunnel that he was too exhausted to walk down.

Shane had texted the night before that he and Nate were going to visit their siblings at college. Israel was hurt they hadn't asked him to join—not that he would have been able to miss this final, which had been scheduled earlier than most. Either it hadn't occurred to them that he'd want to see college too— maybe even more so since he didn't have an older sibling—or Nate was still angry at him.

Peter hadn't responded to his last email, either, and Israel couldn't help rewriting the message he'd sent over and over in his mind. He should have come up with another lie to keep the man talking.

"Five minutes left," his teacher called.

"¡Coño!" Israel swore under his breath. Econ was the one class that was actually relevant to what his dad wanted him to study, but it was too late; he still had ten questions left. His only option was to skim the rest and start bubbling in answers. Israel imagined his father, as disappointed as he'd been that day Israel had told them about his dreams in the car—hard-eyed and shaking his head.

After school, Israel went directly to his car, hoping he could get out of the lot before Izzy found him and asked what was wrong. He had to try to repair the situation with Peter.

Israel drove to Lara's house and crouched in his seat, reading the Remembered Souls forum for two hours until Peter's small silver pickup finally pulled out of the garage. Again, Israel followed. This time to a taco place nestled in a strip mall, indiscernible, as far as Israel could tell, from every other taco place in the state. A man with clear-framed glasses held the door for an old woman hauling a plastic bag filled with tinfoil-wrapped tacos. A mother and three kids trotted toward the restaurant.

Peter climbed out of the truck, wearing cheap jeans belted tightly at the waist and a checkered button-down that was a size too large. Israel took a deep breath and got out too. If he was going to end his nightmares, if he was going to have a chance at a normal life in college where he didn't have to explain to roommates why he woke up gasping for air each night, he had to do this now.

Inside, the three kids and mother had piled into a booth. Two had crayons and were scribbling on a paper place mat. Peter stood near a sign that said PLEASE WAIT TO BE SEATED, scrolling through his phone.

"Excuse me, Peter? I'm Israel Castillo. I emailed you about your dad."

The man almost dropped his cell, but he caught it and clasped it between his hands like he needed to pray. "How did you know I was here?" he hissed, as though someone in the restaurant would overhear them. "Did you follow me?"

"Please, I just want the chance to talk to you. I don't mean any harm."

"A table for two?" a waitress with red lipstick asked, already gathering the menus.

"Yes," Israel said.

"No," Peter said at the same time.

The waitress didn't notice or mind their disagreement. She waved them toward a booth with the menus.

"What can I get you to drink?" she asked.

"We'll need a few minutes," Israel said, sliding into the booth. His hands were clammy and left a smear of sweat on the hard plastic.

Peter stood stiffly, arms crossed, his eyes darting from the waitress to the kitchen and then to the door as though he were looking for an escape. "You're a stalker. I should call the police."

"I'm not a stalker." His heart was pounding so loudly he thought Peter must be able to hear it, but he tried to keep his voice calm. "Let me just explain: I have this dream—"

Israel stopped as the waitress plopped a basket of chips and a small stone bowl of salsa on their table. She seemed unbothered by the fact that Peter was still standing. "Just give me a holler," she said, turning to the table with the three kids.

"What kind of sick joke is this?" Peter whispered.

"Look, I know my email seemed crazy, but it's not a joke. There's a lot of us who have memories from another life. I'm in this group online, Remembered Souls, and they're the ones who helped me find you." He left out the part about how he was trying to find out what he hadn't gotten right in the last life—Randolph's life.

"What do you want, kid? I don't have any money."

"Please just tell me about your father." There must have been something about how Israel said it—he was sure he sounded desperate—because Peter uncrossed his arms and sat.

"Fine. Truth is, I didn't know him that well."

"That's okay," Israel said, trying to be gentle. "What do you know?"

"He and my mom met at the racetrack," the man said, his voice warming some. "She took his bet. And she always liked to say he bet on her."

Israel smiled. It sounded like a well-rehearsed story, like when his mother told the story of his and Izzy's birth—how he slipped out nice and easy, but Izzy fought the whole way.

"With one stroll through the stables, he could tell when a horse was favoring a leg or missing a glint in its eye. It wasn't a perfect system, obviously, but he won often enough to make it exciting. He took me, sometimes." Peter looked wistfully at something behind Israel.

"You said he was a vet, right?" Israel asked as though he hadn't memorized Peter's emails to him.

Peter nodded. "He always smelled like cow shit and was tired all the time. He probably drove a hundred and twenty miles a day to visit all the ranches. There were days when he didn't get home until after Mom had put me to bed. If he was back early enough, he'd come into my room to tuck me in before he headed into his home office to make phone calls and answer emails." Peter smiled, but the expression surprised Israel with its sharpness. "Sometimes I'd hear him leave in the middle of the night because there were emergencies. My mom was always trying to get him to hire a young vet to help out, but he said it would slow him down."

"My dad is a workaholic too." Maybe the similarity was significant?

Peter went on as though he hadn't heard Israel: "I respected him because he worked hard and I admired how much all the ranchers needed him. But respect and admiration aren't the same thing as closeness, I suppose."

This had to be the thing Randolph hadn't gotten right in his life; he hadn't prioritized being a father to Peter. But what could Israel possibly do to correct this if Randolph was already gone?

"Tell me your dream again," Peter said, interrupting Israel's thoughts.

Israel did, trying to tell it as linearly as possible and with more detail, so that it was the story he'd asked for instead of the nightmarish images that hurled at him while he was asleep. Peter blinked rapidly the whole time, like he was fighting back tears.

When he was done, Peter shook his head. "That's not how it happened," he said.

Israel's stomach felt like it dropped to his feet. "What do you mean?" he asked nervously.

"He wasn't getting medicine for me. I was away at camp. For a whole month. When the accident happened, my grand-parents came to pick me up."

That couldn't be right. The rush to get medicine was the foundation of the dream. "But maybe you were sick and he was going to mail you a prescription?" Israel sounded stupidly hopeful, yearning almost. *Stop it*, he told himself.

Peter shook his head. "I never got sick the whole time I was at camp. I'd remember."

"So would I," Israel said, more sharply than he intended. This man may have lost his father, but at least he didn't have to relive the accident every night. He didn't have to suffocate in his dreams, holding on to the things he loved: his wife and son. "Maybe I could talk to your mom," he said. "She might remember why your dad was getting medicine."

"No. Look, you better stay away from her or I really will

call the police. She doesn't like talking about him." The man took a chip and snapped it aggressively before dropping the pieces back into the basket. "Here's my theory: I think you came across the story from an old newspaper article or something when you were a kid, and it got, I don't know, like, stuck inside you somehow."

Israel tried to remember the first time he'd had the dream, but the memory was fuzzy. It was so long ago. Could it have been something he'd read? But no, that didn't make sense. "The first time I had the nightmare was before I could even read," Israel said, but he knew he sounded weak. There weren't enough shreds of him left to hold up much of a defense.

"Someone told you. Had to be." Peter brushed his hands together as though the case were closed, and a few small chip crumbs fell onto the tabletop.

"Look," Israel said, inhaling deeply to steady himself. He had to try again—had to convince this man that it was true. "When I was little, my family tried to come up with every excuse in the book for why I could remember this. But I remember too much, too well. And the accident happened before I was born. While I was being born, actually." It was Israel's only ace.

"Okay," Peter said, but Israel recognized the tone. It was an Izzy kind of *okay*. Peter wasn't any closer to believing; he wanted to placate Israel.

"I can't explain the medicine thing," Israel said, "but I can promise you that your dad was thinking about you. Your literal names: Peter, Lara, Peter, Lara. It's how I found you."

"That's another thing you got wrong," Peter said. "My father never thought of me." He pushed himself out of the booth.

"You're just going to leave?"

"I don't owe you anything, kid," Peter said.

"You haven't even eaten." His voice was pleading.

"Lost my appetite. I think it's best we don't talk again." He threw down a few dollars, and nodded a goodbye at Israel. As he opened the door, the bell tinkled above his head, and it felt like too jolly of a sound, because Israel knew that when the glass door swung shut, it closed on his hope, too.

"Are you going to order?" the waitress asked him. Up close, he could tell that her lipstick was bleeding into the fine lines around her mouth.

Israel managed to shake his head and stand. As he opened the door, the bell was quiet. He looked up at it, wondering if he was supposed to make anything of the silence. Maybe Peter was right. Maybe the dreams weren't actually real. Maybe he wasn't either.

In the car, he clicked his seat belt into place and felt a ripping sensation in his chest. His body began to rock with silent sobs, the belt tightening against his waist. He slammed his forehead again and again into the steering wheel. There were no tears, but his mouth made wet gasping sounds. What was he thinking? He couldn't fix a life that had already been lived. Even though he could unbuckle himself and get out of the car, he was trapped—just like Randolph had been.

His phone dinged. It was Izzy.

```
Are you all right?
```

Just stop, he texted back. He was about to toss his phone
onto the passenger seat, when a notification from Remembered
Souls caught his eye.

If Peter wasn't going to help him make sense of the dream
or escape it, there had to be something else Israel could do.
There was one last person who might be able to help.

OtherPlanes.

Israel opened a direct message and took a shot.

```
Hi. You don't know me, but I've been
following you on this group for a while.
I think I need your help. Please. I can't
keep dying every night in my sleep.
```

CHAPTER THIRTY-ONE

SHANE

....

Twenty-three days before

SHANE WAS STILL hungover when they returned to the island in the late afternoon. After dropping off Nate, he thought he saw someone—Cass?—seated on the curb by his own mailbox. Was she waiting for him or was it a mirage from all the alcohol sweating out of his body?

It was Cass, though, dressed in warm-up pants and a T-shirt with the sleeves slightly rolled. All the volleyball girls copied Cass's effortless tuck, filling their school's hallways with lean, bronzed arms. He had loved this, the way the world seemed to mold itself around her, taking her shape everywhere. Now it would be an endless reminder of her.

She stood when he got out of the car, flattening her hands against her thighs like she was trying to smooth her warm-ups. There were tears welling in the corners of her eyes, and his own eyes stung, as though he were her mirror.

"You weren't at school."

The heat made him feel like vomiting, but he knew they had to finish this conversation once and for all. He sat down on the curb where she'd been sitting. She remained standing, blocking the sun, which made him grateful. Her hair was pulled back tight like she wore it for volleyball, stretching the skin across her cheekbones.

"Nate and I went to visit Meg and Aaron," he said.

"Yeah? You don't look great," she said.

"We partied a little hard."

She lifted her chin as though the news were difficult to hear. He wondered if she could tell he'd kissed someone. "You called last night while I was asleep," she said.

"Yeah. I mean, I don't really remember, but I think I wanted to say sorry. For what I said in the cafeteria on Monday," he said. "That wasn't okay."

"Thank you. I appreciate it."

He looked at her, really looked at her. But for the first time in a long time, he couldn't read her face. "Why are you here, Cass?"

"I guess I wanted to try to apologize too and see if there's somewhere for us to go from here."

Just a few days ago it was the only thing he'd hoped to hear. That she still wanted him. That they could still have another chance. But now . . .

"Come on, Cass. You and I both know that we don't have a future. You're going to college, and now I know I'm not."

"We could do long-distance like we talked about before."
She didn't sound very confident.

He raised his eyebrows. "Do you really believe that? I mean, no offense, but you couldn't even do long-distance for a weekend."

She crossed her arms. "You act like I've never been around other guys before."

"So there was something special about this one?"

"No, that's—"

"So he wasn't special?"

"Why are you twisting my words? It was a mistake. But I don't want either of us to make the mistake of doing senior year without our best friend."

"You weren't and aren't my best friend, Cass. You were the love of my life. There's a difference." Shane closed his eyes to keep the tears in. He had to ask her now, to know the truth. "Did you know that I—" It was hard to say the words. "I struggle with reading. Did you know that?"

He reopened his eyes. Her shoulders and chin had dropped. She looked terribly old, like her face had been carved out of ancient wood. "Yeah," she finally said.

"If you knew, why didn't you try to help me?"

He could tell she *knew* she could have done something more: talked to his parents or a teacher at school. Sure, he may have hated her for it and they may have broken up then, but, also, he wouldn't be staring into this black hole of a future.

"I tried to help you study and do homework all the time," she said.

"You know that's not what I mean."

She wiped her face on the edge of her T-shirt, revealing a stretch of her abdomen that he still wanted to touch more than anything. "Before this, I've never seen you unhappy. In all the years we've known each other. The happiness, the confidence, the easygoing everything's-all-right attitude, it lulls people into thinking everything actually is all right."

He was silent. What was there to say? Shame is heavy? It binds you?

"You have to take the mask off once in a while. Let people see deeper. And that's something only you can do." She took a shuddering breath. "The question you really need to be asking, Shane, is why *you* didn't ask for help."

She was right, of course, but it was all too late. It didn't matter anymore. It was easier to blame her for his failure than to turn the mirror on himself. He stood, brushing the gravel off his pants, ready to draw the final line between them, to cleave off the piece of himself that was left.

"Cass," he said, and took a deep breath. "It's time for us to say goodbye." And he meant goodbye to all five years. Goodbye to his best love. To a body he knew as well as his own. To that first kiss that peeled him from the inside out. To laughter, ringing through a new house.

Cass left without a word.

JANIE'S NOTEBOOK

....

THE EULOGY I WANTED TO WRITE

HOW COULD YOU?

How could you ignore me for years?

How could you hurt your mom like that?

How could you let me walk away at the party?

How could you leave after you saw how my mom leaving destroyed me?

How could you kiss me like it meant something?

How could you see magic through all the mud?

How could I?

How could I put up with years of you ignoring me?

How could I pretend like it was all okay?

How could I be too scared to say I love you?

How could I keep whatever was happening to you a secret?

How could I walk away at the party?

How could I miss everything you were telling me?

How could we?

CHAPTER THIRTY-TWO

JANIE

....

Five days after

IZZY IS LEANING over the bow. Cass grips her by the life vest straps. We're all probably thinking about the navy training accident where the older brother of a girl in our grade fell in and was struck by the boat. Did his family think he'd become a dolphin too?

I cut the motor, feeling nauseated from fear and seasickness. "There's no way I'm moving until you sit," I say, knowing that I sound like a parent.

As the boat drifts and loses momentum, the dolphins disappear farther away in the green depths, probably off to find a more exciting boat.

"Why did you do that?" Izzy shouts. "Speed up. We're losing them." Her eyes are wide in desperation, and she's shuddering violently like she's cold, shaking the boat with her.

"We can't keep racing them," Cass says, and pulls Izzy

toward her. She combs her hair out of her face. The tenderness of the gesture makes me ache. It's something my mother would have done. She was always sweeping my hair aside and tucking it behind my ears, before running her finger down my nose and touching the tip with a *boop*.

After she left, it took me a whole year of slamming locker doors and snapping at people who stared to feel ready to talk to my mom. By the end of that year, I still had Nate—outside of school, anyway—I'd made friends with Marisol, and I'd discovered pot. I'd begun to feel sturdier, to sleep, and to rebound with my grades and teachers at school. So I told my dad that I'd talk to her if he promised to be there the entire time.

"Janie?" she said when he handed me the phone. Hearing her voice peeled the scar tissue off, and I started to silently sob.

"Janie?" she said again. There was doubt in her voice, fear, too, like it was all a cruel joke.

"She's there," my dad said in the background, loudly enough for her to hear. "Just talk."

So she did, and I listened. She told me about the rabbits who were getting to her vegetable garden, a gym she was trying, and her newly adopted cat, Beauregard.

We still haven't seen each other in person, but we do this once a week now, her talking and me mostly listening. When she asks me questions, I stumble over the words, as though I can't remember what order they go in. But each time she says my name, the wound hurts a little less.

"Janie." It's Cass's voice now. "Hello?"

"What?" The minute the word is out I realize I snapped, and shake my head in apology. "Sorry."

"Take us back," she says. "Please."

I nod. Izzy has collapsed onto one of the benches. Her hair is wild from the wind, and the life vest—the blue one intended for my mom—makes her look small. It's the most vulnerable I've seen her.

"How do we get them back?" she asks. Her voice is small now too. "They figured out how to do this. There must be a way to undo it."

I pause, thinking a moment. She clearly needs to believe this but also to accept that they're gone. "Maybe they don't want to come back?" It comes out like a question. Cass shoots me a look that says: *not you, too.*

I'm not saying I believe her, but it is nicer to think that Nate is beneath the waves than to think of him in a coffin. If there's anything I've learned from growing up in my family— and from my relationship with Nate—it's that there's a lot we can't see. I thought that my parents' fights were normal, that all families had resentments simmering between them. I didn't notice the rift until we were tumbling into it.

Izzy starts crying, her eyes squeezed tight, her mouth stretched into a dramatic, downward arch, her whole body heaving. Cass strokes Izzy's back. I don't understand how someone so generous and patient with Izzy can be so short with me. I'm not sure what I ever did to her. I'm not sure why I put up with it either, but somehow, it's become a habit. Putting up

with unkind things because I want something for myself—
Nate's attention and love, Cass's kindness and adoration, Izzy's
sharpness and bravery.

I take us back to the dock. Theo spots us from the bait shop
and comes out.

"Did you find what you were looking for?" he asks as we
climb out of the boat.

Izzy looks at him fiercely, setting her jaw, and I recognize
the expression from my own past. She could explode, a flurry
of fists and insults.

"Nate said that the ocean is magic," I say. Cass looks
irritated and Theo appears puzzled, but the statement
interrupts Izzy, who swivels toward me with an energy that
makes me unsure if I'm about to join her pack or be hunted
myself.

"That was in Aaron's eulogy," she says. "But what does it
mean?"

This makes me stammer because I don't know. I liked to go
to the ocean because he loved it and I wanted to be with him.

I shrug weakly, and just like that, her attention flits away.
It feels like the sun going behind a cloud.

I drop Izzy off first. She doesn't say anything to Cass or me
when she gets out of the car. Simply stands and faces her house
like she needs to power up before she goes in.

"Why do you think they did it?" I ask Cass as we drive
away.

"I think—" She falls quiet, and I steal a glance. Her eyes are wet with tears. "I think I hurt Shane enough that he didn't care anymore."

It's so honest that my truth spills out: "We were close. Nate and me. No one really knew."

I expect her to roll her eyes, but she doesn't. "I'm sorry," she says like she believes me. "Why didn't anyone know?"

"I don't know," I say, because I can't say, *He was ashamed of our friendship. I'm awkward and weird-looking and even my own mother doesn't love me enough to stay.*

"Nate could be—insecure," she says. "He *needed* to be sarcastic to protect himself. It was part of his foundation almost, right alongside being popular and good at soccer."

"And I don't fit in with that." I imagine my tissue pulling away from my muscles, my muscles unwrapping themselves from my skeleton, revealing bleached dry bone. It hurts to be this bare.

She's silent again, and I know this is an acquiescence. There were times that first year where I wondered if I had it wrong, if our conditional friendship was Nate giving me a sort of grace to be a wild person at school and someone different at home. But maybe I wouldn't have punched walls if I'd had him helping me at school in the first place.

"I know who taught them to fly—the guy whose plane they stole," she says. "I saw the pilot's name on Israel's iPad." She pauses, and I can tell she's deciding something. "Do you want to go with me to talk to him?"

"What about Izzy?"

"I don't think she's ready." She takes two measured breaths, like she's trying to stop crying, but her voice quivers anyway. "I'm worried about her."

"Do you think—" I'm not sure that the words are coming out right, so I start again. "Do you think that if you figure out what they were doing, it could help her?"

My eyes are on the road, but I can feel her watching me. "Yes," she says. "And me."

"And me too," I say.

She nods. "Yeah, you too." She says it so gently it feels like my mom saying my name.

CHAPTER THIRTY-THREE

IZZY

....

Five days after

I DON'T WANT to go inside. I'd rather walk back to the marina and watch the ocean with the binoculars until it's too dark to see. Then slip into the water, test its so-called magic, and swim to the boys. But, even from the driveway, I can hear Luna whimpering. She darts down the stairs to our lawn as soon as I open the door, pissing on the grass like a drunk boy.

Israel found Luna's mother near one of our dad's work sites when we were twelve. She'd made herself a cave under an abandoned tarp and was nursing four pups. Luna was pudgy and white while the other three puppies were lean and mottled gray like pigeons. He took them home, and eventually sold off all but her.

We didn't realize Luna was deaf until the Centenos almost ran her over backing out of their driveway. She'd found a chicken bone and was happily crunching it to bits when they braked hard and leaned on the horn. So Israel taught her tricks with hand signals. If he made a gun shape with his hand, she'd fall onto her side. If he brought four fingers to his thumb like a bird beak, she'd bark. *Come*, he'd say by curling his fingers toward his upward-facing palm.

I'm following her around the yard now, flapping my fingers closed to beckon her inside. She's ignoring me purposefully, planting her butt between the two of us so that I have to make eye contact with the star of her anus.

"Damn it, Luna," I say, trying again to shuffle in front of her face, but she bounces around again, showing me her wagging tail. She probably wants to play. If Israel, the giver of treats, isn't around to throw her slimy tennis balls and tug on her rag toy, I'm next best.

I touch my mouth, the signal for food, and she conveniently sees me. She practically gallops back up the stairs to the house.

"I guess you're my responsibility now."

Inside, she points her nose at her empty bowl. If Israel were planning to leave for good, wouldn't he have left his beloved dog with someone who gives a damn?

I dump a cup of kibble into her bowl, and she gobbles it up like it might vanish if she doesn't hurry.

"Bela?" my mom calls. "Bela?"

I groan. "So I was chopped liver before, but now y'all need me?" I say to Luna, who doesn't look up from her bowl.

My mom is back in her bedroom cave. She's closed all the

vents so the room feels like a sauna. The blinds are shut, casting everything in fuzzy daytime shadows: the dresser, a rocking chair piled with funeral clothes, and the bed, where my mom's head is barely visible above the comforter. Even from the doorway, I can see her hair is unwashed and matted with sweat.

"Mami, it smells like a gym locker room in here. We need to air it out."

"No, tengo frío," she says.

I don't know how she could be cold in such a stuffy room. I perch on the edge of the bed.

"Bela, Bela." She grabs my hand and grips it to her chest. "I need to ask you something."

I expect her to ask me why Israel did it. Dolphin or not, we'd both agree he ran out of our lives.

"¿Fuimos buenos padres?"

It's heartbreaking the way her voice tremors. Were they good parents? Sure, I resented how they favored Israel because he did better in school, but I never doubted their love for me. We didn't have a lot of toys growing up, so my mom invented games—who could build the tallest towers with cans, who could cook the best meal with mystery ingredients like sardines and olives, who could memorize all the words to a song and perform it. She would leave work to bring me malta and saltines if I was sick. My dad would make our favorite empanadas stuffed with shark meat. He bought me my first video camera, so I could play director and boss Israel around.

"Yeah, you still are good parents," I say.

She shakes her head at this—not as though she's disagreeing about her parenting, but like she isn't a parent anymore. The headshake stings.

"If we were such good parents, why didn't he leave a note?" she wails.

"Well, he didn't know he wasn't coming back," I say, though I'm not sure that's true.

She looks at me dully like she doesn't remember why I'm here. Did Israel know he'd take our parents with him too—burying our dad even deeper in work and our mom in this gym-smelling cocoon? Did he know and do it anyway?

"You should eat something," I say, because food is the one way our family takes care of each other.

"No tengo hambre," she says peevishly.

"I'll make you a plate," I say, even though she's clearly not hungry.

In the kitchen, I throw out a few containers of untouched funeral food our neighbors brought. I manage to assemble a plate for her from the leftovers that are still good, and heat them in the microwave. I shoo Luna off the nest she's made on the living room couch. A few dog hair tumbleweeds stir and settle as I walk by, so I turn on the robot vacuum, which Luna hates. She clings to my heels as I climb the stairs with my mom's plate.

Mom's back is turned to the door now, and she's pretending to be asleep. Luna nudges her with her nose.

"Mami, you know I still need you, right?" When she

doesn't move, I try one last time in Spanish: "Todavía te necesito."

She still doesn't roll over. So I leave the plate where Luna will undoubtedly get to it. I don't hang the funeral clothes or open the vents or crack a window.

If they aren't going to parent me, I won't daughter them.

I retrieve Israel's iPad and the shoebox from my closet, where I've been hiding them in case the police return to search his room again.

I climb onto the roof. Seated and finally alone, I let the exhaustion from the day seep into me: the final funeral, the boat trip, my mother's dismissiveness.

Cass and Janie may have been impressed by the dolphin show, but they still have doubts. I could take them out every day to see the boys, and they wouldn't be any closer to actually believing. There's no way to prove it, and even if I can—what does proving it do? I can't change what the boys did. My only hope is to figure out how to talk to them like the old man talks to the whale in Janie's script.

I lift the binoculars toward the ocean, but it's gotten too dark to see much. The ocean is almost the same navy as the sky. The beach looks empty. No dolphins.

What my mom said haunts me: Why *didn't* he leave a note?

I've already spent hours on the tablet, reading every single text and message stored there, taking screenshots of his browser history so I don't mess anything up, and opening all the apps. His electronic life was huge and boring. The only relevant thing I've found is the email thread with Peter.

"What should I do next?" I ask the ocean. "What would you do next?" Despite his insistence to the contrary and my parents' opinions, Israel and I had plenty in common.

Easy. I'd find my wife and son.

I check the photos I took of Israel's history. He'd searched their names a month before the crash. I navigate to the pages he clicked and stare at the photos he must have found: a stern silver-haired woman, a pale man with a rat face. I pin the woman's address on a map. Did he actually go there? The Israel I knew was so cautious, but this Israel who learned to fly a plane? I don't know.

I open a window to compose an email from his account.

Hi, Peter, this is Israel's twin, Izzy. I'm not sure if you heard, but my brother was in a plane crash. Can we talk?

CHAPTER THIRTY-FOUR

CASS

....

Six days after

THE DIRECTIONS ON my phone lead us to the mainland. First there's a stretch of outlet malls and big-box chains, followed by treeless subdivisions, and finally miles of cattle ranches, their longhorns watching the highway with what looks like boredom.

We miss the drive and make a turn at a ranch a couple miles down the road. We slow when we get back to the dot on the GPS map. It's a dirt drive, marked with a small blue sign: Gerard Township Airport. When we turn, it feels like we are entering some postapocalyptic future. Nothing but dust, dirt, and a few sun-strangled plants for miles. There are three small hangars—all a faded silver—as easily from this imagined future as from some distant past. The middle hangar's door is wide-open and two trucks are parked nearby. An old man in coveralls sits in a lawn chair outside, his legs kicked out, eyes closed, and a newspaper unfolded on his chest. He doesn't stir as we climb out of Janie's car.

Another man emerges from the hangar. He has a gray goatee and a single slim gold bar earring. He's dressed in a short-sleeve plaid shirt, ratty jeans, a red baseball cap with a torn brim, and brand-new-looking cowboy boots with teal stars cut into the gold leather. They're dressy, like the kind of boots you'd expect to see on a teenage girl at a country concert.

"Here for lessons?" The man's voice surprises me with its thinness.

"Are you Bradley Simpson?" I ask.

The brim of the man's hat is so curved you can't see his eyes. "Brad. Who's asking?"

"We're friends of the boys who—"

The man lifts his hand to cut me off. "I spoke to the police three times already."

"The police?" I echo, hoping he'll tell me more if I play innocent.

"I said all there is to say. They broke in and stole my plane."

Janie's attention appears to have wandered, and she's edging closer to the hangar, trying to see inside. Izzy would badger her way in, but what can I do? Channel my mother. Be empathic.

"I'm sure this has been hard on you," I say.

He starts to rock back and forth in his boots. I wish I could see his eyes, but the question seems to have worked. "Hard on me?" he repeats.

It's an in, and I take a stab at it. "Well, you knew them too," I say.

His cheeks pucker like he's biting the insides of his cheeks at this. "As students taking lessons. Perfectly legal business. Nothing more." He catches a glimpse of Janie. "Where you going?" he asks, his voice a high whine.

"I like planes," Janie says as she slips inside the hangar.

He mutters a curse and follows. I do too.

It's hot and dark inside, and there are two white planes lined up like pelicans drying their wings. The plane on the left is much smaller, like it might only hold one person. The other is larger—but not by much. Both planes have maroon racing stripes and combinations of letters and numbers painted on their sides. Janie wanders up to one and pats it on the side like it's a pet. I'm drawn to the empty spot, space for a third plane. This is where Shane stood before dawn that Sunday morning. What was he thinking as he climbed inside?

"How did they get it out?" I ask. "Wouldn't they have needed a key?"

"I don't have to answer your questions. Unless you're here for lessons, you need to leave."

I'm about to give up, to turn and leave, but Janie pulls open one of the plane doors, and he spins toward her. She climbs into the cockpit. "Yes," she says. "We're here for lessons."

The man traces his goatee over and over, his forefinger on one side of his face and his thumb on the other. He seems off-balance, unsure. "You're over sixteen?"

"We are," she says.

"It'll cost you." He says this firmly, and I can't help eyeing his boots again.

"How much?" Janie asks.

"Usually between seven and ten grand per person if you do it all the way to licensing."

How on earth could the boys afford that? How could we?

But Janie simply nods. "How do we sign up?"

As soon as we're back in her car, I don't waste another minute. "What exactly is the plan here?"

She belts herself in and shrugs. "If we spend time with him in these lessons, we might be able to get our questions answered."

"Yeah, but how are we going to pay for it?"

"I've saved a bunch for college."

"There's no way we can use your college money." My own college fund is dismally empty; being a volleyball camp counselor for a few weeks out of the summer doesn't pay much. I'll need all the scholarships and loans I can get.

Janie shrugs. "It's not like my dad won't help me out if I need more. Plus, I figure we'll only have to do a few lessons—not the whole process. I should have enough for you, at least."

"Me?" I ask.

"Well, I'm terrified of heights, so I'll only do the ground parts."

She's looking over her shoulder to back out of the parking space. I'm not sure if she registers my shock. "Janie, I can't fly a plane."

"Well, not yet."

"No, but, like, I can't." I emphasize the word *can't* because it's not about heights or knowing how. It's about that moment on the beach that I won't allow myself to replay. It's about Shane.

Janie glances at me and then back out the windshield. "I understand."

Izzy wouldn't hesitate. She'd learn to fly for Israel. For me. I bet I could call her now, admit how Janie and I have spent our afternoon, and she'd jump at the chance. But there's part of me that wants to keep the information for myself, decide how and when to tell her what I learn. Because I want to protect her? Because I want to be the one to hurt her? Because I want to be the one who decides.

We drive in silence through downtown, where streams of tourists with ice cream cones and shopping bags clog the sidewalks.

Janie turns onto my street. "Here we go," she says as though she's a cabdriver delivering me to my destination. And, I'll admit, that is how I've treated her.

"Okay. I'll do it," I tell her.

"Great." She nods, like she expected me to agree all along.

SECURE MESSAGE THREAD

IsC: Hi, my name's Israel. Thanks for letting me message you.

OtherPlanes: I'm Glen. Apologies for insisting on the encrypted app. RS isn't a very secure forum. That's why I never reveal anything about my current identity there. Who knows how the government might try to use people like us.
So how can I help you?

IsC: I guess I want to know how you deal with the memories.

OtherPlanes: Well, in my last life, I didn't care about them. Didn't care about anything except me. This time around I'm using them to live better, to contribute. That's why I'm on RS so much.

IsC: They don't haunt you?

OtherPlanes: I don't know about "haunt." Sure, they can be scary. My last end was pretty violent. But I wouldn't trade them for anything. They make us special.

IsC: I don't want to be special. I just want to sleep.

OtherPlanes: I don't need much sleep myself. I'm a transcriptionist and can work odd hours.

IsC: So there's no way out? I just have to

remember for the rest of my life and try to do better than last time?

OtherPlanes: There's a way out, but it's no guarantee that you won't have the same problem in the next life.

IsC: What is it?

OtherPlanes: The doorway. A portal between lives. Between chances.

IsC: I read your posts in RS about that. It seems pretty terrifying.

OtherPlanes: More terrifying than dying every night?

IsC: Ha. Good point. Ok, so how do I find it? What do I do?

OtherPlanes: You need to learn how to fly.

CHAPTER THIRTY-FIVE

NATE

....

Thirteen days before

IN THE OPERATING room, a middle-aged nurse with a sharp chin and a military-like flattop asked Nate to count down. After five, he opened his eyes.

"Four-three-two-one," he said.

The nurse cocked his head.

"Aren't I supposed to be counting down?" Nate asked, but the words came out slurred.

"It's over," the nurse said. "You're done. We're going to move you into recovery, where your family is waiting."

Nate took stock of his body. His tongue felt heavy and his brain filled with cotton. He couldn't feel his knee at all or it finally felt normal, like it had before the injury when he didn't notice his own body.

"Did they take my knee off?" he asked the nurse.

The nurse laughed and shook his head. "They only replaced your ligament."

"With a dead person's."

"Correct. A tendon from a cadaver," the nurse said.

"Does that make me part zombie?"

"No," the nurse said.

"What do they do with the old one?"

"The ligament? It gets disposed of with other medical waste."

"Too bad," Nate said. Janie would make a weird joke about keeping it, wearing it on the outside of his body like a piece of jewelry.

"Once the anesthesia wears off, we'll get you up and walking. Dr. Dennis wants you using the knee as soon as possible."

"I'll be like the walking dead." The more he spoke, the more limber his tongue felt. He wished he could shake the cotton out of his brain as easily. He felt like he was missing something—what was it?

"You'll be running again before you know it," the nurse said.

That's it: the ability to move like an arrow down the field. The scouts at the camp this summer. His future.

He was worthless now.

"What do you think I should do?" he asked the nurse as he moved Nate to recovery.

"About what?"

"The future."

"What are you, seventeen?" he asked.

Nate nodded.

"Go to college. Make mistakes. Fall in love. Be young." The nurse laughed, like he was remembering his own youth. He pushed Nate into a room where his parents waited. On TV, Judge Judy was scolding a man in a security guard uniform.

"He's awake," the nurse announced.

"I didn't finish counting down," Nate told them. "But they took my knee anyway."

"Not the knee. Just the ligament," the nurse said gently. Then to his parents: "He'll be loopy for a bit while the anesthesia wears off. I'll come back in an hour or so and we'll discuss aftercare and pain management."

"He thinks I should go to college," Nate said.

"Why wouldn't you? They took Aaron," his dad said with a chuckle.

"I know soccer means the world to you," his mom said, dragging her chair closer to the bed and taking his hand. "And I know this is going to be a hard road to recovery. But your future isn't over."

Even drugged, Nate couldn't believe her.

CHAPTER THIRTY-SIX

ISRAEL

·····································

Twelve days before

ISRAEL HADN'T SEEN Nate since school let out over a week ago. If it weren't for Izzy, who told Israel he had to visit after the surgery no matter how guilty he was feeling or how angry Nate still was, he wouldn't be standing at the top of Nate's steps in the rain, waiting for someone to answer the door.

No one did.

Israel twisted the knob; it was unlocked. At first Israel couldn't see anyone from the entryway. The living room was dark except for the light from the TV. As his eyes adjusted, he spotted Nate's hair, slung over the couch arm and shiny with grease. Israel shrugged off his rain jacket and approached Nate's feet. His friend's knee was braced and propped on a stack of three throw pillows, his shoulders propped with a few more, so his body formed a V. There were two plates on the coffee table, one with an uneaten sandwich and the other with browned apple slices.

"Hey," Israel said. Nate's face remained strangely blank. He would have thought Nate were asleep if it weren't for the fact that he was looking right at Israel. "I rang the doorbell, but—" Israel shook his head and started over. "I came by to see how you're doing."

Nate ground his elbows into a pillow and tried to push himself up into a sitting position, but his efforts barely raised him an inch. He sank back into the pillow.

"Do you need help?"

Nate shook his head and finally spoke: "I like it here." Israel wasn't sure if he meant here on the pillows or here in the house. Nate pointed at the recliner, and Israel took a seat.

"So how are you feeling?"

Nate shrugged. "The PT is a bitch."

"Again, I'm really sorry, man."

"I know."

"Do you?" Israel said, a bit afraid of the answer.

"Yeah. I have to move on and figure out who I am now."

"Who you are? What do you mean?"

Nate was quiet for a moment, tilting his head back like he was listening to the rain on the roof. Israel began to wonder if he'd even heard the question.

"I was a soccer player and now I'm not," he finally said.

Israel felt the sickening swirl of the guilt again in his gut. For Israel, soccer was an activity that looked good on his applications, but for Nate, it was something that gave him purpose. It was woven into his DNA.

"It's okay," Nate said, like he was reading Israel's mind. "I deserved it."

"What are you talking about? Nobody deserves that kind of thing."

"I did. I do."

The doorbell rang.

"That'll be Shane," Nate said.

But the girl who'd driven Nate to the hospital, Janie, stood on the steps with a yellow polka-dot umbrella instead when Israel went to open it.

"Oh," she said. "I'm sorry."

"What are you sorry for?" he asked.

"I—I—I live next door." She pushed aside damp bangs.

"I know," he said. Why did she sound so nervous? He'd seen her with his sister a few times too, and she always acted like she was about to jump out of her skin.

"I was just checking on Nate."

"Come on in."

"I better not," she said. The words came out in a rush. Before Israel could protest, she spun quickly and jogged back down the steps. She slid at the bottom, and he thought, for a second, that he was going to have two broken knees on his conscience, but she recovered quickly and power walked through the yard to her own house, her green rubber boots squelching in the mud.

Israel returned to the living room. "That girl Janie was here for you."

Nate sat up now, looking interested for the first time since Israel had arrived.

"She said she shouldn't stay," Israel said.

That deflated Nate again. "Of course not."

"Is she afraid of us or something?"

"She's afraid of breaking the rules, I think."

"What rules?"

"The ones that keep us balanced just so." Nate made a flat plane with his hand. Israel didn't entirely understand, but there seemed to be rules between him and Nate, too, like the rule that they needed Shane to grease the wheels of their friendship.

A few minutes later Shane arrived on Nate's porch with a *clump clump* of his oversized feet. He was drenched, his white shirt transparent, his short hair lying in wet triangles, one dripping down the bridge of his nose.

"God, man, I could have picked you up. Don't you have an umbrella?" Israel asked.

"I forgot it." Shane stepped on the floor mat, shivering.

Nate pushed himself up so he could see Shane from the couch. "Were you trying to drown yourself or something?" he asked. Then to Israel: "He can borrow some of Aaron's clothes."

Israel returned with the largest sweatpants and sweatshirt he could find in Aaron's room. Shane stripped right there on the mat, leaving his soggy shorts and T-shirt in a pile. The hems of Aaron's sweatpants squeezed Shane's calves and the sweatshirt showed a sliver of his belly. He looked like an overgrown child.

This, Nate seemed to find hilarious. Usually, jokes didn't elicit much more from Nate than a wry grin, but Shane's appearance made him laugh so hard he clutched his stomach. Shane joined in, his laugh still the big, sunny gulps that drew everyone in. Israel was happy to see his friends acting carefree, if only for a minute.

When the laughter died, Shane sank onto the floor, folding his knees to his chest and wrapping his long arms around them like he was preparing to cannonball. "Who knew junior year would end with such a shit storm," he said. "Let's hope senior year is better."

"I second that," Israel said.

"You second it?"

"Yeah, like I agree and support your statement. You know, like with motions in a meeting?"

"I know what seconding means. I'm not that stupid," Shane said.

Israel flinched. His friend had never talked that way to him before.

"I'm asking why junior year was so shit for *you*?" Shane said. "I mean, you get good grades. You're going to college. You have a car."

It stung to have his friend go after him like this—to be another person who couldn't really see him—but what could he expect? They only knew as much about him as he wanted them to know. And maybe they wouldn't judge him. They'd all been through a lot lately. Maybe he could tell them the rest.

"I have nightmares," Israel said quietly. "Well, they're actually memories, of someone else's death. And they're getting bad. Or they were always bad and it's getting to me more now because I'm stressed out. Making me feel like I'm going to break. I know, I sound crazy." He said it as fast as he could, hoping that the more he talked, the less likely they'd be to laugh.

But they didn't laugh: Shane looked downward like a scolded dog and Nate squinted at him, as though trying to focus.

"I have a secret too." Shane glanced at the door as though someone might be eavesdropping on them. "I can't really read. Not very well, anyway."

"That's not a secret, man," Nate said, so gently that Israel thought he might cry for Nate. For Shane. For himself.

"It's not?"

Israel had witnessed Shane leaning forward in his desk so that he could see over the shoulder of the person in front of him many times. He'd tilted his own paper too. "No," Israel said, trying to make his voice as gentle as Nate's.

Shane sighed. "Cass knew too. Do you think that's why—why—"

"No way," Nate said vehemently. "That didn't have anything to do with you. That was about her."

"When you said you feel like you're going to break, I feel that way too," Shane said to Israel. "Or I feel like I did break.

And I don't know how to put myself back together. Or if I even can."

Israel nodded. "Every night, I'm this guy named Randolph, who has a son and wife. And I'm in a car, skidding across the pavement, and then it catches fire and I can't escape."

Nate shuddered.

"How do you know it's real?" Shane asked.

"I found him," Israel said. "The son."

"Fuck. Really?" Shane asked.

Israel nodded. "I'm trying to stop the memories. I have to." His voice cracked with desperation, but he took a breath. "And I think I found a way. I just need to learn how to fly." It scared him—being so vulnerable with these two friends, who he'd always thought of as the royalty of their high school—especially after his own parents, their doctor, and Peter had all treated him like he was unhinged.

"How to fly? Like fly a plane?" Shane asked.

Israel nodded.

"I love a good adventure," Nate said.

"I could use an escape," said Shane.

Israel thought of the moment in his nightmare where he pushed the red seat belt button over and over, where he tugged on the fabric. It had never released before, but OtherPlanes had given him back a sliver of hope. *There's a way out.*

And if his friends were willing to help, then maybe it really was possible.

CHAPTER THIRTY-SEVEN

SHANE

....

Eleven days before

"SO WE'RE GOING to a flight school," Shane said as he settled into the passenger seat beside Israel. Nate was already in back.

"Yep," Israel said. "This guy I'm talking to—he's an expert on transmigration—said—"

"Wait. Hold up. Transmigration?" Shane interrupted. Anything was better than sitting at home, trying not to check his phone every few seconds to see if Cass had posted anything on social media, but this still seemed wild.

"Another word for reincarnation. I like it because it sounds less religious."

Less religious? Shane thought transmigration sounded like a cult practice.

"Okay, so how exactly do you get to be an expert at transmigration?" Nate asked.

"Most of us remember a little bit from one past life—usually only our deaths—but he remembers, like, all of them," Israel said.

"And what's flying supposed to do about your dream?" Nate asked.

"I'm trying to find this thing he saw in a past life. A doorway, I guess." Israel spoke with such conviction that Shane twisted in his seat to make eye contact with Nate. Nate, who normally would have raised his eyebrows back at Shane, looked out the window.

People were truly unknowable, Shane was beginning to realize. Everyone held a version of themselves up to the light while the real person crouched beneath. Except for him. Everyone had already seen through to who he was: a fraud, a failure.

They crossed the bridge and drove down a country road for miles, the view occasionally punctuated by iron arches over ranch driveways. HOMEWOOD. CREEK'S END. DOUGLAS RANCH. When Israel's phone alerted them that they'd arrived, there was nothing but a small blue sign. They turned, their tires kicking up dust. The drive cut through a pasture of scutch grass that was more dirt than plant. It felt like they were entering another world altogether: a dry, empty place.

Three silver hangars sat at the end of the drive, a pair of pickups to the side and a small white airplane in front. A goateed man dressed in jeans and cowboy boots, an undershirt, and a tattered red baseball hat stepped onto the plane's wing and climbed out.

"That's the pilot?" Shane asked.

"Brad?" Israel asked when they were out of the car.

The man nodded, a gold bar earring catching the sunlight. "You must be Israel."

"Yeah, these are my friends Nate and Shane."

Brad tilted his head back, as though he wanted to appraise them better from under the shade of his hat. Shane caught a glimpse of his eyes. They were like shallow tide pools: flat and blue with only sand beneath.

"I hope that's okay," Israel said.

"As long as y'all pay." The man waved them into the hangar. "Sorry it's so dark. There's no AC, so I keep the lights off to make it cooler." It was humid inside and smelled dizzyingly of fuel. A white-haired man in coveralls had a flashlight in his hand and appeared to be inspecting the engine of another plane. Shane wandered up to it. It was bigger than the one out front but still smaller than he'd imagined—like a sports car with wings.

"I had a few students before you arrived," the man said, but Shane found this hard to believe. It seemed like these two men were alone in the middle of this plane desert and always had been.

"You boys thinking about becoming pilots?" Brad asked. "As your career?"

They shook their heads.

"Lots want to be commercial pilots, but out here you set your own hours." Brad gazed out of the hangar, apparently seeing something in the drab landscape that Shane could not. "You can work for ranchers or do ads over the beach. Or teach lessons to folks, like me. Your life is yours. You'd like that, wouldn't you?" At this, he looked right at Shane. It sent goose bumps up his arms. Shane was so dependent on others, his life had never felt like his own.

Shane could imagine himself now—not as a commercial pilot, but running a charter service, an island-hopper for the rich tourists so they could avoid the wait for the ferry and the toll bridges. He'd wear white short-sleeve button-downs, a hat like the commercial guys, and a bomber jacket the one month of the year it was cool out. He'd use his hosting skills, serving the tourists champagne when they boarded and promising them a smooth ride. He wouldn't be at anyone else's mercy, and people—if they thought of him at all—would remember him as the charming man who kept them safe. Nothing less.

"We'll go over payment, paperwork, and require-ments for licensure up front and take a tour," the man said with a grin. "And then we'll get started for real next time." Hearing that, Shane was more enthused than he'd ever been for school.

When he got home later, Shane's mom was in the kitchen, clip-ping daisy stems over the sink. Several already clipped blooms stood in mason jars tied with twine.

"Where have you been?"

"With the guys."

She sighed and put down the scissors. "Is this how you're going to spend your whole summer?"

"How should I be spending it?"

"Thinking about your future."

He wanted to tell her that he was thinking of his future, and for the first time, it wasn't with dread. But they'd agreed to keep flying a secret from their families to protect the real reason they were taking lessons—Israel's real reason, that is.

"I am, Mom," he said.

She wasn't done with him, though. She pressed her lips. "I know you're hurting. Heartbreaks are among the worst kinds of pain."

"There's worse?" It was a joke, but she took him seriously and nodded.

"Death is worse," she said, and looked out the kitchen window. He knew she was thinking of her sister who'd died of ovarian cancer a few years before.

"No one is dying, Mom," he said. "I promise."

She gave him one of those sad smiles adults use to mean, *I've seen more of the world than you.* "Don't forget to do your laundry," she said.

"Yeah, yeah. I won't. Oh, can I borrow some money? A check."

"For what?" his mom asked. Shane's parents didn't usually blink when he asked for money. They told him that his only job was school.

But he'd prepared an excuse, just in case. "An SAT prep class," he said, knowing she'd eat it up. He was right. She beamed at him and gave him a blank check from her purse.

Upstairs, Shane downloaded a flight simulator on his laptop. Eventually, Brad had told them, Shane would have to pass a written test, but he decided to cross that bridge later. The next lesson would be on the ground and in the air because, according to Brad, you learned to fly by actually doing it. Shane wanted to be as prepared as he could be.

The simulator directed Shane to select a plane, and he picked a Cessna that looked like one in the hangar. The tutorial, though, was a string of text that appeared on the screen, and he was expected to read it while flying the animated plane. Shane turned the text off. He'd have to learn by trying—just like in real life.

He figured out how to accelerate down the runway, but he crashed into the fence at the edge of the airfield. How did you lift up? He tried again, this time getting the plane to hop a few times on the runway before it crashed. Finally he got the simulated plane off the ground and into the pixelated sky, but he lost his bearings. Which instrument showed him where he was according to the horizon? He couldn't remember from Brad's tour of the cockpit, and he couldn't see the ground. He tilted the nose down and then up, and when he finally found the ground, it was above him. Somehow, he'd flipped over and was upside down. He tried to right the aircraft, but it stalled and plummeted. The simulator screen flashed red as he fell.

He crashed into a stand of trees and the fake windshield cracked.

The simulator reset itself and returned him to the runway. He managed to take off again, and this time he kept his eye on an instrument that showed a little image of a plane on a line that he took to be the horizon. He kept the wings level and pointed the nose above it. The simulator took him over the forest where he'd crashed before, above mountain peaks capped with white snow, and out over a flat blue ocean. He didn't know where he was in the simulated world, but he saw a path into his future more clearly than he ever had before.

He could do this. He would.

CHAPTER THIRTY-EIGHT

NATE

....

Ten days before

NATE WAS AWAKE, but he stayed in bed. He heard his parents leave and, a few hours later, Aaron—off to wait tables at an oyster grill on the boardwalk. Nate's stomach ached with hunger and his bladder felt like a bowling ball, but if he didn't move at all, he could almost forget about his knee. Almost.

The problem had become his thoughts.

I'm worthless.

I deserve this pain.

They were like boomerangs. Every time he dozed off or managed to think about something else, they sliced through him again, hooking his brain and dragging it down.

I was never that good at soccer.

I was a big fish in a small pond.

It was all a pipe dream.

I was worthless then.

But I'm even more worthless now.

He had to find a way to shut his brain off or—or what? He wasn't sure.

I've been so selfish.

All those times I barely nodded a hello at Janie.

When I resented Israel for asking me to teach him.

When I avoided talking to Aaron after he left for college.

Slamming into his crutch at the soccer field and bending his knee in Aaron's dorm had hurt, but also helped somehow. As though the physical pain quieted everything else.

Nate swung his legs over the side of the bed and stood gingerly, testing how sore it still felt from yesterday's PT. He limped from his bedroom to the bathroom, then down the hall to the living room without his brace, trying to put equal weight on each of his legs. His weak knee buckled every few strides, quick collapses that knocked the breath out of him. But the pain worked—momentarily erasing the thoughts that looped through him. Offering a sliver of quiet—a moment where he was only his body. Only that hot, filling hurt.

Finally Nate collapsed onto the couch, his heartbeat knocking loudly in his skull. He touched the skin around his knee. It was hot and puffy.

The doorbell rang. It had to be Janie. Here to take him to his PT.

"Come in!" he shouted. She let herself in. Her hair was in its usual braids, frizzed by the humidity, so it looked like a sandstorm around her head. He wanted to pull off the hair ties and sink his fingers into it. It would be warm, he thought, and moist from sweat.

"You ready?" she asked.

He tried to stand again, but his knee buckled immediately and he fell back into the couch with an *oof*.

"Where's your brace?" she asked.

"I think I forgot it in my room."

She returned with it a moment later and helped him Velcro it on. "Ouch," she said, nodding toward the swelling. "Want me to ask my dad to look at it?"

"No, the physical therapist will ice it when I'm done."

"Okay. If you're sure. Want help getting up?"

He nodded and she slid an arm under his armpit and around his back. She squeezed him to her, so he could smell her cottony scent, and then helped lift him. He wanted to stay like that—in her embrace, half balanced on his good leg, momentarily free of both pain and his thoughts.

At PT, Janie waited in a chair by the treadmill, a book open in her lap. The physical therapist took it easy on him—given the swelling—so he had time to watch Janie flipping each page slowly as though she needed to say goodbye to it before she could move on to the next.

While he was doing knee bends, he caught her looking back at him once—her bottom lip pinched between two fingers. She blushed and dropped her hand.

"I have an idea," she said when they were back in the car.

"What?" He tried to keep the exhaustion out of his voice.

"You'll see."

She drove past their houses toward the south end of the island, where there were relatively few people even in the summer. As they drove, the vacation homes grew larger and farther apart, and finally gave way to the national park—a craggy tangle of black mangroves and seagrasses. The park had one small man-made beach for camping, where several tents quivered in the wind like frightened animals.

She turned before the toll bridge to the next island, parked, and swung open her door.

"Janie, I don't want to be at the beach right now. I told you that the other day."

"I know. I know," she said. "But I thought you might change your mind once you were here. You used to see magic here, remember?"

"I used to pick my nose, too."

She laughed and kicked off her shoes. She helped him pull off his, and stabilized him with an elbow as they walked out onto the beach. The unevenness of the sand made his knee ache.

The sky was blue and cloudless, and the water shone emerald green. It had been so long since he'd felt it swirl, cold, over his feet.

A round white bird hopped nearby, taking flight with a

squawk each time a wave lapped the sand and settling back down with a fluff of its wings when the water receded.

Nate spotted a pink-and-orange starfish, leaned over gingerly so as not to get his brace wet, and pulled the creature from the sand. He handed it to Janie, and felt a zap of electricity as her fingers brushed his. Nate watched Janie to see if she'd felt it too, but she was looking at the starfish, wrinkling her nose as the creature moved its thousands of little tube feet against her hand.

She carefully placed it back in the water and rubbed her hand on her shorts. He wanted to grab that hand and hold it against his throat, to feel the grit of sand beneath the soft pads of her fingers, the shock of being close to her.

But his knee was throbbing, and he didn't think he could stand much longer.

Because I'm weak, he thought. *Weak and worthless.*

He hopped back up the beach and sank onto a dry patch of sand. Janie joined him. They sat in silence a moment, watching an older couple who was holding hands with a toddler, lifting him between them and swinging him over the waves. The toddler shrieked in glee. What was it like to have your whole future before you? To be that carefree?

"Look," Janie said, pointing. There were two dorsal fins, one much smaller than the other, circling offshore. "They're hunting."

Nate was silent, the pain in his knee pulsing with each heartbeat. *I deserve it*, he thought. *After how I've treated her.*

"Hey, Nate." Janie's eyebrows were drawn together in concern. "You seem different lately."

"Different how?"

She cocked her head. "I don't know. Spacey, I guess."

One of the dolphins flipped onto its back and then rolled right side up, wriggling as it tried to catch its prey. It made a wide circle and disappeared beneath the waves. The smaller one—its child?—trailed after. Soon he could no longer see them.

"I'm better than ever," he said sarcastically.

"I know not being able to play soccer has got to be hard."

He nodded and felt sadness drumming behind his eyes, urging him to cry. "People think it's just a game. I mean, it *is* a game, but it was more to me."

"I know it was," she said softly.

Nate swallowed back his tears and tried to feel the magic he'd once felt in the sigh of the waves, the dolphins in the surf, the sun on his back, the heat of Janie's body, so close to him that they were almost touching. Could touch.

But it was gone. Just like everything else.

REMEMBERED SOULS FORUM

....

GULF COAST

BeeHappy: I saw it yesterday! The doorway you were talking about.

OtherPlanes: Were you flying?

BeeHappy: No, I'm a window washer. The scaffolding failed and we were hanging on the side of the building until firefighters used harnesses to lower us to the ground.

CyclistRights: Damn. You okay?

BeeHappy: I am now. Never been so terrified in my life. I was sure I was going to die. That's probably why I saw it.

CyclistRights: Did you think about going through?

BeeHappy: Nah. I got my bees to take care of.

OtherPlanes: You could probably be a bee if you were thinking of one as you passed through. The queen, even.

Hell, I'd look for it again if I weren't trying to do it right this time around and stop feeling so restless. If there's anything we in RS know it's that it doesn't matter if

you leave this life. There are endless lives
to live.

BeeHappy: I dunno. I like this life and I think
other people like me in it. They don't want to
lose me.

OtherPlanes: That's why I live without people.
No chains.

CHAPTER THIRTY-NINE

JANIE

....

One week after

MY DAD IS watching baseball in his recliner. He's been making more of an effort to be home since it happened—though not necessarily to be more sober. He lines the cans up on the counter, his way of keeping track of how many he's had, and once he's snoring, I sweep them into the recycling and put on a movie. I set up my replacement phone, a refurbished device Dad ordered online.

Izzy surprises me with a text: Can you come with me to Honore? I'm meeting someone who knew Is. Don't tell Cass.

This is the second time I've been asked on a secret journey. Both Izzy and Cass could borrow cars from their family if they really needed to, so it isn't just about the fact that I have a car. Maybe they're starting to like me for real.

What would have happened if, one of the times they'd

come to lean on the movie theater's candy case asking for freebies, I'd let it slip that I hung out with Nate almost every day? Would they have believed me?

`Yeah, I'll come`, I text back.

"Dad, I'm going to Honore with Izzy," I say loudly.

He rubs his eyes and stretches. "What?"

"I'm going to drive to Honore with Izzy," I repeat.

"Why?"

"She's going to meet a friend of Israel's who lives there. She wanted company."

"I don't know, Janie." He puts down the footrest of the recliner and scratches the beard hair on his cheeks.

"You don't know?"

"She seems a little—off. Candy told me what happened at her brother's funeral."

"People think I'm a little off, you know."

"It doesn't matter what other people think; it matters what's inside—"

"Exactly," I cut him off.

He sighs. "I don't want to see you hurt again."

Now I understand. This is about my mom and the year after she left. He didn't know what to do with me any more than the school counselors did. "I'll be fine, Dad," I say sharply.

"Okay. Okay." He looks up at me, his eyes bleary from sleep or alcohol or sadness. "You know, you remind me of her."

"Is that a good thing?"

"Of course it is. You're strong and stubborn and smart."

"She left us."

"That wasn't just about her. I didn't listen. I didn't really hear her." He picks up a beer from the TV tray we use as a side table and tilts his head back, but the can is empty, and I can tell this racks him.

"You don't have to protect me, Dad," I say. "I know she had to quit school when she had me and we only moved here so I'd be safe."

His eyes widen as though he's shocked I figured this out. "Janie, none of that was your fault. I don't always understand the choice she made, but I do know she has always loved you. Always."

"Yeah, well, it hurts when you don't get picked," I say, thinking of Nate as much as my mom.

He looks at the can in his hand again and squeezes it so it crinkles. "I know," he says softly. "I know."

Izzy is sitting on the bottom step outside her house, holding a chew toy. A white pit bull is on the other end, tugging and shaking, but Izzy hangs on like it's no struggle. When I pull into the driveway, the dog gallops up to the car and stands on my door.

"Sorry," Izzy calls. "She loved going on car rides with Israel."

She grabs the dog by the collar and pulls it toward the house. Once inside my car, Izzy kicks her sandals off onto the floor mat and puts her legs up on the dash. "Do you mind?" she asks, pointing at her feet.

I pause. It never occurred to me to mind when she takes ownership of the things around her. "No," I say.

She lets her head loll back on the seat while I reverse and head for the mainland.

"You wrote Nate's eulogy for Aaron, didn't you?"

Her intuition surprises me. Does she know me that well? Or Aaron?

"What was he to you?" she asks.

I shrug. "Aaron was like an older brother."

"No, Janie," she says, clearly impatient. "You know I'm talking about Nate."

I pause. My best friend? My first and only love? Someone who broke my heart nearly every day? "I don't know. It was complicated," I say.

I think she'll be unsatisfied and continue to prod, but she doesn't. "It's all more complicated than it seems," she says. "Israel was my twin, but I don't think he liked me much."

I know Cass would say, *Of course he did*, but Izzy is right: Things can be more complicated than they seem. You can love someone and not like them very much. "Why do you think that?" I ask instead.

"He always wanted space. Privacy. I get it, but, like, I spent my entire life with him, too, and I never once wanted more space. If anything, I wanted less space." She's talking fast now. "Janie, if he felt something, I could feel it too. Here." She gestures at her side. "He didn't like that. It felt like a violation to him. So he asked me to ignore the feeling, but it was like ignoring your right hand." Her voice wavers.

"Wanting more space doesn't mean he didn't like you."

She shakes her head as though frustrated by me. "Can't you just tell when a person doesn't like you much?"

"Yeah." I'm thinking of Cass now, how little kindness she spent on me—until I told her about Nate.

"Hey," Izzy says, waiting until I meet her eyes. "I love Cass more than most people, but she can be . . . obtuse sometimes."

I look back out the windshield, feeling overwhelmed by how much Izzy sees me.

We cross the bridge to the mainland. Several trees have been nearly swallowed by the rising water level. They're reaching toward the sky, as though begging to be rescued. "Israel was obtuse too," I say.

She smiles at this, but her eyes are wet. "I need to tell you something, because you're about to find out anyway."

We're on the mainland now. The landscape transitions quickly from vacation homes and wetland to strip malls clustered around highway exits and cattle ranches. The grasses are scrub green and gold and the air through the vents smells damp and earthy. "Okay," I say. I have no idea what to expect.

"Israel remembered a past life. He'd talk about it when we were kids, but he never grew out of it. And this man we're meeting today? He's the son of the guy Israel used to be."

I'm struck speechless.

We're meeting someone who Israel knew from a past life? I didn't know Israel well at all. From Nate's stories, he was the most serious of the group, the most driven as well. Recently Nate had called him the brain of their trio. Shane was the heart. *And you?* I'd asked. *The janky knee?* he'd said with that half smile.

"You're being awfully quiet," Izzy says. "I thought you'd understand because of that script you wrote."

The script? It takes me a minute and then I remember: I'd seen an orca up close at an aquarium on a school trip and thought its eye was haunting—godlike, even. I had wanted to write about the feeling I had when I saw it, that something small could contain the whole universe. There'd also been an old man standing with his hands pressed against the glass and whispering. I invented the part about him talking to his dead wife because I was drawn to the idea that someone could leave you and still be part of your life in a completely different way. But Cass had been right. It was a stupid idea for a school film project with zero budget. How were *we* going to get an orca to do what we wanted?

"I'm not sure what to say. That's . . ."

"Crazy. I know. Do you see why I had to ask you along?"

Maybe it is an insult, but I smile. "Cass would have tried to talk you out of this."

"Exactly," she says, and then smiles back.

All along, I'd hoped Cass and Izzy might help me get into Nate's circles, but I never imagined we'd become actual friends, that it would be like tender blooms in the wake of a fire.

CHAPTER FORTY

IZZY

....

One week after

THE TACO PLACE is located in a strip mall and has four booths and a few small tables. A long-faced sandy-haired man who I recognize from Israel's searches sits in one. He's dressed in khaki shorts and a green polo and liberally seasons a bowl of tortilla chips with salt. It's hard for me to imagine that this plain-looking, salt-loving man was so important to my brother.

"That's him," I tell Janie.

The man hears me and looks up. "Wow," he says. "I can see the resemblance."

This baffles me. No one ever thinks we're twins. Israel was blocky and always had chest hair sprouting out of his collar, unkempt curls, and bushy eyebrows. I tame my hair with serums and a straightener and get my eyebrows threaded into perfect knocked-over parentheses. But maybe there's some similarity that I can't see.

"Considering you're his son, you look nothing like him," I say. I mean it as a joke, but the guy just looks uncomfortable. "I'm Izzy. This is my friend Janie."

I catch Janie blushing out of the corner of my eye.

"Nice to meet you," he says. "If I could express—" He pauses, unsure, but I wave my hand like he needn't bother finishing that sentence, and scoot into the booth. Janie perches on the edge as though she might spring up and dash out at any moment.

"So you met my brother?" I ask, cutting to the chase. "After all those emails."

"He followed me. Here, actually."

My brother followed this man? That sounds like something I'd do. "He told you about the memories, then?" I ask.

"He did," Peter says cautiously, like he's trying to hold something back.

"Did you believe him?" I prompt.

The man looks at the bowl of salsa as though it might save him from answering, but it doesn't and he's forced to shake his head. "He told me he remembered getting medicine for me, but I was away at camp when my dad died. I figure he must have read about the accident somewhere. Like in a newspaper."

I must look like I'm about to jump down his throat because Janie taps my knee with her own, and I think she means *be patient*.

"I wish I could express how large a hole my father created," Peter continues.

I get this. Sometimes I forget the hole that Israel left behind until I hear his name. Or remember his smile, and everything inside me scatters, sharp. Janie dabs under her eyes with a napkin, and I swipe at my own tears.

"Israel was interested in my father the same way I was. And strange as it is, I was so desperate for stories of him, for talking about him, that I was willing to sit here and listen to a kid who had become obsessed with him," Peter says.

And that's why I'm here too—across the table from this bland-looking man. I'm desperate to hear about my brother's final days.

"What did he say to you?" I ask.

"He told me he found me through some online group."

I lean forward, feeling goose bumps spring onto my arms. "A group?"

"Yeah. I guess it was for people like him who think they remember past lives."

"What was it called?"

"Oh gosh. I don't know. Something with *souls* in the name maybe."

In my mind, I scroll through everything I saw on Israel's iPad. Was there anything about souls? Not that I can remember, though there was that one discussion app that I'd mostly ignored. Was it in there? I have to search the iPad again.

"I have to go," I say abruptly.

Peter looks stunned, his hand frozen mid-chip-dip, salsa

dribbling over the lip of the bowl, his mouth hanging open. Janie's mouth is open too. I know I'm being rude, but I don't care. If my brother found Peter through this group, it must have the answers I'm looking for.

"Thanks for your time," I say, as though it's an interview. I nudge Janie out of the seat. "Hurry," I say, like the group might self-destruct if I don't get there in time.

Outside, I tug impatiently on the door handle, and Janie fumbles with her keys. Each time she hits the unlock button, I pull on the handle at the same moment, and it doesn't unlock correctly. "Jesus," I say, and slam my hand against the window.

Janie pales. "I'm sorry," she says, even though it's my fault. She presses the unlock button again, and this time I wait before trying the handle and swinging open the door. Then I throw myself into the seat.

"What's the rush?" she asks as she starts the car.

"I have to find those people Israel was talking to." I pull my phone out and start searching, but *souls* and *groups for remembering past lives* doesn't give me much to go on. There are books and websites, but no groups that I can find. Why should I trust Peter anyway? It's not like he believed my brother.

"Look, I know Peter said the medicine part of Israel's dream was wrong, but you believe all this, right? I mean, you saw the dolphins. They found us, Janie. They did."

She looks at me and pauses like she always does. This time, though, it's not awkward. I get the sense it's because she cares about saying something right. "It's okay to believe Israel even if there's a detail that's not true," she finally says.

I notice she avoids mentioning what *she* thinks happened, but I don't push. I slouch against the passenger door, feeling depleted all of a sudden. "I was jealous of him when we were little," I say. "That he had this thing he could remember from before."

"He was probably jealous of you, too, because you could feel when he was in pain."

I kick my feet up onto the dash. "Thanks," I say. "For letting me believe."

"Thank *you*," she says back.

"For what?" I ask, but she doesn't answer. She turns her head to the side window, and I can't tell if she's crying or watching the strip malls stream by.

As soon as Janie drops me off, I retrieve Israel's iPad from its hiding place and climb onto the roof. I scroll through his apps, finding the one I'd only glanced at before: a discussion app where people can join different topics. The trending posts on the main screen are mostly current events, so I'd assumed he was just reading the news there.

I click the login button and the password autocompletes. The view shifts.

Remembered Souls Forum, Gulf Coast, Closed Group, it says along the top.

This has to be it—the group he mentioned to Peter.

The first thread is entitled *Who I Was Before* and has over five hundred replies. I click on the most recent.

Perci6453: I remember those French weaklings were fleeing from the fight. They were supposed to be our allies. I kept riding Fabek among them, trying to rally their troops, but I got hit by grapeshot. Fabek was hit too, and he rolled onto me. 17 hands high—he was a monster of a horse—and he was on my legs. I tried desperately to free myself, but he was too heavy and bleeding everywhere. I wished I could feed him one last apple, feel his peach-fuzzed lips nudging my hand for more, but his breathing was fast and shallow. Since Charleston, he'd grown thin. We all had. If we weren't cavalry, he'd have been food long before.

I began to sweat and feel nauseous. At first, I thought it was just the heat from Fabek's body and his blood soaking me. But then I found the hole in my stomach. Holes. They smelled like excrement. And I knew that my being was leaking out from them.

I woke once, feeling like I was being rocked to sleep by my mother. I could smell the ocean, but when I opened my eyes, it wasn't the ship I saw, but our manor in Warsaw. I could feel the cold stones beneath my feet, the dusty furs we draped on our furniture, our crest stitched into a faded tapestry. That's the last I remember.

WasAthena: Ok—so you were a Polish cavalryman in the Revolutionary War? Do you remember where you were when you got hit?

Perci6453: Savannah.

WasAthena: Oh yeah, I definitely think you're Casimir Pulaski then. This bio says he was hit by grapeshot and then they brought him on board a ship where he died.

My heart races.

There are people like Israel—a whole group of them. For the first time in days, I feel something like relief. At least he wasn't alone.

I read another:

TurtleDove45: I was at the Alamo, but I didn't die there.

NecklessNick: I thought everyone died at the Alamo.

TurtleDove45: No, I died of pneumonia years later. Isn't it nuts that I survived one of the most famous sieges and my lungs were what did me in?

I slipped in and out of delirium those last days

on my deathbed, waking sometimes to the shouts,
"Viva Santa Anna, viva la República." Those are
the cries that woke me the last morning of the
siege. The sentries had not sounded the alarm
and his men were right outside. I crouched in the
corner with Susanna and Angelina. We were sure
they would kill us like they'd already killed most
of the men.

They didn't.

After I lived through the siege, I remarried. I
eventually saw my grandchildren. And those damn
words were still the last I heard.

The Israel I knew would have scoffed at these posts. He
would have said Perci6453 and TurtleDove45 picked famous
figures from American history because they wanted to seem
important. But what about the Israel I *didn't* know? This
Remembered Souls group member—what did *that* Israel think?

If he found Peter through the group, he must have posted
somewhere in this thread. I scroll back, reading post after post
of people sharing stories of their deaths and other users reply-
ing with questions and guesses, like it's all a big trivia game.
I finally locate his post, written in May, a few weeks before
school let out.

IsC: I died in a car accident. There was a crash,
and my car caught fire. I got trapped inside. I

kept thinking of my wife, Lara, and son, Peter, who was sick and needed the medicine I was supposed to be picking up. Can anyone help me find who I was?

If it weren't for the fact that I recognize his description of the dream, I'd doubt Israel was the author. He never asked for help in his life.

After a little back-and-forth about the details, a user replied to the post with a link to a death announcement for Randolph Ryerson, Peter's father.

The date the man died gives me vertigo. I dig my heels into the shingles so I don't slide off the roof, and read the death announcement again and again. Each time I reread it, I'm convinced I'll find a different date, that everyone is right and grief is pulling me apart, but those numbers are as clear as the three dolphins I saw. As clear as the date on my birth certificate.

That man died in a car and became my brother. My brother crashed into the ocean and became a dolphin.

Does that mean I'm someone too? That we all are? Even Luna, who I can hear whimpering on the other side of the window?

I open the app's inbox. My brother direct-messaged someone named OtherPlanes: I think I need your help. Please. I can't keep dying every night in my sleep.

Again, my brother, asking for help. He was hurting, and he never once turned to me.

He was hurting, and, despite my twinsense, I didn't know.

How could I not know?

I failed him.

The thought feels like a chisel in my throat.

CHAPTER FORTY-ONE

CASS

....

Eight days after

I DREAM THAT I'm flying a plane solo. I look out the front and side windows, trying to find our island, but I don't see any land and I can't tell what is sky or ocean. It's all one terrifying, empty blue. The instruments mean nothing to me, and I don't know what direction to head. Down, I think, is the only option. I've seen enough movies to know I push the handlebar-looking thing in front of me back as far as it goes. I feel the plane tip forward and gain momentum as it dives, my stomach in my throat.

I jerk awake with tears running down my cheeks.

When I emerge from my room, the air smells soothingly of syrup. My mom is in the kitchen, a spatula hovering above a hissing pan. Her fleece robe is knotted over baggy pajama pants.

"Hi, sweetie pie. Do you want some pancakes?"

I nod. "I'll make coffee."

I scoop the beans into the grinder while she flips two pancakes onto plates and adds a pat of butter to each. "Have you worked on your college essay at all yet?" she asks.

"No, Mom. Of course I haven't." I press down hard to grind the beans. How can I think about college again like everything is normal? What happened to it being okay to take time and space to grieve?

"Maybe writing about him, about this, would be a good idea," she says when I release the grinder.

"I don't want to get accepted to college because someone feels bad for me."

"I'm not saying that, Cass. I just wonder if maybe it will help you make meaning out of this."

"Meaning?" Heat rises in my cheeks. "There's meaning behind Shane crashing into the ocean?"

She nudges the plate of pancakes toward me. "I'm not saying out of his death. I mean out of his life. Out of yours."

I glare in response.

"I know it's hard, but it really could help. Just think about it, okay? And while you're at it, one more idea to chew on: What about getting a summer job? Saving up for college?"

"I just wanna coach volleyball camp again at the end of July. I promise I'll save more this time."

She sighs. "It's not just about the money, Cass. I think you'll feel better to have some structure to your day. Something that lasts longer than a few weeks, you know?"

"God, Mom, what is it with you today?" I know I'm

shouting, but it feels good. "Stop giving me advice. I don't want to feel better."

I want her to shout back at me, for us to drown the kitchen in noise, but I only get a look of concern. "What do you mean, sweetheart?"

"You always told me I should protect my heart above everything else, but I protected my heart above Shane's and look how that turned out." I'm crying again, remembering the day he picked me up from the tournament, how he curled inward, enfolded, like one of those slow-motion videos of a cocoon opening in reverse. Later, in the cafeteria when he called me a bitch, I realized the Shane who'd been cocooned away was the one I loved. The one who traced the veins up my wrist and cooked me imaginary food. The one who chased my laughter and kissed me like I was a queen.

I turn on the faucet to fill the carafe, but my mom turns it back off. She spins me toward her and puts her hands on my cheeks so that I can't help but look in her eyes.

"You didn't cause this, Cass. Whatever happened, it wasn't your fault."

"But I knew we'd eventually break up, and I didn't want to be the first hurt, so I hurt him instead," I say, only now realizing how true it is. I regarded the incident with Kendall as a minor tick on the ruler of my life, when, in actuality, it was a self-sabotaging cliff jump.

I drop my gaze, but she taps the bottom of my chin with her finger, lifting it again. Tears sting the corners of my eyes, but she won't let me look away. "When you have a hard practice, you hurt afterward, right? You feel weak and sore, but, eventually, your muscles grow stronger," she says. "Hearts do too."

Even if she's right, there's no way Shane's heart could have rebounded and grown stronger when mine still hasn't. I take a shuddering breath. "Fine, I'll try to get a job as long as you leave me alone."

She smiles and mimes zipping up her lips and tossing away a key.

The Adventure Pier movie theater seems like the most natural place for me to find a job. Izzy and I have spent so many weekend and summer days in the theater's air-conditioned caverns when it was too hot for the beach. I can imagine myself in the same burgundy polo and gold-plated name tag as Janie and filling popcorn buckets beside her. A few weeks ago, just the idea would have made me uncomfortable.

She's at the ticket sales counter when I arrive. I stand in her line and smile when she waves me forward.

"Hey," I say. "Are you guys hiring?"

She widens her eyes at my question, then shakes her head. "All the college kids are back, but maybe in the fall."

"Oh okay." I try to mask my disappointment. "My mom wants me to find a job, but I'll try somewhere else."

"Wait—I was going to text you. I scheduled and put down a deposit for our first lesson. It's at five."

My stomach rockets to my feet with terror. It can't be time to fly yet, right? There's got to be things to learn about the physics of flight and the laws or something first. "What should I tell my mom?" I ask.

She shrugs casually like escaping parents isn't something she has to deal with. "I guess you could tell her you're training for a job here."

I can hear the line behind me grumbling. The ticket seller next to Janie, a big guy I've seen at school, is watching us without really looking. I don't blame him. We are an unlikely pair—the bitch who broke her beloved's heart and the awkward girl who was a stranger to the boys who died. He can't tell that we are the widows.

"Hey, are you having dreams?" I ask, ignoring the watchers. "About the crash?" Just the thought of the empty blue sky makes me shiver.

She plays with the stylus on the credit card machine, twirling the cord. "I wake up a lot," she finally says. "I don't remember having a dream, but it feels like I've just been with him. Like he's in the room. It makes me so—" She interrupts herself with a headshake.

I'm always impatient when Janie doesn't finish thoughts, but I try to be patient this time.

"Lonely, I guess," she finishes.

An older man with wire-framed grandpa glasses appears behind Janie and frowns at me. "Janie, you have a line."

"Neil, this is Cass," she says. "She's looking for a job."

"All full."

"Got it. Thanks." I turn to leave and then stop myself. "Hey, Janie."

She looks at me, face so open that it breaks my heart. I've been such an asshole to her. "Me too," I say.

She looks puzzled for a moment and then nods, understanding—I hope—that we share the aching loneliness of being left behind.

CHAPTER FORTY-TWO

IZZY

....

Eight days after

I TRY ALL night to break into the encrypted app that OtherPlanes directed Israel to without any luck. I fall asleep around dawn, waking up several hours later to Luna at my door and a text from my dad: `Police said we can get Israel's car. Will you come pick it up with me this afternoon?`

Israel's car is a boat-wide sedan from the early 2000s that our dad bought to reward him for good grades. When I asked our dad why I didn't get a car, he said I needed to learn to be more responsible and that Israel would be giving me rides, which was bullshit. Israel had early-bird classes and practice after school, so I always had to walk or take the bus. But now he wants me to drive it?

`Try mami`, I text back.

I log in to Remembered Souls and open Israel's inbox.

My last option is to direct-message OtherPlanes from Israel's account. If he doesn't answer, I'm no worse off.

Hey, so you think souls can move into animals, right? I type.

"Come on. Come on," I say to the screen.

I roll onto my back and stretch a hand out lazily to scratch Luna's head. The iPad makes a whoosh sound when OtherPlanes messages back.

Who the hell is this?

I want to understand how this all works, I write.

OtherPlanes doesn't respond. Luna grows interested in a fly on the chair in the corner of my room and makes soft snuffling noises as she tries to catch it. The fly takes off, bouncing angrily from window to window. Luna lets out a frustrated woof. I'm frustrated too, and want to shake the iPad like an Etch A Sketch.

Hello? I type. Hello? The guy must know Israel is gone, so I try the truth. I'm just trying to find my brother, Israel Castillo, I type.

No answer.

OtherPlanes—I learn by scrolling through his posts—thinks of himself as some sort of prophet of transmigration. He believes people like he and Israel can badger their way into new lives upon the end of their current life. It all sounds like bullshit to me, but my brother messaged him for help, so he saw something in this charlatan.

I stop at a post from over a month ago. OtherPlanes talks about being a pilot and passing through a doorway to become a little girl. A pilot? My hands are shaking, like all that crawling energy under my skin has burst outside. My brother talked privately to OtherPlanes and then started flight lessons. He was looking for this doorway. He had to be.

I pull up a screenshot I took of Israel's search history. *Bradley Simpson, flight instructor.* The school is at a small regional airport almost an hour away. I'll need a car.

I try Janie first, but she says she's at work until four.

`Fine, I'll help,` I text my dad.

A few hours later he picks me up with a large thermos of coffee in his cup holder. He looks weary, the skin under his eyes creased, his shoulders low. Before he says a word to me, his phone rings.

"Aló," he says over his earpiece. He pauses for a moment. "No," he says. "Diles que no." *Tell them no.*

He hangs up and backs out of the driveway without looking at me.

"What was that about?"

"Some güevón trying to give us the wrong tile."

I can't remember the last time I was alone with my dad—if you don't count him dragging me to the parking lot during the funeral. We drive in silence before he clears his throat.

"Bela, can I ask you something?"

"Yeah."

"Was your brother happy?"

The truth? I don't know. There was so much I didn't know about Israel. "I think so," I lie, though I'm not sure why I'm protecting his feelings.

"We—I—put so much pressure on him about his grades." My dad's eyes are glittering, and it softens me.

"I don't think it's ever just one thing," I say. Look at me: I'm sad because my brother is gone, because he chose to leave, because he felt like he had to, because our parents, Cass, and so many others are in pain. They are distinct yet overlapping sadnesses.

We pull into the police station lot.

"I'll go in to get the keys and find out where it's parked," he says, swinging open his door. Before climbing out, he looks over his shoulder at me. "Thanks for coming today. Your mom never answered."

"She's having a hard time," I say.

"There are still responsibilities."

As her daughter, I don't disagree. And yet, as her daughter, I want to defend her. I think of Cass after Israel's funeral, implying that my talk of dolphins was getting in the way of her feeling sadness. "I think grief is one of them," I say.

He turns away, half on the seat, his feet on the step outside. "You're on me now too, huh?" he says. "I *have* to work."

"You don't, though."

He slams the door and heads into the station without

another word. When he returns, he drops the keys into my palm and points to the lot behind the station. "It's back there. Drive it straight home," he says warningly. "I've got to check on the Cooper house."

"Sure," I say. But who would I be if I listened?

I'm almost excited to drive Israel's car until I open the door and am hit with the grassy clean scent of him. Tears spring to my eyes. The driver's seat is tilted back, almost reclining. It certainly wasn't my straitlaced brother who did that. I'd blame it on the cops, but it was probably Shane's doing. He was tall enough to pull that off and had a free pass to drive Israel's car. *I owe him*, Israel would say when I pointed this out. *He's been a good friend*. It was never clear to me why Israel owed Shane for friendship more than he owed me for sisterhood.

I adjust the seat and climb in, at first trying to hold my breath and then gulping in the scent of him. That's the thing I've learned about grief—you both want to escape and to remember everything.

I drive, feeling like my eyelids are windshield wipers in a rainstorm: as soon as I blink tears away, new ones are there, blurring my vision. It takes almost an hour to reach the airfield on the mainland, a field with a long dirt road.

A red hatchback—Janie's car?—is parked between two pickups. What the hell?

I march into the open hangar, but the sight of two white

planes—similar to my brother's that plunged into the ocean—socks me in the stomach. I want to lie beneath one and imagine that it's the morning on the beach, except the plane will climb high and make a wide arc, returning right to this spot.

I almost forget why I'm here, but I spot Janie, still in her work uniform and seated on a folding chair near the back of the hangar, playing with the tail of her braid. Cass, with her glorious hair tied back, is next to her. The instructor I found online is in front of a whiteboard on wheels.

"What the fuck is going on?" I ask.

The three turn, and the man flinches like he recognizes me. Cass looks guilty. Only Janie seems glad to see me.

"We're learning to fly," she says.

"Oh good," I say. "There are some things I need to learn too."

SECURE MESSAGE THREAD

IsC: What happened to the existing soul? The one that was inside Millicent's body before you went through the doorway and took over?

OtherPlanes: I don't know. I think it transmigrated the traditional way, waiting in the liminal space before awakening at another's birth.

IsC: So did it hurt?

OtherPlanes: I don't think so. But like I said before, it wasn't easy to jump into someone fully formed. It might be easier to jump into an animal because their brains are wired more simply. I think, as long as the soul listens to the animal's instinct, the body will live on normally.

IsC: What happens with your last body? The one you leave at the doorway? Does another soul take over?

OtherPlanes: No. Of course not.

IsC: So what happens then?

OtherPlanes: It dies.

CHAPTER FORTY-THREE

SHANE

....

Eight days before

THEY RAN THROUGH the checklist for Shane's first takeoff. Brad beside Shane, his hat off to accommodate the large headset. Shane wished he'd put the hat back on, so he didn't have to see those flat blue eyes. Shane's stomach felt queasy, but he'd run through simulation after simulation until it was easy to keep a fake plane in the air. Brad would be able to take over the controls if anything went wrong.

At Brad's instruction, Shane took a deep breath and pushed the throttle all the way in. They accelerated down the runway, and it felt like driving a car fast down country roads. Shane checked the RPMs, watching the needle on the airspeed indicator climb. He began to lift the nose until the wheels were just barely skimming the ground. Then, he felt it: the takeoff, as much inside of him as beneath. They were in the air and there was nothing but open sky above them. The simulation couldn't give you this feeling. It was the lightest he'd been since Cass.

"Smooth takeoff." Brad's voice was calm in his ear. Israel and Nate—who they'd had to lift into the plane—were on the headset too, but with the strict instructions to remain silent until they were done with the ascent.

Shane continued to climb until Brad told him to level off. He realized he was white-knuckling the yoke, but he relaxed his fingers and allowed himself to look around.

While he'd been focused on the takeoff, the world had spilled out beneath them: a mottled red-gold-green blanket dotted with longhorns and scrub trees. The Gulf glittered in front of him, their island a thin curve off the coast like a fingernail clipping.

The plane seemed to gobble up distance, and the next thing Shane knew, they were over the line of cars waiting for the ferry to another island. Then the green dome of the botanical gardens on the bay side of their island, the neatly parked boats at the marina, and the downtown, crawling with ant-sized people.

"That's my house!" Nate called over the mic. Shane craned his neck and saw Nate's yellow cube in a line of colorful chiclets.

"There's mine," said Israel. His was a crown on the top of a cul-de-sac.

Shane found his own by the shape of the pool, which he and Meg jokingly called "the amoeba." He tried to find Cass's, too, but all the roofs in her condo complex looked the same. It was easier to spot the houses at Seabreeze Cove that he and Cass had christened their own. He could confront them more easily from above—imagine them as toys that he could flick into the ocean if he wanted.

Adventure Pier's Ferris wheel spun lazily beneath them. Shane remembered how many times the height of the ride had thrilled him, but now that feeling shrank in comparison.

The beach, a narrow white stripe, stretched from tip to tip on the ocean side of their island. It reminded Shane of a layer of skin—so thin and fragile that it doesn't seem capable of protecting you from much.

They were over the Gulf in minutes, the waves cresting in white slivers. The water was so much bluer than it appeared from land and Shane wished, suddenly, that Cass could see it like this—blue on blue as far as the eye could see.

"Dolphins," Nate said into the headset. Shane looked out the side window. There was a group of nearly twenty small shadows darting beneath the water. They looked like tadpoles.

"They're great problem-solvers and incredible hunters," Brad said. Shane had practically forgotten he was there. "Sometimes I think it would be a better life. Everything would be so immediate: breathing, eating, survival."

Shane didn't disagree. That's what he liked about flying so far: everything was simplified to a drone, to blue, to a flat map beneath him. He could relax into it, spend his days carting passengers from island to island.

"All right, pull all the way back," Brad said.

"All the way?"

"Yes."

Shane did, until the alarm began to sound—a high whine like a mosquito in his ear. Shane felt them tilt toward the left wing, and the nose of the plane tipped down. The motion made his stomach skip, like they were on a roller coaster. Before him, he saw nothing but blue, reminding him of when, in the simulator, he couldn't tell what was up or down.

"Now, it's counterintuitive, but you can't pull up to recover from a stall. You have to point the nose down."

Shane froze. It felt like they were picking up velocity; the seat belt was cutting into his skin. All Shane could think about was Cass laughing, how she'd tilt her head back, nostrils flaring, eyes downcast so her eyelids almost closed. It hurt. It hurt. It hurt.

Shane watched the altitude indicator. Were they leveling out? Brad was doing it, the yoke moving under Shane's hands.

"It's hard to override instinct," Brad said. "Ready to try again?"

Shane nodded, even though his hands were shaking. He felt like he was in a tunnel with Brad's voice, eerily calm, at the other end. He tried to focus on the controls, the instruments, the horizon. This time, when the alarm sounded, he pointed the nose down. The plane leveled just as it had for Brad.

When it was time to return to the airfield, Shane's heart had settled and his breathing was nearly even. He began to descend and reduce the power as instructed. They sank lower over the gray strip of the runway.

"Pull up some," Brad said when they were close. Shane pushed the throttle in and lifted the aircraft's nose, maintaining the airspeed. They crossed the threshold of the runway.

"Now put her down," Brad said. Shane pulled the throttle all the way out and kept the nose from dropping. "Hold steady."

The wheels bounced. Nate's and Israel's whoops broke Shane from his tunnel. Shane braked, using the pedals now.

"Great," Brad said. When they came to a stop, Shane pulled off the headset and twisted in his seat.

"I flew," Shane said to Nate and Israel, and even though he'd panicked mid-stall, now all he could do was laugh.

CHAPTER FORTY-FOUR

NATE

....

Six days before

"WHY DON'T YOU turn toward the coast and head back to the airfield?" Brad said.

Nate relaxed his grip on the yoke and made the turn. It was almost over. Finally. He'd been trying to listen to Brad the whole lesson, but it had been hard to concentrate. His thoughts kept flapping like wings inside his head, each beat cutting him.

I'm worthless.

I deserve pain.

He dug his nails into his palm to feel their bite, but it wasn't enough to quiet his mind. He *was* worthless—as small as the surfers that carved across the waves beneath them.

He hadn't wanted to learn to fly—not like Israel and Shane—but they'd convinced him to try.

"You might like it," Shane had said.

"You might see the doorway," Israel had added.

He wouldn't make this mistake again. The sooner Nate was on the ground, the sooner he could go home and make slow painful laps around his living room until his brain shut up or he collapsed, whichever came first.

Nate listened to the engine, trying to block out his inner voice with its drone. He'd made it up here somehow. He could get back down.

He focused on the palm trees that looked like green starfish from above, the long roofs of rental party houses, the boats bobbing like ducks in the marina. There were smokestacks in the distance, beside a field of white circular structures used for storing chemicals. One of the smokestacks had a flame at the top like a lit candle.

They flew over neat suburban grids and the brown sweep of ranchland. Finally Nate spotted the runway and lined up their approach as instructed. They began to descend.

"Coming in a bit hot," Brad said. "Pull up."

Pull up—that meant pull back on the yoke, right? Nate knew the answer, but he felt like he couldn't retrieve the information through the steady wingbeat of his thoughts.

I'm worthless.

I deserve pain.

I'm worthless.

I deserve pain.

The runway seemed endless, a gray stripe stretching into some infinity. All around it were empty, flat fields. Nothing, really, for miles. They might as well be landing on the moon.

Except there *was* something in front of Nate—an opening just above the runway. It looked like someone had drawn back a curtain of sky. The darkness beyond it was as flat as the landscape—the most nothing of things Nate had ever seen.

The wings in his head went still, the inner voice silent. This was the kind of place where peace would be entire, where quiet would feel like velvet.

What was it?

"Pull up, damn it."

Nate was vaguely aware of Brad taking over the controls, of putting them down with a jarring slam of the wheels, of cursing at him loudly. When they came to a stop, Shane reached over the seat and squeezed his shoulder.

"You all right?" Shane asked.

"Holy shit, man. You had us scared," Israel said.

Nate felt like he was going to throw up. Had he almost killed his best friends? He pushed open the door and tumbled down. The impact made his knee seize and he cried out.

Israel climbed down and leaned over, his hands on his thighs like he was out of breath. "I really thought we were going to crash."

"We're okay," Shane said.

"Did you see it?" Nate asked breathlessly.

Israel spun to face him. "What? You saw the doorway?"

He wasn't sure *doorway* was the right word. It was like nothing he'd ever seen before. Nate nodded and shook his head at the same time.

Israel frowned, his thick brows shadowing his eyes. "Where was it?"

"Right above the runway. It disappeared when Brad took the controls."

"What did it look like?"

An open curtain that promised a silence and darkness so absolute it belonged to another world? Nate couldn't say that. "Like a tear in the sky," he said. "Magic."

"What's this about a magic doorway?" Brad was behind them, settling his hat back onto his head.

"Nothing," Shane said too quickly.

Brad pulled down the brim, but tilted his head back so he could squint at Nate. His blue eyes were hard and cold. "You're damn right it's nothing. Not when my job is on the line—and, more important: our lives. So next time, do what you're told. If you're not going to listen, these lessons are over and you'll still pay for the full block. You hear?"

"Yeah, yeah, we got it," Shane said.

Nate stopped listening. Even now he could feel the tear, leaking dark and quiet right under his skin. He didn't understand it, but he knew it was the opposite of everything. The opposite of pain and fear and worthlessness. It would silence the thoughts that were drilling into him. Forever.

He'd have to find it again.

CHAPTER FORTY-FIVE

ISRAEL

·····························

Five days before

ISRAEL WOKE UP, gasping and exhausted as always. He pulled his phone off the charger and reread the last messages with OtherPlanes. If he went through this doorway, he'd have to do it alone. Nate, Shane, his sister, his parents—everyone would think he'd died. Even if he left a note, they wouldn't know who he'd become. He'd have to find them from the next life and try to get them to believe him like he'd tried with Peter. If he even remembered this particular past life.

Israel pictured his mother—not the beach-bathing socialite she was now—but back when she'd worked as a hospital scheduler and would meet them at the bus stop in her scrubs. She'd throw tater tots in the oven, and the three of them would "ice-skate" sock-footed around the kitchen while the tots baked. Could he risk giving up the memory of being himself?

But he knew, he could admit, that nostalgia colored the truth. He'd never been that happy boy, smiling and spinning on the kitchen floor. After the tots, he'd always crash, too tired from his nightmares. His mother would scold him for falling asleep and make him do his math homework standing up. He'd snap at his sister, who only wanted him to hurry up so they could play more. And his father, home late from work and tired himself, would yell at them for squabbling.

These nightmares tainted every memory. They constituted every relationship. He was nothing but them.

Will I have nightmares and remember this life in my next? he typed.

OtherPlanes was always online, so it only took him a few moments to respond: Maybe, but that's part of the power of choice. Better make this end a happy one.

There were no guarantees that it was worth it, then. And what did he really know about OtherPlanes? The man thought the government was after him because he remembered past lives. If it weren't for the fact that another user in their group— and now Nate—had seen the doorway, Israel wouldn't trust him at all.

He closed the app and climbed out of bed. His sister wasn't outside his door, but he heard her voice rising angrily, along with their dad's downstairs.

His entire family was in the kitchen when he descended, his dad dressed for work and his mom in a knit beach cover-up, her skin already shiny with tanning oil. Her hands were on her waist and she was glaring at Izzy, who squatted beside the fridge, pulling vegetables out of the bin.

"They got our final report cards," Izzy said over her shoulder.

Israel glanced at his dad, hoping for a smile, but his dad's teeth were visibly clenched. His mustache twitched over down-turned lips.

Israel spotted the torn envelope on the counter, the print-outs unfolded beside it. He grabbed his and traced the list of As down the page until he landed on one B+. Econ. Of course. Izzy's, he saw, was a mixture of Bs and Cs.

"I thought you were getting all As this semester," his dad said.

"Yeah, I thought I was. I didn't do well on the final."

"¿Estudiaste?"

"Yeah, I studied."

"¿Y entonces?"

So? How was he supposed to respond to that? So, he'd been distracted by his quest to end his dreams? So, he'd been hurt by his friends? So, he wasn't strong enough to live with this thing even though plenty of others did?

"No sé," Israel said. *I don't know.*

His dad's eyes narrowed and hardened, and there it was—disappointment sharply carved into the lines beside his mouth—just like that day he'd told them about his dream. The resonance rolled into Israel like a boulder.

"There's still time," Israel said weakly. "I'll do better next year."

"It's all cumulative," his dad said. "This matters."

Izzy fed a carrot into the juicer, and the machine made a loud whine.

"Coño, Isabela, we're trying to have a conversation here!" their father shouted over the noise.

Straight-faced, Izzy fed a cucumber and a piece of ginger into the machine. She grabbed a handful of kale next like she planned to keep juicing until their dad gave up. She winked at Israel, and he backed out of the kitchen. He opened the front door and sat on the steps while Luna galloped down to pee.

Israel hadn't been able to keep his grades up second semester—how was he going to do it another whole year? And four more after that? Colleges weren't going to take econ majors who couldn't do simple supply and demand problems—and the financial firms weren't going to hire someone who couldn't cut it in college.

If he went through the doorway, he wouldn't just escape the dreams, he'd escape the weight of these expectations, too. He'd be free—to be whatever, or whomever, he wanted.

Israel pulled his phone out of his pocket and texted Nate and Shane.

Can you come over this afternoon? We need to talk.

• • •

Israel sat cross-legged on his bed, tossing a stuffed basketball at the hoop hanging on his wall—anything to keep his hands moving and his nerves at bay. Shane was on his back on the floor, catching and returning the ball. He'd shaved his own head—a summer heat haircut, he'd said—which exaggerated his large ears and also made him look like a baby-faced military recruit. Nate was in the desk chair, extending his leg with a grimace and curling it back as though doing his PT.

"I've decided to do it soon," Israel told them. "I don't know what other choice I have to end these dreams."

"Doctors," Shane said.

"Mom took me to one when I was little," Israel said.

"Have you been to any lately? Now that you're older, things might be different."

"They'll just put you on meds," Nate said.

"Maybe that's a good thing," Shane said. He glanced at Nate when he said it like he wanted Nate to hear this too. "There's nothing wrong with being on meds."

"What if you do this and you can't come back?" Nate asked.

Israel didn't tell them about the conversation he'd had with OtherPlanes. They might try to talk him out of it if they knew what he knew. "Wouldn't you rather have a life where the most painful thing in it hadn't happened to you? Honestly?" he asked instead.

"Yeah," Shane said with a sigh, clearly thinking of Cass.

"Yeah," Nate agreed.

"Would you give anything for that life?" Israel asked. His

friends were silent, but Israel willed certainty into his voice. "*I would.*"

"Brad said we need more hours before a solo flight," Shane said.

"He just wants more money," Nate said.

"It's also illegal," Shane pointed out.

"When has that stopped us before?" Israel asked.

He saw a flash of a white T-shirt in the hallway. It was his sister, pausing in the shadows outside his door. She was in her pajamas, her hair wrapped in a towel. Israel wondered if by sitting here, making these plans, he'd somehow called out to her with his body.

He met her eyes, but she ducked away. He heard the click of her door and the familiar sound of documentary narration beginning on the other side of the wall.

"Look, I've decided I have to do this. I just need help getting the plane." He looked at Shane when he said this. "Please."

Shane sat up, folding his long legs underneath him. "Okay. I think we need a few lessons to scope everything out. My parents' treat." Shane smiled mischievously. "Plus, you could use more practice."

"And you'll tell me how to find the doorway?" Israel asked Nate.

"I'll try," he replied.

Israel felt calmer now that his friends were behind him.

Shane snapped his fingers. "We should do it after that senior party."

"What better way to celebrate our ascension than larceny," Nate said.

"To new beginnings," Shane said, raising an imaginary glass.

Or to saying goodbye with a party—a happy memory, Israel thought.

CHAPTER FORTY-SIX

NATE

....

Four days before

NATE'S DAD WAS asleep in the recliner, the TV volume on low. A bearded man in an infomercial tested knives that looked like plastic on large blocks of chocolate. Nate stood behind the couch, balancing on his bad leg, holding it longer and longer until he had to lean against the couch back, panting. The pain was so bright, so loud, that it emptied his brain of everything. But his inner voice always returned.

I have no future. No backup plans.

I'm a terrible friend and family member.

I'm worthless.

I deserve pain.

He thought of the tear in the sky, darkness so thick that he couldn't conceive of a light cutting through it. Nothing could. Not even his thoughts.

Nate's dad shifted in the recliner and made a grumbling

sound but didn't open his eyes. His mom, who'd been working on a grant in the kitchen, poked her head into the living room and peered at him over her computer glasses. "What are you doing?" she asked.

"Knee exercises for PT."

"You going to get the door?"

The door? He'd been so buried in his head, he hadn't even heard the doorbell. "Oh, sorry," he said. He pointed at the quiet TV as though it were an excuse. His mom shook her head and disappeared back into the kitchen.

Janie was on the porch in her work uniform, unbraiding her hair. In the porch light, it was blond and brown and red and gold. The braids had left crinkles with little straight tufts at the ends.

"I need to cut it all off," she said, gesturing at her hair when she caught him staring. Her upper lip and forehead were beaded with droplets of sweat.

"I love your hair," he said, dropping his eyes.

"I love *your* hair," she replied, reaching around to squeeze his bun like it was a clown nose. "You never wear it down." She pulled his hair tie out, and her hand brushed his neck briefly, accidentally. The touch made him shiver. Goose bumps on the corresponding side of his body rose, and he tried to flatten them by rubbing with his other hand, hoping she hadn't noticed.

"Want to watch a movie or something? I brought popcorn." She held up a black plastic trash bag, bulging with leftover popcorn from the theater.

"My dad's asleep," he said. "Your house?"

"My dad's"—she wrinkled her nose—"asleep too. How about the beach again?"

The word filled him with longing for their first summer together. Racing each other barefoot across the sand. Crashing into the waves. The tightness of salted skin. The freedom. Would he ever have that again?

No. He didn't deserve it.

"Come on," she said with a playful whine.

He gave in. Even if it wouldn't be like it once was, he was glad for the distraction.

Janie lit the dark seawall steps with the light on her phone so Nate could navigate down carefully. The beach itself was lit by a half-moon and Adventure Pier in the distance. Every few minutes a chorus of screams erupted from the pirate ship ride.

They sat in the sand, and she flapped open the plastic bag, wafting the smell of butter toward him. He shoved a fistful of popcorn into his mouth. Janie held some flat on her palm, and tossed the kernels, one by one, onto her tongue. He loved how unselfconscious they could be around each other—how easy it was to listen to her openmouthed crunch of kernels and the sound of waves and to say nothing at all.

"I caught most of that new Marvel movie tonight," she said.

He unlaced his shoes, bending his hurt knee uncomfortably, and then worked the shoes off with his toes. "Is that all you do? Watch movies?"

"Well, all you do is watch TV."

"Touché. But I go to parties sometimes too." It felt good to talk about normal things again, to pretend like everything was as it had been. "There's one this weekend. You should come let loose for once."

"Yeah?" Her cheeks were flushed and her lips were flecked with salt. He imagined her fingers slick with butter, and he had an urge to take one and put it in his mouth.

"Yeah," he said, meaning it. On a moonlit beach, it was easy to forget about the wall he'd built between their school and home lives.

"I'll think about it." She tilted her head back and looked up at the sky.

He followed her gaze. "Do you think you'd leave Earth—if you had the chance?" he asked.

"Hmmm," she said. "Would I get to come back?"

He shook his head and swatted a sand fly. "Nope, and because of how long it would take you to get there, everyone you knew at home would be gone."

"Could I take someone with me?" she asked.

"Sure. One person."

"Yeah, all right. I'd do it."

Despite the pier's glow, he could make out Orion's Belt— three stars slung right above them. He'd always thought the other constellations—bears, dogs, and archers—were difficult to decipher, but the belt looked like a belt.

"Who would you take?" He hadn't done this much, but he knew that flirting meant dancing around a subject, each person daring the other to get as close as they could before hopping away.

She flushed again. It had to mean the answer he was hoping for: him.

She tossed more popcorn into her mouth and spoke with her mouth full: "I guess it would depend on what year it was. I don't know who is going to be in my life in the future."

"Yeah, okay," he said with a smile; she hadn't taken the dare.

"So what were you up to the past few days?" she asked in a rush, quite obviously eager to change the subject.

I flew, he wanted to say. *I found a hole in the world.* Instead he leaned forward and kissed her—went right for those flecks of salt on her mouth. They stung the chapped cracks of his lips. He tasted them on his tongue. His hands were on her face, dusting her cheeks with sand.

He could tell she was nervous by the way she was breathing through her nose urgently. Her hands seemed unable to find a place to rest. They were on his shoulders, on the back of his neck, on his waist. He trapped them between his own, wound his fingers in hers. He'd never felt his whole body surge into a kiss before; it felt like jumping into a pool.

He fell backward and pulled her on top of him, her breasts

crushed against his chest. There was sand everywhere—plastering his skin, crunching beneath him, even stinging between his eyelids. He dragged his teeth against her lower lip and squared his hips below hers. His body ached to move more, to pull at buttons and shove aside fabric.

Nate slid his hands under her shirt, working one up her spine and the other up her side. Janie shivered and straightened her back. Her eyes were wide—almost surprised. It was the same face she'd made that day they met, when they dropped their bikes and stood on the seawall, expectant, like anything could happen.

I don't deserve her.

I don't deserve this joy.

The thoughts filled his head until it felt like a frenzied bat nest.

There's no way she'll stick around.

Not after how selfish I've been. Not after the pain I've caused her.

There's nothing for her here.

Nothing worthwhile.

No one worthwhile.

"What's wrong?" she asked.

He realized he was staring at her, a few inches from her face. He sat up, knocking his forehead against her chin. "Nothing," he managed.

"Did I do something wrong?" she asked, rubbing her chin and climbing off him.

"No, I just—" What could he say? He was a liar. A coward. He'd knowingly ignored her at school.

"I just thought we should go slow or whatever," he finished. It was something he must have heard on a movie or TV show.

Janie was silent. He couldn't even go three minutes without hurting her.

He scraped sand behind him into a mound and leaned back against it. "You're going to leave," he said; it was the only excuse he could think of that wasn't the truth.

She looked confused. "You mean for college?"

"Yeah."

"Well, I'm going to apply to a few schools with good literature and screenwriting programs out east. I miss the seasons, you know?"

She made her own sand pile and leaned next to him. She smelled like popcorn, and his lips still buzzed from the pressure of hers.

"Aren't *you* going to leave?" she asked carefully, like she wasn't sure if she was allowed to ask.

I don't deserve to go anywhere, he thought. *I've been such a piece of shit for years.*

"I want to be up there." Nate pointed at a star. She'd be the one person he took with him if he left and could take someone, but of course he didn't say that out loud. And she didn't ask.

All Nate wanted to do was kiss Janie again and to lose his

fingers in the tangle of her hair, but he knew he shouldn't. He'd just hurt her again.

"Nate? Nate?" Janie had turned to face him, crisscrossing her legs in front of her. The moon lit one half of her face but the other was dark. "What's really going on?" Her hair blew into his face, tickling his nose. She brushed it away tentatively. "You've been, like, dropping out of yourself or something. Are you feeling depressed maybe? It's okay if you are, you know. I could talk to my dad and see if he has suggestions of someone you could go see."

She'd tell her dad? He was flooded with embarrassment. "No," Nate said. "There's nothing wrong with me."

"That's what I'm trying to say," she said. "There's nothing wrong with whatever you're feeling."

He stood, wincing as he put weight on his healing knee and brushed all the sand off his clothes and skin. "Let's just go. The flies are biting."

"Okay." She sounded disappointed, but she stood too, and grabbed the bag of popcorn by the neck. The bag, now choked in her fist, made him inexplicably sad: how quickly something that had seemed like a beginning could turn into just another end.

CASS'S COLLEGE APPLICATION ESSAY DRAFT

ON JUNE 22, 2019, I made a plan to write my college application essay. My parents seemed ~~distant~~ **more distant than ever**, and I had just broken up with ~~the love of my life~~ **my boyfriend of five years**. I thought I would write the essay about how the bonds between people change, how there are phases of transition. I planned to ~~wow you with~~ **include** one ~~long~~ **extended** chemistry metaphor.

On June 23, 2019, I witnessed a plane crash. The plane was carrying my ex-boyfriend and his best friends.

Plans change. I can't write that essay anymore.

And yet, ~~here~~ I am, writing my personal statement because the BIG PLAN—that I will go to your college, major in biological chemistry, get a PhD, and run my own lab someday—is expected to move forward.

Life, the endless conveyor belt. Grief, simply the grime ~~gunking~~ **gumming** up the gears. Slowing you down, but not actually stopping the momentum.

What if grief is not supposed to be kept underneath? What if we became like the widows from centuries before and wore it everywhere we went? What if we brought it to our jobs? To school? To the grocery store? What if we allowed the BIG PLANS to change? What if we pressed pause?

Here is the truth: I do not know anymore if I want to be a chemist. Right now I do not want to be anything.

So ~~I guess I should talk about college~~ **what do I want out of college?** I want to better understand loss. I want to read about it. Find it in art. I want to sit in classes with people who have felt things deeply. I want to talk about what happened. I want to be heard.

CHAPTER FORTY-SEVEN

CASS

....

Eight days after

I CAN TELL Izzy is pissed by the way she stares through Janie and me as though we aren't even in the same hangar. I've been her friend long enough to know she'll forget about the silent treatment soon.

She goes straight for Brad, her finger pointing at his chest. "What exactly did the boys say when they were here?" she asks.

Here we are, pretending to learn to fly, trying to build trust until he gives us a window to ask about them. But Izzy refuses to play by anyone else's rules—unspoken or not.

"I know my brother was looking for the doorway," she says.

I have no idea what she's talking about, but Brad's eyes widen with recognition. In seconds Izzy created an opening in the conversation that Janie and I were going to pay thousands of dollars to wait for.

"She and Israel are more alike than they seem initially, aren't they?" I ask Brad, willing my voice to sound as defiant as Izzy's. Izzy is beside me, and I can tell by the way she squares herself and sets her jaw that my question has made her stronger.

Brad ignores the question and turns on his heel, disappearing behind his whiteboard. "Ready for the hot seat?" he calls over his shoulder. We follow him, my heart pounding in my ears. I don't want to be closer to the planes.

"What is it? This doorway?" Janie sounds genuinely curious, and this stops him in his tracks. Is he curious too? We are near the back of the hangar, where flight vests, headsets, and a few sets of keys hang on pegs.

"My brother thought he could go through it into another life," Izzy says—more to Brad than us.

Another life? Like a dolphin's? It still makes no sense to me, but I know the longer we talk, the more answers we'll get and the less time we'll have to fly. "Does any of this sound familiar, Brad?" I ask.

"I don't know," he says, turning to face us. "Maybe. I certainly never saw anything."

"But did they see it?" Izzy asks.

"Once Nate was coming in too hot for a landing and he just froze up, so I had to land for him. He said he saw something that looked like a tear."

A tear? The skin at my hairline prickles. Could all of this be true?

Brad pushes up the brim of his hat to wipe his forehead, and I catch the first glimpse of his eyes. They are blue and empty, like the sky in my dream. They make me want to turn and run.

"Look, whatever the reason, they stole my plane," he says. "I'm still fighting the insurance company about this."

"Can you believe he's talking about the insurance company?" Izzy turns to me, and just like that, the silent treatment is over. Brad's back is to the wall, and the three of us position ourselves in a semicircle. As though reading each other's minds, we've blocked his escape.

"You're talking like you have no responsibility here," I say.

"What about *your* responsibility?" he shoots back. He reminds me of a cornered wild animal, snapping at anything that moves. But Izzy's fury falls from her face, and I can tell his bite landed. I wonder what my own face is doing. If it's betraying my own guilt.

"You're right. We're all complicit," Janie says. She takes a deep breath. "I didn't get Nate help. Even though he was practically shouting at me to."

"I let Israel push me away even though I knew better." This from Izzy, whose eyes have dropped to the concrete floor of the hangar.

This is easy for me; I've known my failure all along. "I broke Shane's heart," I say. "Your turn, Brad."

He clears his throat and looks around like someone else might be hiding amid the planes. "Israel was the one looking for it, I think," he says it low, practically a growl. "I only over-heard them talking about it."

"Did you tell the police?" I ask.

He shakes his head.

"So Israel was trying to find this doorway thing, and Nate and Shane were along for the ride?" Janie asks.

"I think Nate was—" He pauses a moment and rubs his goatee. Janie folds her arms across her chest, hugging herself. I put my hand on her shoulder. "Lost," he finishes, and I feel her shoulder sink.

He turns toward me. "I think Shane wanted to fly. He was getting good at it." At first I find it harder to swallow than Nate's and Israel's news. Some part of me can see it, though: Shane soaring above all of us, those long arms stretched, his head lifted, so that he isn't smiling down on us, but out. Always out.

If flying is something he wanted to do, I wasn't the reason he climbed into the plane.

And I won't be the reason Izzy or Janie or anyone else does either.

"We're leaving," I say.

"But—" Izzy protests.

"No." I'm more sure than I've ever been. I look directly into her eyes when I say it, and, for the first time in our lives, Izzy backs down.

CHAPTER FORTY-EIGHT

JANIE

....

Eight days after

"HEAR ME OUT," Izzy says, her hand pressed against the passenger door of my car so Cass can't get in. "I think we have to go back in and finish the lesson. Just to see if we can find it. The doorway. I need to know if that's what my brother did."

Nate was lost, and I knew it. Brad even knew it. Maybe he'd still be here if I'd told his parents something seemed wrong with him. Or if I'd told him sooner that our relationship made me feel like I didn't exist. Or if I'd told him he offered me safety and peace and an escape from my home. That it wasn't all good or bad, but that it could have been better for both of us.

Who knows—maybe I still would have lost him.

As my dad and that man in the bait shop said: sometimes there aren't answers.

Perhaps it's a comfort to accept this.

"Whether they transmigrated or they died, they're gone

for good, Izzy. And people are so hurt," I say. "I think this is better left a mystery."

"Yeah. Going after them won't bring them back," Cass says. "And I think—I know—we'll end up gone too."

"So you want to give up?" Izzy asks. "Stop trying to find out what really happened now? When we're this close?"

"Yes," I say. It's the most sure I've been in a long time.

"I don't know if this doorway thing is real or not, but I can't get in that plane." Cass's voice cracks into a sob. It's the messiest I've ever seen her—snot bubbling out of her nostrils, tears dripping off her chin. "I can't."

"Cass." Izzy grabs her hand. "Don't worry. You don't have to."

Cass's sobs settle into soft sniffles, and Izzy opens the car door for her.

I wait for Izzy to pull out and follow her down the dirt road. She drives slowly when we get to the highway. I'm slow too, but I easily overtake her and wave. She doesn't seem to notice. I glance back in my rearview mirror and see her jaw working from side to side like she's grinding her teeth. Eventually I lose sight of her altogether.

My dad's car isn't there when I get home, so I flop onto my bed. Yes, it's a comfort to accept that there aren't answers to everything, but what if there are answers I've been hiding from, like I hid all those years from confronting Nate?

I pull out my phone and send a text: `Can we talk?`

My mom calls immediately. "Janie?" My heart still sings when she says my name. "Is everything okay? Your dad told me about the plane accident. I wanted to call but I wasn't sure—"

I cut her off. "It wasn't an accident."

"What do you mean?"

"I think they were trying to leave," I say carefully.

She's quiet, like she can sense where I'm heading with this.

"I was so hurt when you left, Mom. And so, so angry."

"I know, honey. I'm sorry."

"I need to know why. I deserve to know."

"I thought you knew. I left that note."

"I shredded it."

This makes her laugh. It's low and husky, a laugh I hadn't heard in the year leading up to our move. My memory of it is older—from a day at the Ocean City boardwalk when I fed every single one of our fries to a fat pigeon I'd named Harold.

"I probably would have too," she says.

"So why?"

I can hear her take a deep breath. "Well, I didn't feel like my life was my own anymore. I had to build something for myself."

This makes me think of my dad squeezing the beer can when I said it hurts not to get picked. Of Nate's mom, barefoot at his wake. "It *wasn't* just your own. None of our lives are. We can break each other."

"Yes, certainly, we affect each other, but I don't know if I agree about our lives not being our own, Janie. I thought I could be a better mother if I made myself whole again. For myself."

I'm scared of the answer, but I ask it anyway: "Why weren't you whole?"

"Because I gave up my career and followed your father's," she says. "It had nothing to do with you," she adds, like she knows what I'm thinking.

"It had everything to do with me. I'm the reason you left school."

"Janie—"

"Just be honest. I can take it."

"The truth is complicated. All these factors—my career, my dreams, your dad, you—they're all tied together. But I didn't leave because I didn't want to be your mother anymore."

"So then why didn't you come visit?" I ask.

"You adamantly didn't want to see me. I felt like—I don't know—that was my bed to lie in because of the choice I'd made."

"Why didn't you come anyway?"

She's silent a moment. "I guess I should have."

"You still can."

"Okay then, I will."

I wonder what my life would have been like if I'd let her talk to me that first year. Would I already have these answers? Would I have demanded them from Nate back then too? "I guess I shouldn't have cut you out."

"I just hope that I can get a chance to show you who I've become," she says.

"You can't just wait around hoping for chances. Things don't just get better on their own."

"I know. You're right, Janie."

"No, you don't. I knew something was wrong with Nate." Speaking the truth out loud again doesn't make me feel any lighter. "I didn't tell anyone because he seemed so adamant everything was fine."

I expect her to tell me it wasn't my fault, but she doesn't, and this helps somehow. "I carry a lot of regrets too. But usually, in my regrets, there's a kernel I can find—something I'm glad for. It may not make it better, but it makes it meaningful."

I suppose I'm glad I confronted Nate at the party. Sure, I wish I'd said things sooner, that I'd said more, that I'd understood what he was trying to say, that our final conversation had been a happy one. But I did advocate for myself before he was gone forever, and I can close my fist around that kernel and hold it tight.

There's something pushing at the periphery of my thoughts, nagging me: Izzy driving slowly away from the airport, tense and upset. She said Cass wouldn't have to go near the plane, but she didn't say anything about herself. And, because I think I'm starting to understand Izzy, I know she won't stop until she has her answer.

"Mom," I say. "I have to go. We'll talk again soon."

I don't bother texting first. I run outside and jump back into the car. Izzy won't be added to my list of regrets.

AVIATION ACCIDENT PRELIMINARY REPORT

On June 23, 2019, about 5:30 a.m. central daylight time, a Cessna 172M was destroyed when it hit the ocean after takeoff from Gerard Township Airport (T75), Gerard, Texas. The unlicensed pilot and two passengers were fatally injured. Visual meteorological conditions prevailed, and no flight plan was filed for the local flight. The flight originated from T75 at approximately 5:00.

According to the owner, the plane was stored at T75 and used for flight training. Police estimate the pilot and passengers broke into the hangar between 3:30 and 4:30.

Witnesses at County Beach report seeing a low-flying airplane that climbed in altitude over the ocean, lost velocity, and "hovered" before the nose fell toward the left wing. Witnesses report that the plane went into a spin before hitting the water nose-first with a loud "boom."

According to the mechanic who assisted the owner, the plane received a routine oil change the day before the accident. Examination of the airplane by an FAA inspector revealed no mechanical issues.

The owner reported that the pilot had taken five

lessons for a total of five in-flight hours. He stated that the pilot had been trained to recover from stalls and had practiced recovery at higher altitudes only.

All three victims were under 18. The owner retained copies of parental permission forms. Parents stated that the signatures were forged.

Based on witness accounts and interviews with family, law enforcement has preliminarily determined that the plane was stolen for a joyride. NTSB notes no conflict with this conclusion.

CHAPTER FORTY-NINE

ISRAEL

....

One day before

THE DREAM BEGAN as it always did, the feeling of tires as they slipped beneath him, the drumbeat of fear and adrenaline as he slid into the oncoming lane. The woman's face and the round O of her mouth. The shock wave of the impact with her car. The explosive pain in his nose from the airbag. The searing pain in his leg and the ache across his chest from the seat belt. The brief quiet while the world righted itself. The smell of gasoline and a hissing sound. The voices outside calling to him. A loud pop followed by a whoosh. The smoke. The flames. The voices outside the car becoming more insistent, higher-pitched. The sirens. The struggle with the seat belt. The feeling that the front half of the car was folded onto his lap, pinning him so that he couldn't feel or free his right leg. Something outside the car that sounded like a saw. The names, as they always came: Lara. Peter.

If he could interrogate the dream, maybe he would know for sure that it was true, that what he was about to do wouldn't be in vain. *Concentrate on the medicine*, he told himself, at once Randolph and Israel. He remembered a short chestnut horse then, with a small girl on its back, racing around barrels. Randolph knew the mare, Peonía. She had an upper respiratory infection the ranchers called strangles. She would die if he didn't get antibiotics.

He could see Lara for once: her olive skin, the silk scarves she always wore over her shoulders, the crooked tilt of her smile. Then Peter, with his strawberry-blond hair, skinny legs, knobby knees, and hurt blue eyes. Peter in his/Randolph's imagination was running along a lake, flags streaming from his belt as he cradled a football in his arms. Or he was holding a bow, stretching it with all his might, trying to keep his chest flat, his elbow raised. His tongue stuck out as he aimed at the bull's-eye.

The heat in the car rose, accompanied by the terrible stink of melting plastic. The air was thick with smoke, burning his nostrils, his trachea. At the end, there was always a coughing fit that made him see stars, accompanied by a spasm in his abdomen, his body gasping, desperate for oxygen.

Concentrate, Israel thought again. Randolph opened his eyes, despite the sting. In front of him, where the windshield should have been, there was a gaping hole, an image with no data. *That*, Israel/Randolph thought, *is where I'm going.*

Israel woke to something bumping against his door, probably Izzy, collapsing onto his rug in her sleep. He wiped the sweat on his chest and neck off with his T-shirt and tried to breathe deeply until his pulse slowed.

His sister didn't stir when he unlocked his door. The moon from the window at the end of the hallway streaked her dark hair with silver. Her breathing whistled lightly out of her nose. She looked peaceful, curled up like a cat. He often felt so angry at this thing that she couldn't control any more than he could control his dreams that he'd allowed himself to forget it had once been nice to be close to her. They'd crouched together at the beach, hunting for crabs with sticks; they'd traded turns on a bodyboard; they'd built sand forts and plotted attacks on them, on the same side, as they advanced with their shovel soldiers.

Back then, before he'd had a locked door to keep her away, he'd wake from his nightmares with her breath hot on his neck and her arm slung over his shoulder. He'd felt safe. And he couldn't remember when that feeling of safety had transformed into humiliation and irritation.

Israel lay down carefully so as to not wake her. He put his arm on her shoulder and closed his eyes, willing himself to feel safe again, to feel peace, to feel anything but scared about what he was going to do.

Israel woke to the syrupy smell of mandocas. After his dream the night before, he'd helped Izzy sleepwalk back to bed and had returned to his own. He'd managed to doze off, and those few hours dozing had been sweetly empty, like a parting gift from his body.

Downstairs, his dad held tongs over a pan of oil, a white apron knotted over his work clothes as though those could get any dirtier. His mom was juicing limes. Izzy sat on one of the barstools at the counter, hugging one knee to her chest and dangling the other foot. Luna had wrapped her body around the legs of the stool. There was no trace of his parents' disappointment about grades. What gift was this?

"Buenos días, sleepyhead," Izzy said. Israel studied her face, but there was no hint that she remembered him cuddling her in the middle of the night.

"What are you doing home?" he asked his dad. "It's not raining."

"Oh, perdóname, I'll leave," his dad said, pretending to untie his apron. Israel hadn't seen him since the report card had arrived, but he seemed in a good mood. Lit with the sunlight from the kitchen window, the lines on his face had softened. Israel could as easily have been in the kitchen of his childhood as he was in the present.

"He said he'd been missing mandocas and could stand to go in a few hours late," his mom said. She wore jeans and a silk top. Her hair was tied back with a scarf, and she, too, looked like the parent of his childhood, baking tots in the kitchen after school.

"Oh, you've been missing them, have you?" Israel said to his dad. "No one else mentioned them to you, like, a month ago?"

"What? A man can't miss the food of his homeland? I was a child once too."

Israel climbed onto the stool beside his sister. "Hey, I won't complain. Just want credit where credit is due."

"Fine, everybody, it was Israel's idea that I stay home for a morning to make mandocas."

"Thank you."

"Para mi preciosa." His dad set the first plate of fried teardrop-shaped rings in front of Izzy. Israel reached for one and she elbowed him away, leaning forward over the plate so she could guard them with her arms.

"Hey! I thought you only liked healthy food now."

She selected the smallest, palest one from her plate and handed it to him. It was too hot; he wrapped it in a paper napkin so he could hold it.

"What are you two doing today?" his mother asked.

Israel took a bite of the fried cornmeal dough. It was fine to answer with silence if his mouth was full. There was no way he could explain that he'd steal a plane, fly it through a hole in the world, and choose a different life. None of them would understand.

"There's a senior party at the beach tonight," Izzy said.

"You're both going?" she asked.

Israel nodded, mouth still full.

"Pórtense bien," she said. *Behave.* "No drinking and driving."

"Of course not, mami," Izzy said.

She served them the papelón con limón, a sweet and sour concoction made with limes and the same panela as the mandocas.

When the batches were finished frying, they all moved to the table. It was the first time the four of them had sat at the kitchen table together in months. Izzy told a story about a biology teacher at school who'd brought in a tapeworm from one of her cows so the class could see it. A girl in Izzy's class—Israel had a feeling that it was actually Izzy—had joked she would steal it and swallow it to lose weight. But the teacher had thought she was serious and locked up the tapeworm in a metal locker.

"It's certainly the best-guarded tapeworm in Texas," she said.

Their dad kept leaning over the tabletop so he could hear her better, eyes crinkling in the corners from laughter. Their mom held a napkin over her mouth, pretending to be mortified, but she found it as funny as the rest of them.

Israel waited for his future and grades to come up, but they didn't.

Too quickly, breakfast was over. Their mother was going shopping on the mainland; their dad had to check on the cabinet guys. Israel planned to go to Shane's before the party. He might not see his parents ever again—these two people who'd worked so hard to build a life for them on this island. The thought felt like touching a hot stove. He couldn't dare touch it again. He couldn't say goodbye.

"Gracias," he said instead. His dad balled up the apron

and tossed it at him. He brushed out his mustache with his fingers, hiding a smile. His mom ruffled his hair and kissed his forehead.

Izzy didn't move from her seat. She was chewing on an ice cube from her drink, petting Luna—who she claimed she didn't like—and staring at him.

"What was that about?" she asked.

"What?"

"I felt a pang just then. Before they left." She patted her side as though he wouldn't know she was talking about her twinsense.

"Izzy," he said warningly. It wasn't about privacy this time. She'd try to stop him if she knew the truth and could even end up in danger herself. He was banking on her being asleep when he actually flew that night; she couldn't sleepwalk forty-five miles to him.

"Israel, you *can* talk to me; I might be able to help," she said. She wore pj's—cotton shorts, a tank top that said SLEEP in cloud-shaped letters, and fuzzy striped socks. Even without makeup or her hair done, she was starting to look older and fiercer, a woman in a girl's pajamas. But if Peter and OtherPlanes couldn't do anything, what was she going to do to stop his nightmares?

"Later, okay?" he said. "Tomorrow."

"We are twins," she said. "We are made of the same DNA, we grew up in the same house, with the same family. And we barely know each other. Doesn't that make you sad?" It did, of course, but he couldn't let the sadness sink in or she'd feel that, too. If he was going to remember parts of the final moments of this life in the next, he was determined for them to be the smell of mandocas and his parents' laughter.

"Izzy, it's been a good morning. Can we not fight right now?"

"Doesn't that make you sad?" she repeated, following him to the staircase.

She was all spines to the world, but she had such a soft underbelly. She was easy to hurt, and that's how he could protect her and his plan. "No," he said. "Not at all. You just love too hard."

Her face crumpled and he turned away.

Back in his room, Israel pulled out his iPad. He could leave her a message—something she wouldn't see until long after he was gone, when she found the iPad in his hiding spot. He opened the voice memo app. He tried to apologize, but it didn't come out right. He deleted the message and started over.

Again, and again. And two more times after that.

Why couldn't he do this? Each time, his goodbye made it sound like he was leaving a door open for her to blame herself. Just the existence of a message would signal to her that he'd done it on purpose and there was some way she could have stopped it.

Maybe it was far kinder to leave their relationship as is, to let her think that today was a normal day: He was her same prickly, private brother. The death of his body when he went

through the doorway was simply an accident. She'd be resent-
ful, maybe, but not regretful.

He could imagine grown-up Izzy following her love of
movies to study film in California. She'd trade slouchy shirts
for high-waisted pants, red lipstick, and an asymmetrical bob.
She'd simmer with artful moodiness, and all her student films
would be bold, ambitious explorations of grief. Then, on to
Hollywood, where she'd be a force, directing for the big screen.

She'd be all right, and maybe, just maybe, he'd see her
again one day.

CHAPTER FIFTY

CASS

....

Eight days after

"WHERE WERE YOU, Cassandra?" my mom asks as soon as I walk through the door. She's sitting at the kitchen table, her laptop open and reading glasses perched on her nose, probably waiting for my dad to call.

"I told you. Training for a new job at the theater."

"Where's your uniform?"

"Oh. Um, they still have to order it."

"Cass, you're a terrible liar. You have been since you were little." She beckons me to the kitchen table. "Sit. What's really going on?"

I sigh. "We went to see the pilot. The one who taught the boys how to fly."

"What?" She doesn't anger often, but when she does, it inflates her like a balloon: her cheeks puffing, her eyes bugging out. "Why?"

"Honestly, because I needed some help," I say. "I needed to face things, you know? See things differently."

"I could have helped you, honey."

"Could you have?" I say, more sharply than I intended. She's always trying to keep me from making mistakes or failing, but I'm starting to realize that maybe I need to do these things—that I need to reach into the darkness—to learn things about myself.

She looks hurt, her lip turning out, but I can't stop myself. "You only see stuff with Dad one way. You think it's your fault he's not in our lives because you didn't follow him, but he could have left the navy. Keeping up a relationship is on him, too." I nod at the silent laptop to emphasize my point. "When was the last time you protected your own heart?"

"Cassie, I think that's a bit unfair. There's a lot you don't know."

"Well, tell me, then. I'm old enough."

She looks at the laptop like it might ring and rescue us both. "You're right that I probably try to carry too much of this relationship. And you're right that it hasn't been going well." Her voice wobbles.

"Have you talked about . . . separating?" I barely get the word out.

She's silent but puts her hand on mine. The gesture tells me everything.

Even if I saw it from a mile away—even if Izzy did too—I'm

still shocked. "Why haven't you?" I ask savagely, sliding my hand away.

"We're still working on it and thought maybe we should wait until you're in college."

This infuriates me. They were going through the motions of being a couple—barely—for some arbitrary milestone? "Why? It's not like it will be magically easier on me because I'm out of the house. You might as well not waste the time."

"It's not a waste. There's good between us," she says, tears welling in her eyes. "A lot, actually."

Her sadness deflates me. "But will you be happier apart?"

"I don't know, Cassie."

I think of Shane, flying because he could, because his heart had already grown stronger. "You know what I learned today?" I say. "Shane liked to fly and was actually good at it."

Her eyebrows pinch together like she's confused. "I'm glad, honey."

"I guess I'm trying to say: don't wait to be happy."

She smiles weakly at this. "You're so grown-up."

My phone rings, Janie's name displaying on the screen.

"I think she went back," Janie says as soon as I answer. "I think she's flying."

I look at my mom, and I can tell she's worried, that she wants to say no to the question I haven't asked yet. But she nods because she understands that this is what makes us good—any of us, all of us: the care we take of each other.

CHAPTER FIFTY-ONE

NATE

....

One day before

NATE'S MOM'S EYES were glued to him during dinner. She spun her gold wedding band, working it up and down her finger to reveal a thin tan line.

Eat, he told himself, but a moment later he realized his fork was still hovering in front of his mouth. His brain was a bat nest again: a million copies of the same thought flapping against his skull.

I'm worthless.

I deserve pain.

Aaron was saying something about a customer who was trying to sue the restaurant where he worked because she'd burnt her mouth on a fried oyster. Their dad rubbed his arthritic knuckles and rolled his eyes at the tourist. His mother seemed to be waiting for Nate to do something. *Laugh*, he told himself. It came out in a rushed huff of air—not a laugh at all.

"The fuck, Nate?"

"Aaron," his dad said warningly.

"What are you doing tonight, honey?" Nate's mom asked him.

"There's a senior party. On the beach," Nate answered.

"There won't be any drugs or alcohol?"

"No." He caught Aaron smirking at him.

"What time will you be home?" his dad asked.

"I'm sleeping at Shane's." Another lie, of course, because he couldn't say they were going to steal a plane so Israel could find a doorway to another life.

Nate pictured the tear he'd seen, its rich, ripe darkness. It pulled at him—a magnet. What if—Nate wondered—he went instead? What if he disappeared inside? Everything would be so quiet.

His mom leaned over the table and grasped his hand. Hers was warm, damp, and dotted with sunspots. He could feel the cold metal of her ring, the lines on the inside of her palm. For a moment her touch grounded him and cleared his head. He could ask her for help, but what would he say? That his thoughts were too much? That they were hurting him? How stupid was that?

His tongue felt like it was cemented to the floor of his mouth, his throat closing.

"Be careful," she said, releasing his hand, and the moment slipped away.

• • •

At dusk, Israel and Shane carried the keg down to the beach and left Nate with the plastic cups. The dance team had arranged ten brightly colored coolers around the firepit as benches. Half of them were scrawled with the last names of well-meaning soccer parents—*Turner, Freeman, Hastings, Guerrero, Tran.*

Seniors arrived in carloads, jean-shorted and with folding chairs slung across their backs. They unpacked hot dogs, bags of chips, and mixers onto three rickety card tables. They kicked off shoes and hopped from blanket to blanket, admiring each other's tans, pedicures, new swimsuits, and mirrored sunglasses.

Nate used to be like them: lost in his little life, unconcerned because the future was glittering and endless like the ocean. But now?

There is no future.

Marcus hauled the wood to the pit and handed Nate the lighter fluid.

"Do the honors," he said.

Nate poured the fluid, tossed a match onto the wood, and watched the fire flare up, hot and bright, before it settled into a small glow. Someone clapped.

He spied Janie's red hatchback as it parked along the seawall. She got out slowly, walked over to the meter, studied it for a moment, and pulled out her phone. Her hair was loose and wet, wrapping around her neck in the breeze as she finished paying the meter. She pulled blankets out of the back seat of the car and stacked them in her arms, watching her leather sandals as she climbed down the stairs. As she hit the bottom step, Janie looked up hopefully, still pinning the blankets with her chin.

I don't deserve her.

I don't deserve anything but pain.

Nate crouched down so people couldn't see what he was doing, and grabbed one of the logs at the edge of the fire. It seared—a firework of red in his brain—and the inner voice fell quiet. He looked at his palm and poked the red welt. Another firework. Another moment of silence. It felt like relief.

When it was dark, Nate sat on a cooler next to Marcus and Tien, who were roasting hot dogs. He pushed the skewer into his toes, trying to keep his face still while the prongs pierced his skin. This way, he could keep his head clear enough. He could make it to the plane and take it for himself.

Someone stepped between him and the fire. It took Nate's eyes a moment to adjust, to make out the hair dried to a nest of flyaways, the loose T-shirt with oversized lettering: CAPTAIN OF MY OWN SHIP.

"Why are you ignoring me? Is this about the other night?" Janie said loudly.

Nate stood abruptly, grabbed her elbow, and drew her away from the fire.

She yanked her arm back. "You invited me here. I thought things were going to be different."

"I can't escape it," he said. Even now the thoughts were

there, slinging themselves against his skull: *I don't deserve her. I'm nothing.*

"Escape what?" He could see the fury rising in her cheeks, the tiny capillaries on her nostrils becoming redder. "This double life you've built?"

"I'm scared," he managed.

"Of what?" Her eyes were searching his face like his mom's had at dinner.

He had to push her away. Keep her safe from him. She'd be hurt, but maybe it would protect her from a bigger heartbreak.

"Of what people will say," he said, looking down so he didn't have to see the pain on her face.

"I can't pretend anymore," she said. She sounded tired but not weak. "I'm done."

He wished he could say goodbye, but he knew it was better this way.

"I understand," he said.

She turned and marched toward the liquor.

He tilted his head back and found Orion's Belt and Sword. Could she leave if she knew she wasn't coming back? he'd asked her before they'd kissed.

Now he had to ask himself the same question.

And something else, too: Could he do it alone?

CHAPTER FIFTY-TWO

SHANE

....

One day before; the day of

SHANE HAD STUDIED the hangar combination lock and ordered a lock cutter online. He'd carefully observed Brad attaching the tow bar to move the plane and had figured out which set of keys belonged to which plane. The plan was for Nate and Shane to wait an hour while Israel flew, in case he couldn't find the doorway and they needed to sneak the plane back into place. If he didn't return after that hour, they were supposed to head back to the party without him and pretend they didn't know where he'd gone.

The theft would be the easy part. The harder part would be seeing Cass.

Once they settled the keg Meg's friend had bought for them into the sand, Shane tried to be the host he'd been at his pool for so many summers: he teased his teammates, flirted with underclassmen, poured drinks. But as soon as Cass skipped down the stairs, her hair springing and lit gold in the setting sunlight, he felt like Humpty Dumpty again, teetering right on the edge of the wall.

She wore her black bikini with a white, slouchy-neck tee over it, torn jean shorts, and beaded sandals, which she kicked off as soon as she hit the sand. She didn't seem to notice where they landed—a surprisingly carefree move for Cass, even a happy one.

Israel jerked his head in her direction. "Go say hi," he said. "Or you'll end up obsessing all night." Shane thought he'd probably be obsessing about her all night whether he greeted her or not, but he still walked over.

As he approached, she dug through a cooler and withdrew a can of soda, flicking the can sweat off her fingers as though she were doing a spell.

"Hi," he said.

"Hi." She looked like she might be about to smile, but she bit her lip instead.

"How are you?"

"Okay," she said. It was an overly bright okay, a puffed-chest but empty okay. "How are you?"

"Okay," he said back, hoping she knew it meant *I understand*.

Izzy appeared, eyes narrowed. Before he could say more, she took Cass's hand and spun away with her. Cass glanced over her shoulder once, a quick under-the-eyelashes flit, and every part of Shane lifted because he knew at least she had loved him, at least it hadn't been fake.

Unlike the rest of the night.

For now he had to play the part of old Shane. He organized a hot dog–eating contest—roasting up to five on a skewer at a time and shouting a count as people smushed them into their mouths. He let Marcus talk him into a keg stand and then a game of flip cup. He shotgunned beers with Israel and Nate, chucking the tabs into the ocean for old time's sake when they were finished.

When it was dark, his friends turned off the speakers and splintered into small groups to listen to music on phones. The island police department—ten middle-aged men who Shane wouldn't trust to investigate a candy bar theft, let alone anything bigger—usually ignored beach parties as long as they avoided noise complaints and kept off the roads.

He swam on beer through pockets of tinny cell phone music, through humid clots of bodies dance-kicking sand into the sea. No matter how much he drank, he was always aware that he was in a fish bowl—watched by everyone—and that Cass was perpetually swimming on the other side.

Nate had fallen asleep outside the firelight. Shane wasn't sure how he'd done it, with so much laughter ringing out, with the crash of waves, with all that was before them that night. Perhaps because he wasn't obsessing over an ex-girlfriend like Shane.

It was three a.m. when Israel roused Shane with a bottle of water in hand. Nate was already awake, his head tilted up toward the stars. The beach was silent, the fire almost dead. Shane could make out the mounds of sleeping bodies under towels and blankets. He had fallen asleep in the open, and he could already feel bites rising on his cheeks. Nate pulled back the hood of his sweatshirt. His hair was matted, but he looked more alert than he had during the party. There were dark rings under Israel's eyes, like he hadn't slept at all—or ever, really. In the light from his phone, he looked terribly worn, and Shane realized for the first time that he actually believed his friend: Israel *had* lived a whole life before.

Nate was silent on the ride to the airport. Shane drove, and Israel sat in the passenger seat, reciting the same questions they'd already gone over.

"What happens if there's an alarm system?"

"There isn't. Nate checked."

"Cameras?"

"Negative."

"What if we can't get the garage lock open?"

"It's a cheap lock. We'll be fine."

"What if we can't figure out attaching the tow bar?"

"YouTube."

"What happens if someone is there?"

"We run."

Nate's forehead was pressed against the window, but Shane caught his eyes once in the rearview mirror. His friend smiled, that old smile that was hardly a smile at all.

There were no streetlights, so they drove with their

brights, casting the fences and sporadic trees in an eerie white-blue light. When they turned off the main road, Shane put on the dim fog lights and slowed to a crawl. One thing they'd forgotten to take into consideration: none of them had flown in the dark before. But Shane didn't bring it up; Israel was already too nervous.

When the headlights lit the hangar, Shane let go of a breath he hadn't realized he was holding. Brad's truck wasn't there.

Shane cut the lock and lifted the door with a crowbar until he could squeeze through and open it from inside. The screech as the door lifted made every hair on Shane's body stand up.

The planes—lit by their headlights—looked like ghosts.

Shane grabbed the keys from the peg and pointed at the one that was theirs. It took longer than expected to attach the tow bar and drag it out.

By the time the plane was ready on the runway, the sky had lightened to dark purple with a few blue streaks. The hour they'd planned to wait for Israel was going to put them dangerously into full daylight territory. But it was too late to turn back.

Israel took the keys and a deep, shuddering breath.

"Are you ready?" Shane asked.

Before Israel could answer, Nate smacked the keys out of Israel's hand.

"What the fuck?"

Nate dove for the keys, the fastest he'd moved since the injury. Israel grabbed Nate's wrist, but even with his bad knee, Nate managed to twist his body away, clutching the keys to his chest and using his back to shield them from Israel, like they were on the soccer field.

"I have to go," Nate said, his voice coming out in huffs as he struggled.

"Nate, no!" Israel yelled. "You don't understand what this doorway is."

"You owe me," Nate growled back.

"Please. This dream has haunted me for as long as I can remember. I need to escape." Shane could hear the tears in Israel's voice.

It had been easier to imagine a world without Israel, who he'd only been friends with for a few years, who had always seemed to Shane like one of those people on the brink of brilliance or something darker. But he couldn't imagine a world without Nate—this person he'd known even longer than Cass. He'd been the first to understand what Shane needed and to provide it.

Shane grabbed their shoulders and tried to pull them apart. He managed to pivot Nate so he was facing him. "You might not come back," he said.

"I don't intend to," he replied.

Shane pried the keys out of his fingers. He'd never been good at anything before beyond hosting parties and making friends, but he was good at flying, and if anyone was going to be able to keep them safe, it was him. Otherwise, his friends would find another way to do this—with or without him.

"There's no way I'm being left behind again," he said. "I'll take you both to where you need to go."

VOICE MEMOS

....

Deleted

....

4 files

New Recording 1

Izzy, I'm sorry I pushed you away. I know you wanted us to be closer. I guess I just wanted some space and for us to be our own people. No, I'm not saying it right—

New Recording 2

Izzy, I wanted to say I'm sorry for causing pain. The dream destroys everything in its path and I need to get away from it. I don't know if this will work or not. But I think it's my only option. So please tell Mom and Dad that this wasn't their fault and I love them. I—

New Recording 3

Izzy, I'm sorry for everything. I'm leaving, and I don't know if I'll be back. All I can do is hope that if you see me again, you'll know me. You always believed. Mom and Dad are going to be sad for a while, and I'm sorry for that, too. You're strong, though. You'll be able to hold them up. I've always admired that about you.

Oh, and please take care of Luna. I know you think she's annoying, but she's a good, loyal friend, and I know you could use another one of those.

New Recording 4

Izzy, I love you. I hope you know that. I wasn't the best— *<muffled sob>*

I can't do this. I don't know how to say it.

CHAPTER FIFTY-THREE

IZZY

....

Eight days after

BRAD STEPS OUT of the hangar when I pull up. He doesn't look surprised to see me back so soon.

"I'm ready," I say.

He nods like, *Of course you are.*

We strap in and he walks me through the checks. I'm moving my body as instructed, but I'm not listening; I'm trying to feel Israel. That morning the plane went down, there was the jolt of pain in my side, but I didn't feel his absence. Now I'm not sure I felt a presence, either. If I concentrate, I can feel my shorts' waistband, the cotton of my shirt, but nothing under my skin. Has there ever been? Have I ever been quiet enough to feel anything but the worst?

Brad has me accelerate down the runway and pull back, lifting the nose when instructed. It's easier than I expected, and I feel weirdly calm. The view shifts from dirt runway and dried grasses to a pale blue sky stretching as far as I can see. A fluffy cloud hides the sun, and the light peeks around it, highlighting the edges in gold. If I believed in heaven, this is exactly how I'd imagine it.

I remember the plane that terrible morning: how it climbed and climbed until it stopped. I glance at Brad and pull back harder.

"Steady. Ease off the yoke," Brad says, but he sounds bored, as though he's not fully paying attention. We're probably still as low as the boys were that morning. I could stall us just like they did before Brad could react. See the doorway myself.

The choice to follow my brother, to finally know once and for all, is mine.

Israel made this choice because he was hurting every night. I know it. My body, so often dragged from bed, is certain. But now my mom can't leave her room. My dad can't come home. Israel may not have known that would happen, or he did and he still went through with it. Because he finally trusted me like I'd been asking him to for so long. To go back to the house and feed Luna, and help my mother bathe, and ask my dad to put down the work.

That morning of the party Israel said I love too hard. He meant it as an insult, but I don't think it is. I want to be a person who loves fiercely, with everything I have.

Even if the person I love most of all is gone.

Something sears along my right side, sharper than any pain I've ever felt. Tears spring to my eyes and I make a *guh* sound like my breath has been knocked from me. I realize the iron-hot sear isn't because Israel is hurting. No. The searing pain I feel is because he has been severed from me. Because I let myself feel it—finally and truly.

"I want to land," I tell Brad breathlessly. "I don't want to do this anymore."

Israel made his choice, and I make mine: I choose my parents. I choose Cass. I choose Janie. I choose senior year and all the years that follow without my brother, no matter how painful that may be.

"But we just took off."

"I don't care. I want to go home," I repeat firmly.

He shrugs and directs me through the turn and descent.

Even though I didn't see the doorway, I think I can feel its gravity lifting the hairs on my arms ever so slightly as we land. And I wonder if I'll always think about it, if I'll ever try to find it again, or if I'll wait until, one day, it finds me.

CHAPTER FIFTY-FOUR

SHANE, NATE, ISRAEL

....

The day of

THEY FLEW FROM inky darkness toward the pink glow of the rising sun. Shane was at the yoke because he was the better pilot. Nate was in the passenger seat because he'd seen the doorway before, and Israel sat in the back because he wanted to be able to jump out alone if he spotted the doorway. Let his friends recover and carry on.

When they saw the coast's knot of lights, they dropped in altitude. They skipped over the empty ferry and the bay to their island. They dropped even lower, the trees so near they imagined being able to hop into them and scrabble through the branches. They flew over a cruise ship sitting dark at the port, the pillared courthouse and Gothic-style cathedral at the heart of the island, the haunted McAllister mansion, which had stood defiantly through three hurricanes, the downtown with its taffy factory and lines of tchotchke shops.

And their beach. The strewn shapes of their friends, like starfish at low tide. Could they make out Janie, a blanket tented over her head; angel-armed Cass; and Izzy sprawled on her stomach—not called, for once, by her brother's nightmares?

"How do we find it?" Shane asked Nate.

Nate shook his head. His friends weren't supposed to be with him. Even if he wanted nothing more than to find the doorway again—to envelop himself in silence—he couldn't hurt them. It was his life that was worthless—not theirs.

"Climb," Israel said over the headset. "Hard."

Shane climbed high. Above them, the sky was still bruised purple. Gravity pinned them to the backs of their seats. The alarm whined.

They tipped, left wing down first. Then cartwheeled forward.

Nate felt weightless, free. It was what he'd wanted, but not like this. Not with Shane beside him. Israel behind. Janie on the beach below.

Israel's stomach skipped into his throat. He saw a streak of black so thick it seemed like syrup, hovering where the ocean should be yawning below them. The air shivered around it. He knew the nightmares would go away if he were inside. Everything would. He simply had to choose a quiet life without dreams.

He grabbed the latch, picturing the most peaceful life he could imagine—a giant live oak that sat outside the McAllister mansion, casting dappled shadows on the lawn. The tree had been there before humans, when the island was a sliver of wild forest and swamp ruled by ancient alligators.

A small cool hand on his stopped him from pushing the door open. He thought it must be Shane's or Nate's, but when he looked down, there was nothing there. Yet he felt the pressure—a familiar weight.

Izzy's hand.

He'd resented her twinsense for so long and now here it was, with him.

He tried to see the beach, tried to find her with his eyes, but they were falling too fast. She had never turned away from him—no matter how hard he pushed. He'd deleted the voice memos because he was trying to spare her feeling that she could have helped. But what if he had actually let her try to help him? What if he had trusted her with this? And his parents, too? What if that was how he made things right in this life? By connecting with his family in the way Randolph hadn't.

"Get us out," Israel said to Shane. "Stop it. I changed my mind."

To Nate, it looked as though the sky had split like the skin of an overripe fruit, but instead of sweet-smelling flesh, there was a hard darkness inside. He could feel its pull. He imagined plunging into it like you dove into the ocean. Everything would become remote—waves scraping the sand, the voices around you, the sky above. It was peaceful under the water, but only because it wasn't permanent, because you could break the surface and feel the relief of everything rushing back. He could try again to tell them—his mom, Aaron, Janie. And even if he couldn't tell them and his tongue split at the effort, he knew that they'd see what was happening to him, that they'd understand, before it was too late. He just had to cling to hope a little longer.

"We have to go back," Nate said.

Shane tried to point the nose down as he'd rehearsed with Brad, but it was too late. He was too inexperienced. They were too close to the water. Brad had said flying would make Shane's life his own. He'd thought that, as a pilot, he wouldn't need to cheat. He wouldn't feel like less than the person he loved. He'd be able to choose his own future.

"I can't!" he shouted.

The plane screamed toward the black hole. The green water gathered at its edges.

In the building wave, three gray shapes streaked forward. When the wave crested, they leapt over it and into the darkness.

EPILOGUE

JANIE

....

Eight days after

THE SUN IS setting when we reach the island again—not even an hour after Cass and I stood, hands clasped together, watching the plane land and Izzy spill from it, her arms already open to us. We texted our families that we were okay and drove straight to the beach with the windows rolled down, the wind drying our faces.

We stop at the memorial with its wilted flowers, crosses, and stuffed animals. Someone has tucked small American flags into teddy bear arms, as though even this memorial should be part of the approaching Fourth of July celebration. Izzy picks up a gray bear with fur that's been matted by rain and sea salt—and hugs it to her chest.

On the beach, there's no evidence of what happened here. No Solo cups, volleyball nets, indentations in the sand from the keg. There aren't broken wings, laughing seniors, or dolphins.

The ocean—Nate's magic thing—has washed everything clean.

"I'm sorry they're not here," Cass says.

"Me too," Izzy says, a little sadly. "I'd still like to believe they were, though."

"Me too," I say because dolphins live free, baptized by the waves.

Izzy drops to the sand and kicks out her legs. Cass sits beside her, leaning back on her hands.

It's a Texas sunset, which manages to bleed from yellow to peach to purple to navy like a watercolor painting. I cross my legs and throw my head back. A few stars are already visible in the dark half of the sky, gauzy in the fading light.

"Janie, tell us the story of the man and the whale," Izzy says, rolling onto her stomach so that we can see her face. "From the script."

I close my eyes a moment, trying to remember the scenes I imagined when I was writing it so many months ago.

"There's a man," I begin, "who loves his wife very much, but she dies suddenly of a heart attack. The man falls into a deep depression and his son encourages him to take his granddaughter out because being around her and doing something might help him feel better. So he takes her to the aquarium. And there's an orca there. The little girl says, 'Look, it's Grandma.' The man is charmed by his granddaughter, but then he looks very close, and he sees it is actually her—his wife. Her soul is visible through the eye of the whale. And she seems to recognize him, too, because she just floats there, looking right at him. At the end, he goes back without his granddaughter so that he can talk to his wife alone."

"What does he say to her?" Cass asks.

"Well, I don't know; I didn't write that part into the script."

"It's not too late," Izzy says. "Make it up now."

I pause, but they don't seem impatient with me. "Well, I suppose he says he's sorry for the times he hurt her and that he loves her."

"Do you think she says anything back?" Cass asks.

"Obviously, she says it in whale so he can't understand," Izzy says.

I laugh.

"So how does it end again?" Cass asks.

"With a wide shot of his silhouette being swallowed by hers as she gets closer and closer to the glass," Izzy says, and I'm surprised she remembers this so clearly.

"Yeah, because it's a mystery bigger than us." I gesture at the sky above us, the ocean at our feet, the place where the boys left this life and became something new.

Cass looks at me, her eyes tawny and gentle in the dusky light. Izzy does too, not bothering to wipe away the tears sliding down her cheeks. We are quiet, listening to the rhythmic *shush* of the waves. And for the first time, I feel like we belong— to each other and to this strange world.

Acknowledgments

SINCE THE PUBLICATION of *We Speak in Storms*, I have met so many teachers, librarians, and booksellers who work incredibly hard to connect young people with books they'll love. Thank you for helping to make the world a better place one reader at a time.

Thank you to Julie Henson, Rebecca McKanna, and Cassandra Sanborn for offering their wisdom and insight on so many drafts of this novel. From the start, you have been the champions Izzy, Cass, Janie, Nate, Israel, and Shane needed.

Thank you to Liza Kaplan, for her enthusiasm and thoughtful edits, and to the teams at Philomel and Penguin for their bookmaking magic. Thank you to my agent, Sarah Davies, for being an advocate and adviser.

Thank you to Sean Killian, Jim Hitchcock, Melissa Johnson, Martín Maldonado, Maria Maldonado, and Molly Erickson for giving their time and expertise as I was researching everything from flying to ACL injuries to mental health.

Thank you to my colleagues, friends, and family for their patience and support as I built this book. Thank you especially to my mother, Mary Lund, for being a first reader; to Thuy

Nguyen, for her graphic design prowess; and to Sarah Murphy, for creating educator resources for my novels.

To my partner, Johnny Acevedo, thank you for being my personal publicist and bookseller; for enduring early-morning wake-ups and long weekend hours; for providing countless meals, coffees, and pep talks; and, most of all, for loving me to life. I couldn't do it without you.

AUTHOR'S NOTE

Days after I began writing this book, my mother's cancer came back, blooming across her skin. At the same time, climate change was constantly in the news: a countdown to the end of our planet popping onto my phone screen. Somehow these two griefs became entwined, and I started to feel paralyzed by everyday decisions. All I could think was nothing matters, nothing matters, nothing matters. It all ends. I had panic attacks—short bursts of terror that left me gasping for breath—as I stood in elevators or rode trains. I slept with my head tented under blankets through fuzzy winter daylight or I didn't sleep at all.

I have felt like this before: when I was sixteen, when I was twenty-five. I still wear those dark periods like scars inside my body, feel them stretch and ache in memory.

Because our society has become better at talking about depression in the past decade, I recognized its face. I knew the shape of it. So, this time, I managed to ask for help.

When I sat in a therapist's chair and told her my story, she made me feel like I mattered, like I was important, like I was welcome here.

I wrote *The Sky Above Us* inside those difficult months, and outside of them too. I hope that, in reading this novel, you will know that you are not alone in whatever you're experiencing; that there is a person out there who will really see you; and that it is okay to ask for help for you or for someone you know.

You matter. You are important. You are welcome here.

If you or someone you know is struggling, please consider this list of resources as a helpful guide:

The Trevor Project
thetrevorproject.org
24/7/365 Hotline: 1-866-488-7386 or Text START to
678-678

National Suicide Prevention Lifeline
suicidepreventionlifeline.org
English: 1-800-273-8255 / Español: 1-888-628-9454 /
For Deaf and Hard of Hearing: 1-800-799-4889

The Jason Foundation
jasonfoundation.com
1-800-273-TALK (8255) or Text Jason to 741-741

The Jed Foundation
jedfoundation.org
1-800-273-TALK (8255) or Text START to 741-741

American Foundation for Suicide Prevention

afsp.org/find-support

American Association of Suicidology

suicidology.org/resources

Crisis Text Line

crisistextline.org/selfharm

Text CONNECT to 741-741

National Alliance on Mental Illness (NAMI)

nami.org/Find-Support/Teens-Young-Adults

1-800-950-NAMI (6264) or Text NAMI to 741-741

**Substance Abuse and Mental Health Services
Administration National Helpline**

samhsa.gov/find-help/national-helpline

1-800-662-HELP (4357)

Families for Depression Awareness

familyaware.org/help-someone

National Safe Place

nationalsafeplace.org/find-a-safe-place

Text the word SAFE and your current location (address, city, state) to 698-66. Within seconds, you will receive a message with the closest Safe Place location.

ReachOut.com

au.reachout.com

The National Association for School Psychologists

nasponline.org/resources-and-publications
/resources-and-podcasts